ARRIVING HOME
Copyright © 2023 by Chelsea Lauren

ISBN 979-8-9864995-8-1

Cover Design by Brittany Evans @ BEDESIGNS.CA

Editing by Represent Publishing

Arriving Home

A Lake Juniper Novel

Arriving Home

A Lake Juniper Novel

CHELSEA LAUREN

Note to Readers

This story touches upon alcoholism, drug use, and manipulated abuse. These are brief parts of the novel, but please take caution if these subjects may be triggering to you.

Chapter One
Elijah

This is dumb. Ridiculous really. How is it that my self-confidence became so low I booked an outrageous writing retreat, stuck on the top of a mountain, with no service?

"Book yourself a writing event. Go to a convention or a retreat. Take a trip that surrounds you with like-minded people. Writing can be such a solitary event. Even if you're at a retreat and writing solo, you'll at least be around others doing the same thing. Maybe you could talk to the writers about reviews from such a personal book."

My therapist's words repeat in my head, and have ever since she mentioned this a month ago. As if the universe was shoving signs in my face, I found a writing retreat on Juniper Mountain, right behind my home. Just an hour's drive in elevation. The retreat was at Enchanted Juniper Resort, deemed in the top five most romantic resorts in New England. Number one in Maine. So I figured, what the hell. A romance writer with writer's block at the most romantic resort? I'd be a fool not to go.

What I hadn't expected was how realistic the photos on the website were compared to the resort. Evergreen trees tower around the property, heavy with snow from the night before. The path from the parking lot to the resort curves around a medium-sized frozen pond. The storm two days ago helped coat the ground here, but it's clear it was already packed with a couple feet. It should be a prime snowboarding season this year. Juniper Mountain Ski Resort is just fifteen minutes west from here.

The resort seems quaint on the vast property, sitting slightly higher than the parking lot. It's decently sized though; the website said it has twenty guest rooms. There's thirty writers here, but some are sharing rooms.

I hate the comradery as soon as I walk through the resort doors. A high-pitch laughter echoes amongst the chatter. I'm greeted with stained chestnut walls, similar to the outside, elegantly decorated for the holiday season with garland and pine wreaths that perfume the air. The atmosphere is reminiscent of a log cabin in the woods, but it's amplified with pristine cleanliness, offering a brighter, more romantic element in the woodwork compared to a darkened cabin. While it's a five-star resort, it doesn't give off a posh, rich vibe. A more lived in, welcoming bed and breakfast. Perfect for those who like people. But me and my social meter? We're a force to be reckoned with.

Writers are already gathering in what looks like a living room with a few sofas and sofa chairs. The fireplace is blazing. From my careful studying of the schedule, I remember there's a welcome drink and hors d'oeuvres in a few minutes. I made sure to arrive at the very last moment.

"Elijah Evergreen! What a pleasure." A middle-age woman with a short black bob comes over to me, grinning. She has a clipboard, presumably the woman in charge of the retreat.

I push my shoulders back, adjusting my posture, and throw on a smile. A portion of myself already diminishes. I offer a hand, much to my displeasure, but my mom's trained me well. "Hi, it's lovely to meet you."

"Jan Terrance. Pleasure is all mine. I was so excited when I saw you signed up for the retreat. I'm sure the other writers will be as well. All you have to do is check in at the desk; they'll give you a room. In five minutes, we'll be starting the welcome event right over there." She points toward the living room area. "We'll do an icebreaker, then we'll go through the schedule and events."

"Thank you." I nod and side step to the reception's desk.

Reception is simple, and the closer I walk to the hallway with the guest rooms, the quieter it gets. Music to my ears.

Navigating the resort seems easy; the dining room and bar are immediately to the left of the living room, or what they call the den. Then, there's a conference room, or so the map tells me, and a spa on the first floor. A grand staircase decked out with garland and poinsettias leads to all the guest rooms on the second floor.

When I open the bedroom, I'm greeted with a large king bed, with what looks like the coziest down comforter. A desk rests against the wall with a window above it. I have a view of an evergreen forest.

I sigh, parking my suitcase next to the dresser. I'll settle in later tonight. This place is no doubt stunning; a picture-perfect inspiration for a romance novel. I just hope it's enough to break my six-month writer's block. I'm on a self-imposed schedule I created a few years back. One that's allowed me to support myself with just my writing.

One that has me dropping stupid money on a resort so close to home.

I open the welcome folder, specifically created for the

retreat by the resort. There's a daily schedule and an overview of the week, a menu of the curated meals for the week, and a menu we can order room service from. The Wi-Fi password has my heart aching. When service disappeared on my drive up, I was kind of excited to not have the choice between sinking to my demise or ignoring the world all together. I shove the paper to the back of the folder, noting it's there for my weekly therapy session; otherwise, I need to pretend the outside world doesn't exist. The folder also contains information and bios on all the writers. We were asked to submit the information as a way to network and make it easier for us to remember each other. I recognize a few names, but I've never read their books. The retreat didn't have any restrictions on how many books you've published, but you must self-publish.

I'd like to sink into the bed with my laptop and try to grab inspiration without depletion, but I force myself to put the silly rectangular name tag on my maroon sweater. I promised my therapist I would give it a shot.

The den is packed when I arrive, everyone seated in respective chairs or couches that frame the stone fireplace. It almost seems like the furniture was rearranged to accommodate us. A large Christmas tree is decorated with gold baubles and white lights near the front of the room. The back of the room is nearly all windows, with a cushioned bench that runs the length of the wall. I'd like to sit there, separate myself from the other people, but Jan calls my name again, motioning for me to take her seat while she stands in front of the roaring fire.

A few writers wave and smile, as if I know them. I double down on my mask, presenting best-selling author, Elijah Evergreen.

As Jan speaks, I sink into the back of the couch. I need to find a way not to attend the write-ins or conferences. Just glancing around the room, it's clear everyone's excited and desperate for every word spoken. I'm not the only one who looks like they are in their thirties, but most are upper middle-aged, and from the way it sounded in here earlier, it seemed many were friends. I'm one of five guys. It's not that I'm better than any of them. Particularly if a few lousy reviews are demolishing me. It's more that I struggle to write when I have to mask because of my ADHD, and if I am already struggling, I don't need the added reinforcement from strangers.

"Elijah." I blink, moving to the edge of the couch at attention. Everyone's eyes are on me. "Would you like to introduce yourself?"

I swallow, unlocking the file cabinet in my brain that stores my programmed response to my bio. I quickly note everyone is holding a beverage and small plate but me. There's a bar cart near the arched entryway to my left and a table of hors d'oeuvres. Silly of me to think it would be a community event to grab everything once the welcome event started instead of beforehand. If I had the foresight to grab a glass of wine, it might be easier to process the stare down.

"Hi, I'm Elijah Evergreen. I'm a full-time romance author, best known for my six-book Hemlock Lake series. I'm currently drafting a new series. I'm a Maine native, Christmas is my favorite holiday, and when I'm not writing, you can find me on Juniper Mountain snowboarding or hiking."

"Gosh, I would love to pick your brain. Hemlock Lake is so romantic," a woman around my age says. Her bright blue eyes are captivating with her dark blonde braided updo. She has a beige sweater underneath overalls. I capture her look for a best friend side character. "Are Ansel and Arlo a part of the new series? If not, I petition for at least a sequel."

My heart beats faster and I twist the ring on my pinky finger. I was foolish to think I'd be anonymous attending an event near my town.

"They are," I offer with a smile, but nothing more.

They were supposed to get a sequel this fall, but my life

flipped upside down and delayed the writing. And now, I'm not sure I believe in love.

"Your newest book, *Don't Forget to Breathe...*"

My lungs constrict as I search the group for who spoke. A middle-aged woman with curly brown hair continues to speak. "That book might be your best writing yet. The honest portrayal of a narcissistic lover. The steamy scenes that have you falling for the lover, understanding why the main character is captivated while you're also begging him to leave."

I grip my thighs to keep from twisting my ring too much; I can't have it loosen and fling off my finger. I haven't come across a reader for this book in person, aside from Jemma, my best friend. But she lived through the breakup with me. She was the only one who could offer pointers on how to make the story better from a realistic lens.

"Will we see more writing like this? It's so different from your happy ending romances."

"No." It's all I can say, unable to force a response beneath my metaphorical mask as I weigh the pros and cons of flight or fight.

I don't miss the awkward silence, but Jan is quick on her toes, moving onto the next person, allowing me to drown in my misery.

At the end of the event, we're told dinner will be in two hours. We're free to roam the property, use the amenities, and make the place our home. The staff ensured they wanted us as comfortable as possible, and if we needed anything, to just ask. I beeline it back to my room, but I know I can't stay there. If I allow the chaos erupting in my brain to get the best of me, I'll either head home tonight or I'll be locked in this room the rest of the trip. All I know is I want everyone else to get settled before I explore on my own. The two women from earlier cemented my need to not be involved in the writing sessions. I don't want input or feedback. I just want to break the damn writing curse and get back to my life. The biggest draw to a retreat was taking away my mental load of planning meals and cleaning. Its discounted all-inclusive package should free up more space to create.

I open my phone app, scrolling through my notes to find my list of things that help calm me. My mind is minorly disrupted at the moment, so I zero in on a latte. It's a low energy activity. All I have to do is walk past four guest rooms down the twenty-step staircase, take a right, and then an immediate left through the dining room door. I don't know what the interior looks like. But I convince myself there will be coffee. One, it's a writer's retreat—we need it like an IV drip—and two, making ourselves comfortable would mean consuming food and beverages when we need and not just at the designated times.

I'm in the dining room without remembering how I got here, staring at a long table decked out in a white tablecloth. Our welcome dinner will be community style, and that makes me want to fake an illness. The volume of chatter, utensils, and scraping of plates can be overwhelming. I'm hoping it's just for tonight, as two- and four-person tables exist around the dining room.

"Sir, dinner is not for a couple hours," a young man, maybe right out of high school, tells me as he folds a napkin without looking.

"I know, I uh—" I grip the strap of my laptop case across my body. Maybe we are supposed to use room service when there is not a scheduled mealtime. But the view from the dining room overlooks the ski slopes and a portion of my mind relaxes at the sight. A coffee and writing right beside the window could be enough to get me through the rest of the night.

"Jeremiah, I need you to—"

My head swings to the right, taking in a bar countertop, an

espresso machine, and a breathtaking man in an apron. A swing door closes behind him, presumably leading to the kitchen.

"Hello, you must be a writing guest," he greets me, walking the length of the counter and coming around it.

"I was just telling him it isn't dinner time yet," the young man confirms, and it makes me want to slink back to my room.

"I don't want to be an interruption," I mumble.

The guy with the apron smiles with a soft chuckle, his hazel eyes crinkle. "Nonsense. We want you to make yourself at home. Are you here for a snack or beverage? Dinner will be in two hours, but we have food available all day."

I catch the young man's shoulders sinking a little, but the other man's gaze is too intense to question whether he is upset with me.

"Jere, once you're done with the table, please grab the place cards, and then I need you to help Susie with the appetizer."

Jeremiah grins, his demeanor shifting entirely. "Like her sous chef?"

"Like both of my sous chefs." The man winks, and Jeremiah looks like he wants to run off to not miss a single moment of cooking. "*After* the table. She isn't starting without you."

Suddenly, the man's gaze is back on me and I note the slight pocket of relief I feel. *Chef Austin* is embroidered on his thick, brown strapped denim apron. I imprint his hazel eyes, easy smile, and authoritative kindness in my mind, storing it in my character profiles.

"I'm Austin, the chef here. And you are?"

"Elijah." I smile small, one that isn't entirely weighed down in falseness. If I have to interact with anyone, it feels safer to have a non-writer in my presence.

Austin's smile grows. "How may I help you?"

"May I get a latte if I'm not too much of an inconvenience?"

"Of course, let me know how you like it, and you can make yourself comfortable at one of the empty tables, or you're welcome to take the mug with you."

I glance back out the window to remind myself why I think this dining room might help. Maybe I can start with a brain dump of snowboarding memories, and it could turn into a novel once I access my dopamine.

"Come here." I follow his footsteps as he walks toward the window to a two-person table on the far left of the dining hall, up against a column. "Best seat in the house." He pulls a chair out for me, and I awkwardly sit. "You've got the peak of the ski resort, and there's a frozen pond."

It's a small pond compared to the other one I walked past earlier. The sun is setting, so I won't have much longer with the view, but this should be good for now. Just need a ruse to fool my mind.

"Thank you." I don't miss the way his eyes circle my face and I will my heated cheeks to remain neutral in color. "May I have an oat milk latte with a dash of hot chocolate?"

"Coming right up."

I set up my laptop as he walks away. With a blank document open, I think of Jemma as I gaze at the ski paths. When I left my ex, I couldn't speak. Even though she was part of the reason I had the courage to leave, I couldn't explain to her what went down at first. Jemma has a history with a manipulative asshole too, so she was the one person who could understand, but I still needed time to process. So instead of questioning me, she took me snowboarding until I was ready to talk. When I wasn't ready to talk, I wrote it all down.

And now, that power of mine has vanished. Like he stole that piece of me as well.

A mug sets in front of me, and I glance up at Austin's friendly face. "Here's to your inspiration. Don't hesitate if you'd like anything else." He turns after flashing a bright smile, and as I take a sip of the latte, I note a dash of cinnamon added. A phenomenal touch.

Chapter Two
Elijah

In order to convince myself to book the retreat, I made the promise that I didn't have to attend any events unless it involved my meals for the day. What I hadn't anticipated was the probability of being cornered to not only attend an event, but speak at one. I never prepared a dialogue to get myself out of it.

At breakfast, Jan asks me if I want to speak about character development to a few of the newbie writers before a write-in session.

The worst part of me wants to know whether I'll be compensated, since this is a spur of the moment request. My assistant has tried convincing me to teach writing classes, as a little extra income. Problem is, I have zero interest in standing in front of a room where all eyes are on me. I'd rather be behind my screen with the ability to shut off the devices when they scream negativity. And even that I can't do well.

The best part of me knows I should do it. I started out wanting to consume anything I could from authors I admired. And well, I've always wanted to get to where I am. A place where people are passionate about my writing and want to learn from me. I'm making it, and I can't take advantage of that. I just wish I could curate the questions about my writing to stay within my Hemlock Lake series.

I'm not an awful person. Just a socially anxious one.

My people pleasing always kicks in, though; which is how I find myself in the conference room. It isn't your typical white-washed boardroom, which is a relief. That doesn't give off romantic vibes. Rather, it's the same stained chestnut walls with garland and white lights hanging from corner to corner. There are rolling chairs positioned around a rectangular table, and a whiteboard, but similar to the den, there's another window bench, showcasing the frozen pond I could see from the dining room. Bonus, there are deer.

When I agreed, I searched through my memory of the guest list, trying to remember who said they were just starting out. I could only think of three guests. It eased my anxiety enough to step foot through the door. I could talk to three people. But I should have expected more than half of the group to show up since they all seemed to love being around one another.

Everyone is mingling when I arrive, laughter coming easily to them. It pushes me further into my mind. I wish I could reach for my phone, send a quick message to Jemma, and ask her for advice. She's good at regulating me. If she were here, she'd tell me to find a reward for myself. This is a temporary inconvenience and it might help inspire me. But what can I reward myself with once I complete the task?

Austin's smile comes to mind. I'm quick to push away my sinking thoughts; instead, I zero in on the latte in my head. Finish this task, grab a latte, and free write.

I can do that.

"Could you explain your process of how to create villains in a likable way?" Jan asks.

She's been prompting me with generic questions for the past twenty minutes, some dipping into how to keep characters consistent in a series. I'm grateful for the structure instead of free balling it.

I inhale soft, deep breaths to break up the cluster of anxiety in my chest.

"From the outset, we should hate the narcissist in your latest novel. He's abusive, yet the sex scenes have your readers, me included, fawning over him. It's a dynamic that's difficult to achieve in writing, especially in today's world. It could be beneficial for our writers here to learn more about that process."

My vision blurs momentarily, and I sit at the head of the table, allowing the anxiety to course through my bouncing leg. The last thing I need to do is pace. What is it with these people's interest in this novel? Why couldn't they join the other reviewers who say it's trash?

I don't have a technique for writing the complicated human brain. My brain is complicated, and I write.

"What are you going to do? Cry to your mom and dad? Newsflash, they love me."

I rid the memory from my mind. James, my ex, was right. I have confirmation in person that people fall head over heels with a narcissist, even when the evidence is cut and dry.

"I think," I start, swallowing the phlegm building in my throat, "it's important to recognize we're all human and have flaws. There's always a reason for something. So with empathy, if we can understand how a person operates and what they might have gone through, it's easier to create a forgivable character. Connection is important. Find a redeemable quality and focus on that."

I push myself to stand, pressing hard onto the table to

avoid showing my shaking hands. "If you'll excuse me, I just had a thought for a scene I've been struggling with. Best of luck with your writing."

I grab my laptop bag and dash out of the room. It's one of my favorite tricks; no one ever wants to squash my inspiration. Seven times out of ten, I use it to just get out of a social situation.

I make it to the dining hall door before I grip the handle to balance my lightheaded form.

What the fuck did I just say? That James is forgivable for his actions? If we can understand his abuse, that makes it okay? The thoughts make me queasy. That wasn't what I meant.

It isn't forgivable what he put me through.

Leaning my head against one of the French doors, I inhale for five, wait, then I exhale for five. I repeat the process a few times until I'm suddenly falling. Darting my eyes open, hands grab my shoulders, steadying me upright.

"I'm so sorry!" I recognize Austin's face before his voice. Once I'm balanced, he creates distance between us, but worry is etched across his features. "I didn't realize anyone was there. Are you okay?"

My well-being is a layered question. Even more complicated is why are the passageways in my lungs expanding?

"I'm good. Just uh, lightheaded. Needed to lean against the door for a moment."

His eyes search my face before he gestures me into the room. "Have a seat wherever you'd like. Let me get you something."

The dining hall is empty except for the two of us. I settle into the seat from the night before, but this time, I watch Austin behind the counter. He's making me coffee, and something is going into a small oven they have out for us to see. While a hot meal is served every morning, they also have a fully stocked pastry case.

He moves with ease; this is his territory. When he turns, he has a plate and a mug in his hand. A smile lights up his face as our eyes connect. I want to be embarrassed. Shy away from his glance, but his poise is captivating. The scent of the savory croissant hits me first, then the plate and latte are set down.

"I don't know if you eat meat, so I warmed a spinach and cheese croissant, but this should help fill you up. And then the latte can help with your blood sugar." My stomach growls, thankfully internally, as the steam enters my nostrils.

"Thank you. This smells amazing." I sip the latte first, closing my eyes as my favorite beverage coats my throat. "You remembered." *Even the cinnamon.*

"My specialty." He grins, then hovers awkwardly for a moment.

I should bring this up to my room. He likely has a break at some point and doesn't need to feel obligated to wait on me. But the draw to the view has me wanting to try to write again. Maybe today will be the day I put words down.

"I have to go do something, but the dining hall doors will remain open, so feel free to sit here for however long you want."

"Thank you," I say softly, pushing away the unreasonable thought of wishing he might sit down next to me.

"My pleasure." He squeezes my shoulder, lighting my skin on fire, before walking toward the French doors.

I follow his movements, and he pauses at the door, glancing back with a smile. Then, he disappears.

Before diving into the croissant, I pull out my laptop, opening to the damn blank screen, and freewrite the sensation his hand left on my shoulder.

Chapter Three
Austin

Elijah. I love the way his name sounds from my lips, even if I haven't addressed him by his name yet. He is consuming my mind, and I don't even know why. Maybe it's because he's different. The other writers are eager to participate, ready to make connections, traveling in packs. And Elijah, he seems to want silence, avoiding group interactions where he can, as if he didn't actively choose to purchase this retreat. Maybe it's because he chose my dining room as a safety zone. I remind myself it has nothing to do with me, but hey, a whole resort and he's in the dining room more often than not? Maybe it's just plain and simple: it's been too long since I've been attracted to someone.

Whatever the reason is, it distracts me. We're both out of our elements now. The writing retreat has an event called *Create Your Own Cocktail.* Our bartenders create a specialty cocktail for a writer's main character. They'll get the recipe and the drink to have for the night. It's apparently been a big hit; my sous chef Susie couldn't stop talking about it earlier. She writes the recipes while the bartender establishes the concoction. I was asked to join tonight to help write recipes, as there are two bartenders this year. The retreat is maxed out, and it would take too long for one bartender to go through thirty people.

Our bar is attached to the dining room, but a separate room. There are a few tables and chairs, a couple couches that face one television. It's off by request, but usually the channel can be chosen by the guest. The board game collection is the least immaculate thing about this resort. They are board games donated by the staff, which are in used condition. None are destroyed, as the owners have class, but while popular, they don't fit the design.

As the writers wait their turn, most are invested in games with one another, relaxing into the night. Elijah, on the other hand, has joined the event, but his laptop is still with him and the crease between his eyes has deepened. His dark hair has been hand combed enough, so the longer hair on the top of his head remains positioned to the right. As if on cue, he tugs at his hair before rubbing his hands over his eyes with a sigh. He has a glass of wine, which he must have grabbed prior to the event starting, but it's barely been touched. He's been watching the group. Honing in on a person, typing a few words, then moving onto someone new. I want to distract him, get him outside of his mind, but I can't decide whether that's imposing. I don't want to spook him.

The event continues, distracting me, as it's easy to fall into the comradery of the group. The guests are loving the bartenders' recommendations, some already established cocktails, others brand new, or at least, to my knowledge.

The volume heightens as drinks are consumed, and by the tail end of the event, a middle-aged woman comes back up, even though her cocktail has already been made.

"Hi! Would I be able to describe a character for Elijah?" she asks the bartender, still drinking her drink.

I glance past her, noting Elijah's still here. His bearded

chin rests in the palm of his hand and he's staring down at his laptop. More than half his wine is gone now.

The bartender agrees without a thought. They don't care what cocktails are created and for whom. They just have a job to keep the guests happy, within reason.

"Okay, so the character is this sexy, dominating man. He's the center of any room he's in. A narcissist for sure, but where he lacks, he makes up for in the bedroom. He's exhilaratingly devastating, yet he keeps you coming back for more."

The bartender grins, immediately naming ingredients and pour amounts, keeping me focused on the recipe card. "This is the Sazerac Cocktail. A spin off the old fashioned with a kick because of the absinthe."

If heart eyes were real, this woman would have them. She's about to take the beverage, but I reach out my hand, clasping the glass.

"Would you mind if I deliver it?" I ask. I don't know what I'm doing. He didn't ask for this, and I shouldn't interrupt, but I need to be closer to him.

The woman pauses a moment, glancing between me and Elijah, her lips upturning as she contemplates. "Be my guest."

I walk away so she can't change her mind. Before I reach him, I turn back and catch her watching us. I shake off the view, focusing on my goal. Get Elijah to smile.

"Hi, there."

He doesn't stir until I'm sitting across from him, sliding the beverage over. That's when I notice the earphones.

"Oh, I'm sorry," I say, even though he likely can't hear me. I'm about to stand up when his eyes lock onto mine and he smiles. It's a soft smile, but enough to awaken the butterflies.

His hand touches his right ear, pulling one earphone out. I don't miss the slight wince as he does so. "Noise reducing earphones," he says, then replaces it. "I can hear you just fine. I'm just sensitive to noise, and well—" He gestures to the writers who are now a bit more relaxed. Some are competing in board games while others are just talking . . . excitedly.

I glance around the room, just as a person stands up and cheers. They've had a couple of their character's cocktail. "Why are you still here, then?"

"People watching." He looks at the drink next to him. "This is?"

"The Sazerac Cocktail." I place the ingredient card on the table and slide it toward him. "A woman made it about a character of yours. Some narcissist."

His face twists as he reads the card. He glances at the beverage before scanning the room. He then lifts the beverage, sniffs it, frowns, and places it back on the napkin provided.

"Want it?" he offers.

I shake my head. I try to avoid hard liquor. I'll have a mixed drink now and then, but no dark liquor, and I definitely stay away from absinthe.

He ignores the drink, picking up the last of his wine and finishing it. "Do you, um, have your phone on you?"

I blink at the question; confused by my luck. We've barely spoken, and he wants my number?

"My assistant will kill me once she hears a cocktail was created for my character and she doesn't have a picture to promote."

My interest has been piqued. Has he made a career out of his passion? He has an assistant, and another writer knows his work? Some writers described their characters as "I believe they are like this" whereas this writer could describe Elijah's character so definitively.

"I don't. I keep it in my room when I'm working."

He nods, but he's distracted, glancing over at a table where the woman is, as if he knows it was her who asked. And maybe he does; he was watching everyone.

He stands, grabbing the drink and the card, and walks

toward her table. Her eyes light up, and she asks a question that has him shaking his head. After a bit more prompting on her end, she playfully rolls her eyes. She brings the drink and card to the bar, then snaps a few photos, likely capturing the liquor bottles in the background. Once she's satisfied, she takes a sip of the beverage, grinning after she swallows. When she finishes tapping away on her phone, Elijah comes back to his table.

"What did she ask you that you didn't want to do?"

He sighs, closing his laptop. A rush of adrenaline courses through me. Could it be that he wants to hang out?

"She wanted me in the photo, but I like to keep my personal life and business separate."

"Don't writers often pull from personal experiences, though?"

His face flushes, and not in a good way. I want to reach out and comfort whatever is happening in his mind. He's left me momentarily as he zones in on the laptop.

"All the more reason to not let the readers know what's personal." He then stands, grabbing his laptop and empty wine glass. "I need to head to bed. Goodnight, Austin."

It's my turn to sigh as I watch him walk into the hallway. I should have kept the conversation to small talk, like what his favorite winter activities are. Simple, non-issue questions.

A quick glance at the clock tells me I need to head to bed, too. It's nearing ten, and I usually like to be in the kitchen around five in the morning.

After a quick shower, I grab my phone, intending to check my work email and learn more about Elijah. The staff received an email with the bios and links to all authors attending the retreat. Mainly, it was there to provide good customer service and was helpful for our avid readers. But as I fall onto my bed and click on the screen, my reality comes crashing back down.

Day one of my mother's daily text messages until Christmas Eve. A reminder of what I owe her. I respond with a simple, "okay." Enough to get her off my back momentarily. My bank account has what she's asking for. Another perk of this job. But it'll sink me nearly back to zero.

Liza, my best friend, sent a "you've got this" text message shortly after my mother's came through. As if she set an alarm to remind her of this routine. She probably has. It's all goddamn clockwork. Four times a year, my mother counts down the days until my payments are due. Liza's inspirational words are referring to me staying strong about not paying my mother this Christmas. Each quarter, Liza's increasingly more vocal about how I need to stand up for myself. So much so, it's created a barrier between us. Despite her hating my mother, she isn't prioritizing space in her home this Christmas for me, because *she* can't stand up to her own family, even though her home *is* my home when I'm not working.

It's an issue we've never run into before. Up until this job at the resort, I've had an apartment, worked overtime, paid my mother quarterly, and then worked myself to burnout throughout the holiday season. My mother always wants me to move back to my hometown, or at least stay and visit. Working throughout the season gave me a valid excuse to pay and run. Now, I have no crutch. With eight days off around Christmas, 192 free hours, there is no way I'll be able to lie to my mother. And I cannot, under any circumstances, stay with her. But I also can't stay with Liza, because she and her husband host Christmas for both sides of their family. They have for years. They'll be packed like sardines in their home, so there isn't even a corner for me to crash in.

My phone buzzes. Liza sends over a link to the best all-inclusive resorts for Christmas.

> I'll treat you to any one of these if you
> promise not to give in to your mother.

I power off my phone with a sigh. I don't have the energy to fight a losing battle. Liza won't ever understand. She couldn't. I have to give money to my mom. There is no other option. I can't run away from my problems. All I need is a stable, distracting base—an obligation to return to—surrounding the moments of weakness.

Chapter Four

Elijah

The subdued chatter combines with the screeching of chairs. The sound is deafening, an obnoxious reminder I left my earphones in my room. Breakfast has come and gone, and my cursor still haunts me. I *have* written a great description of how Austin's hand on my shoulder felt the first night. And I've written half-assed character descriptions of the writers last night.

But try as I might, I cannot form a story. I don't like to outline my books. I feel it stifles my creativity. So, naturally, I can't even write based on what past me wanted to do for the new series. I *know* how it should go, but the plot points have vanished.

Today's day three of the writer's retreat and I haven't experienced the workshops nor any write-ins since they asked me on a whim to host a class. Instead, I've remained a recluse; something my therapist is sure to ask about this week during our virtual session. I have deemed this location overlooking the ski slopes in the dining room my spot, though.

The thing is, I never intended to attend a lot of the workshops, if any of them. I can't distract myself with them when words aren't being written. But when Jan pressured me unexpectedly to host a class the first full day, I felt less of an obligation to people please. If I'm taken out of my comfort zone, it's hard for me to maintain my mask of a neurotypical human. And when I'm feeling less than confident, continuing the false barrier is more exhausting.

My writing well has been dry for months, and it was only made worse when *Don't Forget to Breathe* came out two months ago. The topic is drastically different from my sweet, sometimes spicy, small town romances. This novel handles serious life matters, explicit sex scenes, and is nearly verbatim factual. I wrote it to heal, and because I'm still trying to make a living with writing, I couldn't let the words go to waste. I had to publish it. In retrospect, a pen name might have been the best move.

A pen name would have kept writers at this retreat from talking to me about the book. So casually speaking of being attracted to an abusive narcissist. I know it means I wrote the book well, showing the spell I was entranced by, but now separated from the relationship, seeing the support makes me want to puke, then scream, before falling back into the worst part of myself.

My assistant has been great at filtering traction about the book. Only four people know this book is based on a true story. My assistant, so she can filter the negativity, Jemma and her fiancé, and my therapist. I didn't anticipate anyone knowing my name here. Maybe I was naïve.

Despite my assistant being amazing, I have little self control sometimes. And while I had been struggling with writing, the lousy reviews I came across on my latest novel is more of the reason I'm here. I barely read reviews. After a bad review over a silly marketing mistake for my debut novel, I made a pact that I'd write for me and no one else. But in my lowest moments, my fingers have a mind of their own, and suddenly I'm scrolling through one star reviews. Usually, they are ridiculous and I can roll my eyes. But when someone points out how naïve the main character is? How dumb they must be to not see the signs? How *weak* and *pathetic* the character is? Those eat at my core. Because I ask myself those questions every single day. How was I so pathetic and weak?

A steaming latte comes into view, placed beside my laptop, startling me out of my thoughts. Austin's hand unlocks from the mug handle and he takes a seat in the chair next to me. His warm generosity has formed a character in my head, and I wish it would stick. I need a nice character to write.

"Are you doing okay?" His voice is gentle, starting off as a whisper to full volume, as if he doesn't want to disrupt me, even if his actions already have. "The rest of the writers have already left for their activities."

"I'm not here for the activities," I say, reaching for the mug and taking a sip.

He's been consistent with making a latte that compares to Isabella's Coffee in the village of Lake Juniper. I don't need a second cup before any words are written—I try to use it as my reward—but I'm off-kilter here, and caffeine is a coping mechanism.

Austin's slightly more green hazel eyes are taking me in; my entire setup. I'm curious how he perceives me. How I compare to the other writers here. I didn't book this retreat just because my therapist recommended me to. I truly hoped a change of scenery would help. So I booked it to be away from home, in a new space, with this vast mountainous view from the dining room that is perfect. My eyes shift to the grand window. At the height of the resort, the ski paths are distinct down the mountains, but we are far enough away that the people look like ants. Minimal distraction. It feels like it's just us and the mountains for miles.

From my home, I'm at the base of this mountain, and have

the snow-coated trees as a view from my office window. But there is something incredible and empowering being near the peak. As if time momentarily stops while here, and being strong on my "no Wi-Fi" rule, time has slowed.

"I'm not a writer, so I might not understand, but is there a purpose in booking this place without partaking in what you're paying for?"

I focus on him again, trying to rephrase his question in my mind in a way that maybe isn't him judging me. My therapist tells me I tend to feel judged by others, but only because they are my insecurities. Case in point, just because I had the money to do this retreat, it doesn't mean I should have wasted said money. I could have sat in my home having a pity party for free, instead of $350 a night.

"I'm paying for the silence," I say, narrowing in on my mocking word document.

"Noted." I catch his shoulders falling out of my peripherals. "Sorry for intruding."

While his entrance was gentle, the chair screeches as he pushes back to remove himself from the table. I watch as he retreats, picking up the remainder of the empty dishes from the surrounding tables.

I sigh, leaning back against the wooden chair. My words weren't intended to be rude, despite consciously knowing they were. I just . . . I don't do well with unscheduled interruptions. I barely know him. Yes, we had the smallest of insignificant small talk last night, where wine coursed through my veins, softening my edge. And thankfully so, because being presented with the beverage designed after my ex wouldn't have been good sober. But what have I possibly showcased to this chef that he'd want to get to know me? The loner pathetic writer with a blank screen.

He wants more than just to be nice. Being nice would have been placing the coffee next to me and walking away. No, his intentions were to have a conversation. Get a connection. I write about it all the time. Despite knowing how these situations go, the circuits in my brain can't form a sentence to retract or clarify my statement before he's back behind the coffee counter. He never even glances back.

And that's one of the reasons I don't know how to meet someone or participate in groups. Reading social cues, accepting people into my space when I don't anticipate it; none are strengths, but writing used to be mine. Me, the words, and my characters. They provided me stability and zero judgment.

Now I'm not so sure what they provide.

The clattering of dishes and muffled voices snap me out of a trance. My eyes water as I blink for the first time in a while—I don't even know how long ago I zeroed in on a specific tree outside in the middle of the window.

I rub my eyes before massaging my face and letting out a deep sigh. My document is still blank. I swipe my mouse up on the screen, checking the time. I've been sitting here for nearly six hours. *What a goddamn waste of money, Elijah.*

"Hey Elijah!" a loud, enthusiastic voice greets me from my right.

I have no choice but to turn and offer a smile. As I twist, I stretch my shoulders, releasing a few cracks from my position.

Kim, the woman who created a drink for my narcissist, is coming toward me. She's holding a bowl of food that I have to admit smells delicious.

"Hi." I force a smile.

"I just wanted to say that I'm a big fan of your work. I'm dying to find out what happens between Ansel and Arlo. I mean, they have to get together, right?" Kim glances at my screen once she pauses, and I immediately shut my laptop to avoid her judgment. I'm confident I am the only one without any words written.

"Thank you."

I released a novella of their story last January, nearly a year to date. I had planned to release their sequel in July, and then a holiday romance with them or spin-off characters. Instead, I broke up with my ex and couldn't seem to write sweet romances; love isn't sweet *or* romantic. Every day, I have countless messages of people asking when a sequel is coming. I had been so proud of the cliffhanger I wrote, confident for a moment in time that I'd be able to follow through. Now I'm overwhelmed by the pressure.

"Sequel information is top secret, but I'm glad you like the novella," I tell her.

I wish her compliment weighed the same as any negative review. My glorious mind has a fun way of adding extra stress to each person who loves Ansel and Arlo. Another reminder of how I'm failing my fans. My therapist says my fans are just eager and excited; it shows I'm doing my job right, that they aren't reading a book and forgetting about me. But I'm fearful the damage has been done. This could be the end of my career.

"Excuse me for interrupting." Austin's confident voice sends a shiver down my spine. He isn't afraid to take up space; I always wondered what that might be like. He comes into view with two steaming hot bowls. "Elijah and I have a meeting scheduled." He places one of the bowls in front of me and one to my left.

Kim glances between the two of us. *I'm just as confused, woman.*

"Are you taking meetings?" Kim asks suddenly, a smile growing on her face. "I'd love to pick your brain. You're the most successful one here, aside from our host."

My failed knight and shining armor scrunches his face

with a wince. A slight twinge in my stomach has me shifting in my seat.

"I am not. He's making up an excuse to have lunch with me." I sneak a glance over at him, and a smile forms on his lips.

"Guilty as charged." Austin's cheeks warm as he lifts his hands.

Kim's smile grows, and she winks toward Austin. *The hell?* "I'll see you two around." She rushes off to a packed table and starts talking animatedly to the group.

"Sorry," Austin's voice starts, and I shift toward him. He's sitting beside me, like he was this morning. Just now, he decided he can interrupt my silence. "I might be overstepping, but I think you need a break and I'm going to demand you take one."

I swallow, slightly uncomfortable with the rush of warmth spreading through me at his gaze. He's asking me to challenge it, dismiss him like earlier, but I hate making decisions. When the choices are made for me, it's hard to say no, and I hate how attracted I am to that.

He's portraying a quintessential love interest, but in real life. He has to have a flaw because perfection only exists in novels.

"Thank you," I say softly. I place my laptop in my backpack on the floor before pulling the bowl toward me. It smells phenomenal. It looks like ratatouille. And if it is, he can have all my time.

"Also, I'm biased and I want you to taste this."

I'd rather taste something else.

Oh my god, brain. You don't even know this man.

I study the food to avoid making eye contact.

"But if you hate it, that's cool, too." He laughs awkwardly.

I'm ruining everything.

A gentleman brought me lunch, to make sure I was well-nourished, and I'm struggling to look at him. I can't remember the last time a man did something for me *just because.*

"Or, I could leave you alone . . . I just figured since it wasn't exactly silent at the moment that maybe you'd like a break, but that's presumptuous and you don't even know me. I'm sorry."

The damn chair screeches back again, but this time, despite my racing heart and flooded ears, I have enough courage to reach out and grab his hand. It's warm and soft, making me want to caress the top with my palm, but I hold back my impulsive thoughts and force myself to make eye contact. My insecurities must be oozing off onto him, erasing his confidence, and I can't have that.

Those hazel eyes of his seem to hold so much patience.

"Please stay . . . if you want."

His body relaxes and he offers me a small smile, turning his hand within my grasp to shake it properly. "Let's start over. I'm Austin, the head chef of Enchanted Juniper Resort."

After a shake, I let go of his hand. "I'm Elijah, and I'm, well, an author." I laugh out a breath and allow myself to sit back against the chair. I love and hate the freedom I feel with my laptop hidden.

Austin takes a seat, stirring his spoon in his bowl, and my stomach growls. Thankfully, not loud enough for him to hear, but a reminder that despite being in the dining hall all morning, I only had two lattes.

"Are you just starting out writing or are you well-seasoned?" he asks before taking a bite.

I smile to myself at the chef pun. "Well-seasoned, I suppose. Been publishing for seven years now."

"Wow, that's amazing. It's cool to see this retreat has a variety of writers. They host it every year, they said, but this is my first time working here. Have you been before?"

"No," I say.

"What inspired you to book this one?" His eagerness has me glancing over at him. He's so full of life, despite having worked all morning.

This is the pivotal moment in a novel where I'd lay my heart out to him, but that is if I'm writing a book. That isn't actually how romance goes. Right?

Instead, I change the subject because I don't do well with rejection and *what if* he agrees with the bad reviews?

"How long have you been a chef?"

His face shifts from confusion to lighting up. "Around nine years; went to culinary school for four and then have been working since. Started in a cafe as a barista until I could find a place that would take me as a sous chef, bounced around a few places and ended up here, head chef."

I nod. I don't know how to make it as a chef, but they are popular in the romance field. I could definitely learn a thing or two from him for character inspiration. "What's it like working here?"

"Love it so far. Best job I've had." He beams. "I don't know about the writing process, but how has it been going for you?" His voice sounds genuine, but I don't know how to tell the difference between customer service and friendship. Does he want to have a conversation or is he just looking for raving reviews because he's the new chef?

I shrug, starting to shrink at my failure. I'm wasting money and this is my last full week before I have to go visit family for Christmas, which usually hinders my writing. They'll feed into the reviews by reminding me I don't have a partner and I'm the only one of my siblings without a family.

Stop your moping. You have a perfectly fine person right in front of you. You can't be angry about not having a partner if you barely give anything to interactions.

To avoid answering, I take a bite of food. I have to hold back a moan. I can't allow him to see my weakness. I don't want him bribing me with food to hang out with me. But after another bite, it's like my body is regenerating. Maybe it wasn't the smartest to skip breakfast this morning.

"Have you walked around the resort at all? Taken in the sights from outside? It's quite stunning here."

I look at his bright eyes. He's holding back a smile as he glances down at my dish, but he doesn't mention it. He's about to suggest what he considers a brilliant idea. I shake my head, and that sets his body into action. He sits straight, raising his hands up in front of him, as if preparing for me to attack . . . and I guess, maybe that's fair.

"Just hear me out. Maybe you're struggling with writing because you're not allowing yourself to embrace the inspiration around you. You booked this retreat for a specific reason. And while I love having you as a guest in my dining hall"—My heart skips at "love." Has he been watching me? Or is it some cheesy line to make me feel good?—"I don't believe this table is why you booked the trip."

I stare at my food, pushing it around the bowl. My anxiety festers in my gut. This table has been an emotional support for me these past few days. It has the perfect view of the mountain, and I can sit with my back facing everyone else.

"When lunch is over, I have a break for two hours before I have to prepare dinner. I was going to use some of that time to walk to my favorite spot and relax for a bit. Would you care to join me? It's a little brisk out, but it isn't windy today like it was yesterday."

This is the moment that I'll follow him on a romantic walk through the snow, we'll laugh and nudge each other. Maybe one of us will fall in the snow and the other will try to help them up, but we'll both end up on the ground, miraculously not wet, and start kissing and making snow angels. Even if we don't know each other, every romance story knows the snow is magical.

"How about we make a deal?" he says.

I look up and his face is more subdued at his suggestion. *Had I been silent for too long?*

"You take a chance that I might be correct and come with me. You have the opportunity to ditch at any moment. If you don't enjoy yourself, I'll stop bothering you."

I'm not sure why he's chosen me to bother in the first place. Bother isn't the correct word. But out of twenty-nine other retreat members, why is he singling me out?

"And if I do enjoy myself?" I ask softly. I don't want to. I don't want to admit that I might enjoy myself. I love walks through the snow, though. I know how much fresh air and movement are good for activating my brain. I explore daily at home. So why haven't I done it here?

A smile grows on his face and he leans forward, arms resting on the table. "Then you get to tell me why you booked a retreat and aren't participating."

Chapter Five
Elijah

Austin had started with a tour around the main grounds of the resort, claiming I needed the entire experience, clearly confident in his ability to entertain me. I wouldn't ever walk away from him. I'm not rude; it's just possible I may shut down involuntarily. And I really didn't want to be honest with him.

We're the only two people outside; the sound of the snow crunching beneath our feet fills the silence. Thankfully, I had the wherewithal to pack boots. The resort is literally dropped in the middle of a forest, as if the contractors had to get the trees cut down to place a building. Sparkling snow covers the trees perfectly, some weighed down entirely, so if you touch a branch, an avalanche of snow will cover you.

We pass the snowshoeing experience, which leads into the forest, a mini sled-riding hill, and numerous fire pits scattered around the property. Really, it's the breathtaking view; everything is covered in a couple feet of packed down snow for miles. It isn't the dirty, black snow from the village streets or the slush puddles in parking lots. It's the crisp, silencing snow.

What all great Hallmark movies wish they could produce on set.

We walk past the frozen pond I've admired from the dining room; it glistens against the afternoon sun. I pause for a moment and Austin patiently stands beside me. This would be the perfect backdrop for the holiday romance I want to write, but I feel like I can't do that until the sequel of the other book is written. I pull my phone out of my pocket and take a few photos, so I can reference them once I'm home. I walk around the pond, getting an image of the log cabin resort.

"Want me to take a photo of you here?" Austin asks, and I startle, gripping my phone from falling.

I'm more taken aback by him suggesting I might want a photo of myself in a new location. Is it okay to ask? I used to always want photos of my adventures, as memory keepsakes, even if it was a new restaurant I visited. My ex was adamant about how silly it was. If I "didn't remember the experience, it wasn't worth remembering" is what he repeated until I stopped asking.

"No, thank you." I offer a small smile, hoping there weren't too many seconds between his question and my response.

"Okay, how about a photo together?" My brows furrow. There's a small part of me excited about the prospect of a photo with him. If anything, he can be an inspiration for a novel if I never see him again. "If not for you, for me? So I can say I met Elijah, the author?"

Sure, yes, photos with me as an author, not as the awkward human I am. Photos with purpose I can do. I've had my fair share of meet ups with fans. I rarely go to conventions as the crowds overwhelm me, but I have done some traveling. More so, I used to book events at bookstores when my ex had to travel for work. I always went on his business trips, and the events had given me a purpose. They usually had a good turnout, but he never knew that. I would tell him a few people came, took a chance on me, I handed him the "few bucks" I made, and he'd tell me what a waste of time the events were. Truth is, though, he had rather me there than exploring the city alone. So as long as he had been able to look up on the bookstore's website to confirm I was actually at an event, he allowed me to continue to "waste my time." I was always back in the hotel before him, too.

Austin comes in close, holding his phone out. "I brought it just in case you needed any pictures for your assistant." I swear I catch a wink, but I'm distracted by him flipping his camera so we can see ourselves. His arm wraps around my waist, and I stand straight, holding my breath. He's able to angle the camera so the pond and the trees are behind us, and he takes the photo. He drops his arm, and I'm able to breathe, but he doesn't step away. It's official; it's the first photo with a man I'm attracted to. I have exactly one selfie with my ex. My mom has a few photos that she's taken over Christmas, but I made sure he never saw those. He hated having his picture taken.

"This is perfect. Want me to send it to you?" He's grinning down at our frozen faces. I was so focused on my own thoughts that I barely noticed my smile. I seem tired, but I don't look unhappy or unpleasant. Rather exhausted by the world around me. Austin, on the other hand, has flushed cheeks and the tip of his nose is red. His lips are slightly glossy, and I look over at him, noticing he must have recently put chapstick on. My mind flashes over how fun it'd be to peck his lips, stealing a bit of his chapstick, tasting him momentarily. It's a scene I've written before but haven't experienced in years.

"May I have your number?" I blink at his question. "You know, the photo?" He tilts his phone in a gesture.

Right. Of course. The perfect sly move to have contact

with me. But I rattle off my number, anyway. Regardless of his motives, I want that photo in my possession.

We continue our walk, and Austin tells me about the resort; how it's often booked for romantic getaways. It's advertised like that on the website, one of the reasons I thought it might be a good fit for my writing. They have an entire full-service spa, breakfast, lunch, and dinner served, and seasonal activities. According to Austin, the retreat is scheduled this week because the two weeks leading to Christmas are slow in this area. They close after the retreat and reopen December 27th. He's been told leading up to New Year's Eve is packed, and the rest of the winter, they have steady business.

"I bet a lot of proposals happen here." We round a corner, and there's a hot tub oasis right outside the back of the building. It looks like there are four or five hot tubs, each with vine-covered privacy walls. String lights hang above each hot tub, as well as around the vines. They look so warm, but I'm sure even more inviting with the moonlight.

"I already have two proposals on New Year's Eve that I have to prepare meals for. It's an add-on package where the chef will create a customized 4-course meal after an intake of favorite foods. The freedom to customize dishes is one of my favorite things about this job. Other places, I was watched like a hawk. The fact that this resort trusts me to make a dish of my choice for someone's important night? I'm flattered but also wildly overwhelmed."

I love how he is so comfortable sharing information about his life. He casually speaks, as if we hadn't just met. And maybe that's how dating goes. I mean, you have to get to know the other person somehow, right?

This is not a date.

"You get the week leading up to Christmas off, right? So that'll be nice?" I manage to ask, and I hate how I minimized his stress. Yes, time off is great, it gives time to prepare for the busy season, but that doesn't get rid of it.

Our gloved hands brush as I accidentally bump into him. I didn't realize we were walking so close to one another, but I suck at walking in a straight line.

"Yes." He smiles easily. He doesn't move away, and neither do I, but I press my hand against my leg. "Once this retreat is over, I have to clean the kitchen thoroughly and then place orders for the food I will need during the week of New Year's, but I leave here on December 19th. Though most of it falls on my normal schedule, so it isn't much of an additional break."

I only lift my brow, hoping he'll take it as a sign to explain his meaning.

"I operate on a two week on, one week off basis," Austin explains. "I live here when I'm working, and then head home when I'm off."

I stop my tracks, thinking of the logistics. One, I assume he's single, which also keeps him off the market for me. It would be so hard to be with someone who was never home at the end of the night, but two—"Are you paying for rent to live somewhere for one week a month?"

"Oh, god no." He laughs. "My friend has a shed converted to a studio apartment that I rent out. She rents it out the weeks I'm away and blocks off my time off. There's been some issues where I have to stay in her home with her husband, but for the most part it's a sweet setup. I just pay the week I'm there."

The thought of it feels so unstable. Not having a place to call my own. Knowing strangers are sleeping in the bed I usually do . . . I don't mind traveling, but only because I can come back to my sanctuary at the end of the trip.

"It's definitely not for everyone, but I'm enjoying the schedule thus far."

I nod and give him a smile. He doesn't have to convince me. Everyone's life is different.

Austin leads us along a secluded path behind the resort. His chatty self silences once we become surrounded by trees. Instead, the crunch of snow and the slight pitch of the wind swirling between branches consumes us. It is peaceful here; I've been stubborn, searching for my silence in the wrong area. The trees get more congested and we have to duck around some rogue branches. We come to a small opening in the trees. There are a few boulders scattered and a wooden fence protecting the drop-off. My gaze scans the entire area; all you can see for miles are thousands of snow-capped trees. Like a winter wonderland postcard. The ski resort is to the left of us, but not visible, as is Lake Juniper village, farther down the mountain. Here, we've reached the peak and are overlooking the valleys of other mountains in this range.

If it wasn't so cold, this would be where I'd love to sit for hours on end. I breathe in, filling my lungs with the crisp winter air. It's my favorite way to clear my head. I close my eyes and breathe out until the very last breath is gone from my lungs.

Austin comes up beside me, where I've positioned myself, gripping the fence with my gloved hands. "I discovered this place in autumn, and just as you'd expect, it was gorgeous. I had never seen foliage so spectacular."

I open my eyes and gaze over at him. The sheen from his lips has disappeared; they are becoming dry with his words, but his lips are still delectable. His nose is more pink now and his eyes are glossy from the wind, but they have a happiness that didn't exist in the dining hall. A rejuvenation of sorts, and I understand that well. I won't admit it to him, but I feel more relaxed and grounded. I always am when I'm out in nature. He's truly stunning against the backdrop of winter.

"It's breathtaking," I say, darting my eyes a second too

slow to admire the view again. I catch a smile out of my periphery.

"Stay right there, looking out at the view." He steps back a bit, and I want to question why, but his phone comes out of his pocket.

I count the trees as I try to not look staged. It would be a great photo for inspiration.

"Now turn around." I do as he says, stuffing my hands in my pockets, and notice his phone is still positioned to take a photo.

"Austin, I don't need—"

"You look beautiful," he interrupts my words, and I lock eyes with him.

"W-what?"

"I said," he smiles, this time focusing on me, "you look beautiful."

My face warms and I can't help the embarrassed smile that appears. *Who is this man?*

"Perfection." He beams, bouncing back over to me. Austin shows the first photo of my back. He positioned the frame perfectly so I'm on the left-hand side, and the rest of the photo is the backdrop. Same goes for the next few. The man spammed his phone with me facing the camera. The last photo is zoomed in on me from the chest up, some trees visible in the background, but he captured my goddamn blush and smile.

I want to be angry that he tricked me, but honestly, the photo looks like I'm at peace. And maybe for a smidgen of time I am. He also photographed my shocked face when he told me I was beautiful, but god, the intensity of my gaze on him, what I've written in books . . . that gaze is fucking real.

And it makes me absolutely terrified.

"Just to be clear," Austin says softly. "You are beautiful. That wasn't a trick." He winks, then walks back toward a few boulders, brushing the snow off with his gloves.

I appreciate his reassurance. Though, it has me questioning how much of an open book I might be. I had worked so hard to close my emotions off from the rest of the world. Has therapy made me soft?

Austin sits, then taps a spot next to him, and I do as he suggests; sit on the freezing boulder. I'm not so sure I want to be out here anymore, but leaving now cuts off all communication with him, according to the plan. I don't want to stop speaking with him all together. I have enjoyed myself exactly like he said; he could be a good muse. I just need some time to recharge and process what's already transpired.

"So, tell me, what brings you to this retreat?" His words are soft, somehow making this moment feel more intimate. His body heat radiates next to me as he leans in to tap my shoulder.

"I wanted to check it out." I shrug, and I'm not lying entirely. "A romance author at a romantic retreat, couldn't ask for a better location."

"Sure, it's the perfect location. But I don't buy that as the full story."

"Why not?" I blurt. He fucking smiles, and I shove my hands into my jacket, hovering forward against a breeze filtering through.

"Because you wouldn't have spent your entire time in one location. A romance author looking for inspiration likely would have already explored these grounds. Unless—" his eyes light up and I hate how his smirk erupts butterflies in my stomach. "You're attracted to me, and I've become your inspiration."

"W-what?!" I exclaim. He catapulted me hundreds of feet from my comfort zone. Even if that was true, which it's not, what have I done that's given him the impression I might like him?

Austin laughs, shaking his head. "I'm just joking. By all

means, you're allowed to be attracted, but I don't believe that's why you're in my dining hall."

"It's dumb, that's why. Not worth the conversation." I wish my mind could think of something to switch to, but it's frozen right at this moment, my fight-or-flight out of operation.

Austin's hand rests on my back and he turns toward me, just enough to almost touch my knees. The urge to lean a millimeter closer, to absorb his strength, frightens me.

"It's not dumb," he says. "Something is keeping you from writing, and if you don't face what it is, you might go home with no progress and that might make it worse."

Well, fuck his awareness, I sigh. *I know all that, which makes it worse.*

"Did you have a bad book sale? Did something happen personally? Maybe people didn't like your last book?"

I stare out at the view, trying to keep my head level so my tears can't build up too far. This man is dangerous. My therapist and best friend are the only ones who know why I'm really here. My family and friends believe I'm doing research for a book. It's not like the excuse is wild; I have gone on location for research, but most of my books take place in my village, requiring me to walk five minutes. Not drive an hour and spend more than my mortgage on a week's trip away.

The hand on my back remains, sometimes moving up and down. It's so gentle and caring, and there must be a catch. There's a pit of worry in my stomach, but instead of asking him what he wants from me, I sink into his touch and my knee rests against his; neither of us remove the pressure.

"I had a few bad reviews," I breathe. It sounds so pathetic when I say it out loud. But even if the reviews weren't on a personal book, my rejection sensitivity disorder would make it hard to move past the negativity, which is why I often ignore reviews.

"Okay, that's good info to work on. Are you someone with a lot of reviews or is this one of few that might be detrimental?"

Well, now I can't be honest. This latest release already has over a thousand reviews, only a hundred of those are advanced readers. There are a good share of one to two stars, always will be, but the book sits at a 4.15 star average. And while I want to say that's bad, I know it isn't. It's just the rest of my books average 4.87 and up, and I hate how I can't unread the words in my head. They fester, making me second guess being vulnerable.

"Whoa," Austin breathes beside me, and I glance over; my stomach flips as I'm suddenly transfixed on his cell phone. He has my Amazon author page open, with the ability to see all my releases and the number of reviews. "You're popular."

My face warms because I feel weird bringing attention to it when so many other authors similar to me aren't able to support themselves writing when I can, but it's more than that. I feel exposed. I hate when people read my books around me or search through my pages. I know it's on the internet and I don't give much personal information out, despite my readers begging to know more about me, but particularly in this moment, I wish I could shield him from filtering the starred reviews.

Wait, I should have privacy. The Wi-Fi tower won't reach out here.

"How do you have service? And how do you know my last name?"

"Right next to a tower." He points behind us slightly to our right, and if I squint between the trees, I can see a large cell tower. *Of course.* "All employees have a list of guest names. You agreed to it in the contract you signed. It's mainly so we can provide great customer service by already knowing your name and face, but we have a lot of readers on the staff who are excited to read books by authors they've met. I just searched my email to find yours."

Right.

"Alright, show me the damage. What book and what review is stunting you?"

I sigh, seeing the offending book at the top of the page. There is no going back now.

"*Don't Forget To Breathe*. There's a one star by Trish Jans."

"Oh, she did you dirty if you remember her name."

The thought twists in my stomach. It's more than the words on the screen.

It only takes him a moment before he's reading it, and then searching for other reviews. I try to focus on a tree out in the distance. Reminding myself of how small we are in the expanse of the universe, sometimes it helps calm my overactive mind. Other times, it reminds me how it is bullshit. Because I'm living and breathing in this moment, and I don't need to minimize how a situation feels to me. I'm allowed to feel it.

After five minutes of excruciating silence, he turns to me.

"Okay, so her review isn't great, and there are a few others that don't like the darker romance, but it's clear this book is different from a majority of your work. That doesn't mean it's bad, it just means some people only want sweeter stories. A majority of the reviews talk about how well you portrayed the main character's struggle, how real and heartbreaking it was. Maybe you caught some readers off guard, but honestly, it's on them for thinking they'd get sweet love with this book cover."

I push off the boulder and walk to the lookout again. He doesn't understand. I can get past the reviews from readers telling me it wasn't the book they expected, because yes, this book cover is black with a deep purple highlight, with two shirtless male models, one dominating the other, trying to kiss the man who lay slack in his arms. My other covers are colorful with illustrated characters. My *issue* is with the criticism from a lived experience.

"I'm sorry," he starts, his words closer with each step, "I don't know you well enough to understand how this affects you, but I'd like to." Austin's hand rests on my arm, giving it a small squeeze. I want to step away, release myself from his touch, but my body is frozen.

"Why?" I ask softly. "Why, out of everyone here, have I been singled out?" I was hoping that by attending a retreat with others, everyone else would receive more focus, and it would distract me from my mind.

"Well, if you haven't noticed, you're one of two around my age, and if my gaydar is correct, I think you might be one of the only ones who isn't entirely straight. I feel like your books now confirm that theory. It also seems you've been struggling with something and I wanted to see if I could maybe put a smile on your face."

Observant. That's a quality I haven't had in a man. My mind panics at the immediate thought. I can't . . . The last thing I need is a man.

"This review," he whispers, massaging my arm up and down, and I hate how my body sinks into his touch, "it's more than just the review. She struck an insecurity, and it's festering."

I spin toward him at his words, doing my best to keep my mouth shut, but my eyes narrow. "H-How—"

He shrugs, turning toward the lookout, dropping his hand from my arm. There's a sudden coolness and I grip the barrier in front of us for balance.

"Before this job, I had another, more prestigious gig," he explains. "I got a review from a food critic on my grandmother's recipe. It was mine and my grandmother's favorite recipe of hers. I had struggled for years to perfect it, and when I did, I got the guts to premiere it at this restaurant. While most reviews raved about it, there was one review that had me immediately taking it off the menu. I haven't made it since."

My brain immediately wants to tell him it was just one review. That their words over many don't matter. But I stop myself from being hypocritical. Apparently, it can matter.

"How long has it been?" I ask.

"Almost a year."

My eyes nearly bug out, but I try to keep my face neutral. I can't afford to not write for an entire year. I'm already going on seven months of writing and deleting and nearly throwing my laptop out the window.

"So you pulled the recipe and then also got a new job?" I ask, and he lets out a laugh.

"Yes, but the new job was in the making. I'm not advising you to pull your book and find a new career."

"No, but I suppose a new book is the same. Each new book is a new job within the same career. You're still a chef." The words fall out like I've known it all along. I've never really thought about writing like that, though.

He turns his head, locking eyes with me. "You're right." Maybe we aren't so different.

Austin's eyes twinkle, and the world around us starts to glow with the setting afternoon sun. He's incredibly handsome, even with his hat that keeps wanting to slip off his head from his unruly hair. I have the urge to touch his arm or pretend to move hair away from his face, just to touch him, see how he might react. But the review and my ex's words halt my movements, because *what if* I'm wrong?

"I'd love to try your grandma's recipe sometime," I say.

What the *fuck* am I saying? That's like giving him permission to read my book, for him to tell me it doesn't suck.

Because what if he thinks it does? The thought has me gripping the barrier so tight I'm going to lose circulation in my fingers. That feels much worse than a faceless reviewer on the internet.

Austin's face drops for a moment, and his eyes search mine, holding me captive as he glances back and forth. The seconds tick by and I hold my breath.

Fuck. Did I just ask him out?

I open my mouth to retract my statement because I can't start a new relationship. I'm too vulnerable to not be foolish again.

His lips curl up, and I shut my mouth. "Maybe. We'll have to see."

I exhale, another pocket of peace opening within me. If he can debate the thought of making his grandmother's recipe again, I can be bold.

A meal doesn't equate to a date. Just two individuals working through fears over food.

"I just need to know I can trust you. That working through the insecurity is in a safe space."

I nod, breathing in. I understand completely. I won't open up about what's bigger than the reviews before the trust is mutual too.

I capture this moment in my mind; the golden sun highlights his olive skin, defining his cheekbones, giving his eyes a greenish tint. There's a hint of a smile with the twitch of his lips. It sends a spark straight through my heart, piercing open an overwhelming desire to protect this man.

Chapter Six
Austin

Wood fired chicken, roasted asparagus, and fingerling potatoes are on the docket tonight. A meal pre-chosen by the resort, but one that might stay a permanent staple when I curate the menu. I'm psyched to have a wood fire oven at my disposal, being able to create meals more than just pizza. Though adding in some flatbread pizza options for lunch wouldn't be a bad thing.

My stomach growls as the finalized meal settles deep in my nostrils. In just a few moments, Jeremiah, Susie, and I can break to eat before we shut down the kitchen for the night.

"We're all set, Boss," Susie, my sous chef, says, nodding toward the lined plates her and Jeremiah were finishing off.

I should correct Susie, telling her she can call me Austin, as she's a few years older than me. But the sound of "boss" hasn't gotten old, and I can't imagine it will anytime soon. It adds an additional pep to my step. *I've made it.*

My eyes glance over each of the thirty plates, ensuring they have everything set accordingly. I smile to myself as I situate my apron. I really lucked out with my kitchen staff; the three of us are a great team. With a quick once over at Jeremiah, confirming he's put on a fresh apron from his oil spill earlier, he offers me a goofy thumbs up, and we're ready.

"Alright, let's go!" I say, grabbing two plates. Jeremiah and Susie grab plates too, and we file out of the kitchen.

The retreat requested that the tables be set up in one long community-style for dinners. We dispersed them for breakfast and lunch, allowing different groups to form, but the head of the retreat was adamant about finalizing the day with all the writers.

I keep my eyes focused on the people farthest from the kitchen, serving them first, but my eyes betray me; finding Elijah sitting closest to the kitchen. He's created ample space between himself and the writer to his right, his left side entirely open. If I'm not mistaken, his eyes follow my movements, adding a layer of sweat to my kitchen grim. This is my specialty and I want to impress him. I offer him a quick smile before I dash back to the kitchen for more plates.

Once everyone is served, I situate myself near the head of the table, mere inches from Elijah's body. My body absorbs his nervous energy, and I want to whisk him out of the dining hall and somewhere silent. Jeremiah and Susie stand behind me, unknowingly keeping me in check from reaching out to Elijah. I have an overwhelming urge to curl my finger around his, see if it has the same calming effect as before.

"Good evening," I announce. "Tonight we have wood fire chicken, roasted asparagus, and fingerling potatoes. There is enough for more, if anyone is interested. Susie will refill beverages, and Jeremiah will help with any accommodations to your meals. There is no event happening in the bar tonight, but it will be open until ten. As a reminder, beverages can be brought to your rooms and throughout the resort. Thank you and enjoy!"

I get a slew of thank yous before forks and knives start to scrape plates and the volume picks up. Elijah's shoulders tense immediately, his hands remaining in his lap. I lean down, squatting beside him. Susie's doing a similar action while getting a drink order, so it shouldn't look too strange to the others. His eyes instantly meet mine; they are panicked. He doesn't have his earphones in. I can't remember how often he's worn them, but the few men around him don't exactly have inside voices.

I offer my finger toward his lap. He's hesitant before a hint of a smile appears and he tentatively curls his index finger around mine.

"Anything I can get for you?" I ask, only loud enough for him to hear.

He tightens his finger before releasing and shaking his head. "I'm okay, thank you."

I wait until his hands reach for his silverware before I head back to the kitchen. I wish the kitchen had a window for the guests to see into, just so I could keep an eye on him. Instead, we have a window in our swinging door from the kitchen to the coffee bar, giving us visuals of those who come up to the bar, but not really anything else.

I have an all-consuming urge to learn his intricacies. Know his insecurities and discomforts a step before he does, to ensure he's comfortable. Dare I say I want to protect him, from maybe even himself. What a treat it would be to see the peace settle on his face once more.

I force myself to move through my tasks. I eat my dinner, taking out my notebook to jot down changes I would make to this specific recipe, then Jeremiah, Susie, and I start our end of the night checklists. And much to my dismay, I force myself not to check in on Elijah and try my hardest to rid his being from my brain. *Temporarily.* While Jeremiah and Susie tag team dishes, cleaning the countertops and packing up leftover food, I run through inventory, start organizing for breakfast, and then sanitize the kitchen to my liking once they both leave.

Despite the exhaustion nestled in my bones, my mind is invigorated. I order a cranberry and seltzer water from the resort bar, scanning the room while I wait. Elijah has a glass of wine at the table he was at last night. I convinced myself I wouldn't see him again tonight, assuming he'd be overstimulated. I could hear the conversations in the kitchen; the decibel never lowered. It's a pleasant surprise to see him typing away on his laptop.

I pick up my drink, wanting to say hi, but my feet are glued to the floor. If he's in a groove, I shouldn't interrupt and remind him of how loud the room is. Maybe he's blocked it out.

When I convince myself to leave the bar, his eyes connect with mine. He pauses his typing, lifting a hand in a hello. I wave back with a grin, and a smile slowly graces his face. Something has shifted, and excitement flutters through me. He nods toward me, then goes back to his laptop.

I allow the energy of his smile to whisk me to my bedroom. I don't remember the last time I felt intrigued about someone. Wanting to catch their eye every moment I could. It's been a while since I've dated—I've been married to my work—but I can't remember my ex of a year even giving me these butterflies. My crush started with superficial attraction; Elijah's breathtakingly handsome with groomed stubble showcasing his sharp jawline. Now, it has developed deeper with his reserved nature. He's a mystery I'm craving to solve.

I force myself to take a quick shower, rinsing away the kitchen filth before I allow myself to crawl into bed with my laptop. Logging into my work email, I search for the author PDF that'll provide me with a link to Elijah's work. I've never been huge into reading. I haven't found an author that piques my interest more than a movie or show. If I'm honest, it could be that I'm often shattered after a day's work. My energy level to relax is allowing my eyes to watch the romance play out in front of me. If I could get the words on a page to intrigue me, romance novels would likely be my favorite, as I consume any and all romance movies and TV shows.

I had told my best friend Liza when I got the resort job that I'd have more time for reading, yet I've only read new recipes. Maybe Elijah's writing will be different. I've never met an author before this retreat.

Once on his site, I admire his author photo. His hair is slightly longer, seemingly styled by his hands tangling through it. He's sitting at a picnic table in a yellow and blue flannel, during golden hour. The sun glints off a body of water behind him. His smile is captivating. Full, genuine, excited. As if he's reacting to someone behind the camera. My new goal is to unlock that smile for me. It illuminates his face, crinkling his eyes. Erupting shivers throughout my body. I want to know him. His truths; his fears; feel the way his scruff tickles my skin.

I force myself to his "books" tab, shaking my head. I can't get involved personally.

I read through all of his book blurbs. Honestly, I'm still amazed at the number of reviews each book has. He has a successful six-book series, and then two others. One being the book he's stressed about.

I purchase the ebook. Maybe if I know more about the situation, I can help. We aren't dissimilar in our insecurities.

I ignore the slight guilt I feel. Like I'm invading his privacy. But I'm not doing anything wrong. His books are public knowledge, even to the resort. The webpage tells me where my book was downloaded, so I shut off my laptop and grab my phone, ignoring the slew of text messages (more than one from my mom tonight, and about ten from Liza, likely videos for me to laugh at), and find Apple Books on my phone.

My alarm blares directly in my ear. I startle, and my phone slides into my chin. *What the fuck.*

I grab the offensive device, turning the alarm off, and squint my eyes open in the pitch-black room. Memories of Elijah's book manifest in my mind, and suddenly I'm *awake.*

Holy hell. I don't know what time I fell asleep, but once I started *Don't Forget to Breathe*, I was sucked in. I have never read a romance as intense as his. The descriptions and actions had me nearly rubbing one out last night, but I wasn't sure how I felt about orgasming to a book of an author I am trying to get to know. And I have such conflicted feelings. His writing is phenomenal, but it isn't quintessential romance. The main character is in an emotionally abusive situation and the book gets dark; I had tears in my eyes at some points, but then just as it was heartbreaking, the characters were on a level playing ground when they had sex, which made it all the more confusing to my dick.

And if I don't take care of the situation now, I'll be an irritable asshole on top of a grouch from exhaustion. I don't do well with lack of sleep. I made it to the last page, which probably means I got a twenty-minute catnap instead of any significant amount of sleep.

I groan my way up and out of bed, dragging my feet to the bathroom. I shock my body with a cold shower, prioritizing alertness to an orgasm. I'd rather pleasure myself with a memory of Elijah instead of a fictional character.

I'm grateful I'm always the first and last person in the kitchen, allowing me moments to situate myself. Even in my happy-go-lucky moods, I like having the silence to make a latte and sip it as I grab ingredients for breakfast. I find it makes me a better head chef when I'm centered in my kitchen before anyone else is present. This morning though, I'm running a few minutes behind, so I down a double espresso shot before making my normal shaken espresso with oat milk. Maybe the initial rush of caffeine can smooth my sharp edges. It's when my brain doesn't have the allotted sleep I need that my darkness seeps in, one I often easily block out with routine.

But this morning, my godforsaken homelessness over Christmas haunts my mind, and when I try to override the thoughts, my heart races with the descriptions of Elijah's book. I want the endorphins of romance, the sexual tension and love, but the manipulative abuse outshines and suddenly his abusive character has my mother's voice, demanding me to come home, to my rightful plate.

"Boss!"

Room temperature milk splashes against my neck, dripping down my shirt. I blink a few times before seeing Jeremiah and Susie staring at me with narrowed brows, and my latte spilled on the ground.

"Everything okay?" Susie asks, stepping around the liquid and taking the now-empty mug from my hand.

"Yeah." I force a smile. "Yeah, everything's great. Sorry. Didn't sleep well."

Jeremiah is mopping up the spill before I can say I'll do it myself.

"Wanna take over the coffee bar this morning and Jeremiah and I can do breakfast?"

I glance at the counters. The stainless steel island where we prepare most meals is entirely empty. Normally, I have all the ingredients out and prepped before they arrive.

I nod. "Sure. Yeah, thank you. Uh, the recipe—"

"Boss, we got this. Just because your head chef doesn't

mean you don't need a break. Go on." Susie squeezes my shoulder before walking over to the whiteboard where the menu for the writer's retreat is. Below that are a few binders with laminated recipes, just like all the other years she's worked here.

With a sigh, I excuse myself from the kitchen. First, I wipe myself up in the dining room bathroom, then I start with double checking that the prep of the pastry station and coffee bar was completed last night. The different tasks do little to distract my mind.

My mother's words are louder. Harsher. A reminder of why I left, and why I'm still chained to her. Why I can dream of the perfect romance, but I'll never experience it.

Elijah, like clockwork, shows up right as the cafe opens. Before he notices me, I dart into the kitchen, leaning against the wall, the swinging door hitting my feet. His written words take over my mind, and I shiver from head to toe. I rest my head on the wall, shutting my eyes briefly as I try to regulate my emotions. I don't even know what I'm feeling . . . about anything. The sleepless night has my skin prickling with pins and needles. The wrong word or action could send me spiraling until my mind can rest.

I reach into the muddled chaos of my mind, searching for the carefree crush I had on Elijah, before my highly sensitive being consumed a dark book, before my past haunted my morning. I need the simplicity of finding someone attractive. The rush of butterflies his fingertips cause.

I dare a glance out the window of the swinging door. Elijah's at the counter, looking around. He's the only one around. I swear I see his shoulders drop, and just the idea of him feeling alone has me swallowing the confidence to stride toward him.

"Good morning, Elijah!" I greet, trying not to smile too wide, but fail the moment he smiles back. A rush of blood travels south when his eyes connect with mine, and I settle into this feeling.

"Morning, Austin," he says before looking at the coffee menu, even though he's been routine-based. "May I get an oat milk latte—"

"With hot chocolate?" I ask, and I don't miss the way his smile flickers at the recognition before it's gone.

He nods and tucks his hands into his jean pockets. Those hands wrote every word my eyes consumed last night. To imagine those large, yet delicate hands roleplaying those scenes . . . I clear my throat and swivel to prepare his drink, walking through the basic steps of preparing espresso.

I'm grateful my back is to him, so I can breathe through my dick begging for a release I haven't given it. I'm walking a thin line here. I'm not usually behind the coffee counter, giving him his first coffee of the day. I tend to bring his second one over as an excuse to be close with him, not because it's my responsibility.

"How are you this morning? It looks like you were inspired last night." I turn back around as I speak, carrying the latte to him.

He leans slightly against the counter, grabbing the latte. The brush of his fingertips has me inhaling.

"I had character ideas last night, so hopefully the story will come."

My dick twitches, and it takes everything in me to remain neutral. Is there a pun intended in his words? Because I would very much like to read more spicy books of his. Preferably, if I can see whether he's as good in person as his words are.

"That's exciting!" I force out, trying to calm my mind.

Elijah's lips crest over the mug's edge, sipping the liquid. Foam coats his stubble; his eyes close and his Adam's apple bobs with a swallow. A shiver runs down my spine, and I grip the countertop for pressure to keep my knees from locking as his tongue licks the foam from his upper lip.

Jesus Christ, Austin. Get it together. All my brain can imagine is me coating his throat.

"G-good luck!" I squeak. "I uh, I'm needed in the kitchen."

I dash into the kitchen, leaning against the wall again, breathing in. I have three full days left with him. I can manage to do this without imagining him as a walking sex god.

"Boss, you good?" Susie's words interrupt my deep breathing.

Between her and Jeremiah, they have a great start on breakfast. This morning is a buffet style of pancakes, waffles, French toast, bacon, and scrambled eggs. Relatively simple, but from my past experiences, if I try to pretend I'm on my A-game when I'm not, I often burn or undercook something. In my previous jobs, it has never been much of an issue. I could pass my baton of sous chef to someone else in the kitchen, but as head chef, it's expected I exceed every single day. Or, at least, that's what I assume.

But today is one step closer to not having a solution for housing this Christmas break. Experiencing that with the consistent texts from my mother reminding me of her payment, and Elijah disrupting my status quo of no time for romance—the lie I tell myself—I'm not in the right frame of mind to cook. One glance at the whiteboard reminds me of the never-ending to-do list of deep cleaning tasks required to happen before we close for break. The couple of days I'm working after the retreat ends will be helpful, but I'm not good at leaving everything to the last minute. And I'm already stressed about finalizing the two proposal dinners for New Year's Eve.

"Austin?" Jeremiah questions me this time, and I stand straight, walking toward them with a smile.

"Yes, yes. Sorry. Change of plans today if it's okay with you both. I'm going to start the deep cleaning tasks we have, and you two can take care of all the meals today?"

Susie and Jeremiah glance at one another. Jeremiah's smiling face tells me how fucking excited he is about the opportunity to cook. Susie shoots me a look of concern, but with a slight nod, she looks at Jeremiah.

"Alrighty, Jere, time to show me what you're made of!"

"Yes!" Jeremiah throws a fist into the air.

"Thank you. If you need anything, I'll be here." I head into the small office off the kitchen, big enough for a desk with a computer and a few filing cabinets.

Without giving myself a chance to recoup, I grab the to-do list I wrote a couple weeks ago and scan it.

Tending to the drain gremlins is a great place to start.

Chapter Seven
Austin

My body aches and my eyes burn, begging for rest. While I checked off a few big cleaning tasks, contorting my body to complete said tasks, for hours, it wasn't one of the smartest decisions I've had. I never took a break between the breakfast and lunch shift, and Susie kicked me out of the kitchen to rest between the lunch and dinner shift, with a gentle, not-so-helpful reminder that the tasks will be there waiting.

I need to sleep. A nice two-hour rest before I become human again to get through the dinner shift. Susie and Jeremiah can cook it, but I need to show my face and present the meal.

The only thing that had kept me awake was dissecting Elijah's book. I couldn't remember the reviews off the top of my head, and I don't have many books to compare it to in terms of how well written it was, but from my opinion, the negative reviews only make sense if his fans didn't read the book description before purchasing it. And maybe that's what happened. They knew they were fans of his work and purchased on habit. Instead, they should have questioned whether it was the same author. This book cover is a stark difference from the cute illustrated series. These real models show the intensity of the story, and the book description doesn't shy away from the content. If you know what you are getting into, this book is the realest thing I've ever read.

"Hey Austin."

I catch my feet from stumbling over one another at the sound of Elijah's voice. I'm at the grand staircase leading up to the guest rooms. If I pass the staircase and head to the right, I'll go down a hallway dedicated to staff members' rooms.

He's standing at the top of the stairs with the shyest of smiles on his face. He's decked out in his snow boots and winter jacket from yesterday, and it makes me want to grab my own belongings and join him.

"Hi Elijah." I smile at him, feeling a slight energy lift.

He walks down the staircase, and I remain planted in position. I could easily walk away; he might be saying hi in passing, but I don't want a quick interaction. I want to learn more about him.

While cleaning, I kept questioning how personal Elijah's book might be. I don't know him well, or really at all, but there are many similarities between him and the main character.

Like the twist of his ring. His character did it as a stim, or so it was described, but it wasn't just a regular too-much energy stim. More so, a nervous tic. Whenever he felt anxious or scared or unsure of his environment.

Now standing in front of me, I can't help but wonder if he's nervous in my presence. If it's his natural state of being or if something about me causes him to be unsettled.

I remind myself it can't be me because the act of my curled finger around his settled him. On more than one occasion.

The main character in his novel was belittled and manipulated. Consistently told how awful of a partner they were.

How they took up space and were a *waste* of space. Yes, there were multiple heated sex scenes, but just as a manipulative partner convinces someone to stay, Elijah's sex scenes had me forgiving the abuser until his next offense.

Could it be Elijah wrote from a real experience and now the reviews feel like a direct attack?

The thought makes me want to vomit.

"Austin?" Elijah's hand brushes my arm, and I jump. "Are you okay?"

I hope the character isn't a reflection of Elijah. Not because I don't like the character, but because I feel for him, wish he was treated better. The thought that Elijah could have ever felt the insecurities of the character, or even experienced the abuse, heightens my want to protect him.

Show him what romance could be.

Before I can speak, my body reacts and pulls him into an embrace. He stumbles at the movement, but I tighten my grip when his arms consent and wrap around me. He's a few inches taller, so my head rests comfortably on his chest. I find myself inhaling as he does and exhaling, a long, slow breath, sinking into his arms. As if he choreographed the breathing.

I step back, rubbing my face, trying to right myself. My eyes burn at the movement. My body craves the connection.

"I'm sorry," I mumble. "That was unprofessional."

"Nonsense," he whispers. "Sometimes we all need a hug."

I gaze up at him; he's smiling, his eyes soft. His finger is still twisting his ring, but he seems so much more relaxed.

"I am going for a walk. Would you like to join me?"

I can't say no. He's inviting me somewhere, and he greeted me first. I'm not *just* the chef.

It doesn't matter if I barely make it through dinner on my energy level. Maybe Elijah's presence can keep me afloat.

"Yes, definitely. Let me grab my jacket."

With more of a pep in my step, I head off to my room.

With the quickest of movements, I jump in the shower, washing the grime, and spoiled milk from my latte, off of me. I'm cautious of getting my hair wet because I'm not foolish enough to walk outside with wet hair. But in record time, I'm wearing fresh clothes, my winter jacket, and boots.

I grab my phone off the nightstand before leaving my room, just in case there's another moment to capture Elijah in his natural beauty. Clicking on my phone, I swipe away numerous notifications. A harsh reminder I never responded to my mother's message, and it was followed up by a rogue message this morning. The downside of working this job is it can sometimes be overwhelming coming back to the notifications.

I shake off the overwhelm by opening my photo reel. The last twenty pictures or so are all Elijah. I breathe in, letting the anxieties fall off my shoulders, and smile once I reach the stairs again; Elijah casually leans against the railing.

I try to maintain a respectful distance between us as we walk, but no matter how far I veer in either direction, it seems our gloved fingertips keep brushing. We walk in silence, with the crunch of the snow beneath our feet. Without discussing it, we reach my favorite spot, and Elijah leads us over to the boulder to sit, as if this is his spot, and he wasn't introduced to it yesterday.

"So," I start, breaking the silence. I bump his shoulder gently; a shiver rushes all the way to my toes. "Were you able to write today?"

"Sort of," he breathes out a laugh, and I've never heard something so lovely. "You forcing me out here yesterday really helped solidify my characters. I'm still stuck on the actual writing portion, but I did create an extensive outline. I just need to remember how to coordinate words into a sentence."

"Almost feels like having a recipe in front of you, and burning the food despite following the directions."

His eyes light up at the connection, and my body warms. I can connect to his world. "Yes. I can imagine so."

"Are you working on the sequel you mentioned yesterday?" I ask.

"Not a chance." He laughs, shoving his hands into his coat pockets. I want to bottle up that laugh for my dark clouds. I swear his serotonin is rubbing off on me, and the cool breeze awakens my mind. "I *should* be. But two new characters inspired me yesterday, and I rolled with it."

Yesterday. I try to rein in my thoughts as they create a novel about me and Elijah. Those heated scenes in his book now have our faces, playing like a reel in my head. I shift on the boulder, placing my hands in my lap.

What I'd do to help him research for that book . . .

"Anything I can do to help?" I ask before I process my words.

Like take you back to my room and . . .

"I'm just so nervous about writing love on the page." His vulnerability sobers my thoughts. He's zoned out at the view in front of us. "What if it isn't realistic, or it's too corny or it's not enough?"

I have to swallow the shocked laugh that wants to tumble out. His writing is almost too realistic, but it isn't the time and place to express that I read his book last night. Feels like a sure way for him to clam up and skitter.

I straighten, ready to be serious. "How did you write love before the reviews?"

He pauses for a moment. "I always wrote the love I dreamed of, but I uh . . . I don't know if love's real."

My heart breaks. I focus my eyes out toward the trees to keep from studying him and letting him see the tears welling in my eyes. The main character's thoughts and insecurities from the book last night repeat in my mind. The only time the character was praised or shown love was leading up to sex. The partner was so fucking manipulative that the romance did start out wonderful. Sweeping the main character up, believing in this fantastical love. Then, little by little, it was stripped from them. Enough to break them, but need the partner so desperately.

Elijah doesn't need me to analyze his words and put together a puzzle he never asked for help with, but if he had a similar experience to the book, of course, that would shatter his vision of love.

Focus, Austin. Not all fiction is autobiographical.

"If you don't mind me asking, what makes you not believe anymore?"

I've had my fair share of reasons to think love is a joke, but I choose to believe true love exists, and soulmates are real. I eat up romance movies because I don't understand how it can't all be that simple. But I'm also not one to talk. I've been in love once. And even I wouldn't describe it as a life-changing love. More so, a time and place love that I've grown from to lead me to my forever love.

But I continue to believe because I have to. Because it's what keeps me going.

"Bad breakup." He shrugs nonchalantly, gazing out at the view, but his tone is neutral, as if he's said that as an excuse a thousand times before.

"How long has it been?" I ask softly.

"Eleven months." His foot taps in the snow, melting the first layer beneath his boot. Rubbing his hands on his thighs, he gives me a false smile. "Are you doing okay today?"

My heart skips, in the worst way; I've lost him.

"I'm doing okay," I say, swallowing my doubts. If I want to connect with him, I can't hide in my head. "Actually, I wasn't, but being here with you, I'm feeling a little better."

His smile is genuine this time, but his eyes shift back to the view as his body leans toward me ever-so-slightly, brushing my shoulder. I take a chance to loop my arm through his, placing my hand in my pocket afterward, mimicking him. He lowers his arm, providing slight pressure onto mine before he exhales and his body sinks.

I inhale; closing my eyes to stop the tears. The touch overwhelms my senses. I hate how desperately I want to be wrapped in someone's arms. Want to wrap someone in *my* arms. The need to dive into a relationship and treat someone like the romances I watch is strong. But my breakup nearly three years ago reminds me I can't have that. My mother hinders anything serious. And while one-night stands are great in the moment, they leave me hollow in the morning.

He squeezes our arms briefly. A reminder he's here. I open my eyes, but he isn't looking at me. This feels comfortable in the most agonizing love-sick way. I want to woo him. I want to show him my moves; if only to show him love can exist, even if it isn't with me. But he isn't a random guy I've become attracted to. I mean, he is, but I need to be patient. I'm almost certain he's the main character. It aligns with why he'd have a genre shift. Why he'd be hurt about reviews, enough so he's terrified to write. And he confirmed a bad breakup.

He deserves the world, especially if he experienced anything in his novel, and I don't want to blow that.

Make him Grandma's recipe. The thought hits me like a freight train. I can't expect him to open up to me further if I don't extend the trust. I refuse to make it for the whole staff, but maybe I could ask him to join me for a late dinner, once the other writers have excused themselves from the dining hall.

I can't do it tonight. I have to run into town for ingredients during the break between lunch and dinner, as it's my longest while the shops are open.

"Elijah?" My voice breaks the silence, and his arm squeezes mine again. My body warms, giving me the extra confidence to continue. "Would I be able to make dinner for you tomorrow night?"

He chuckles lightly, glancing over at me. "You already do."

I roll my eyes, nudging him. "I *mean*, would you be interested in having dinner with me, after the dinner shift is complete?"

"Oh." He unlocks our arms and straightens his posture.

A breeze brushes through, adding additional shivers to my rejection. I swallow the hollow feeling creeping in. "We don't have to. I just thought it might be nice."

"Sure. I mean, as long as I'm not in a writing wave. I am here to write before anything else."

Guarded. Walls up. I can respect that, but it's fear-based. I'm nearly 100% sure. The *what if* I let my guard down. Of course, he's here for writing, and that's the most important. There's always the ability to reheat the dish if he isn't able to be on time.

My phone rings as I enter my room at the end of the dinner shift. The eagerness I felt to get back to my room and download another Elijah Evergreen novel vanishes. I haven't responded to my mother's text messages, and it's nearly time for her routine one to come through.

I miss the call by the time I make it to the nightstand, and let out a breath the moment I see it's Liza instead of my mother. I almost ignore it—she'd understand—but the phone rings again.

"Hello, Ms. Impatient," I greet.

She cackles. "What can I say? I miss my best friend. Someone who used to respond to me each night, but now he's gone radio silent. Do tell me what your distraction has been."

I place her on speakerphone as I strip down to my boxers. "It's been twenty-four hours."

"Twenty-four hours and I've sent you over fifteen messages and you have multiple breaks throughout the day. So really, it's like you're ignoring me."

"Not my fault you're sending all those messages!" I retort back with a laugh as I climb into bed, situating the pillows behind my back. I sink in, pulling the comforter up over me. Her voice is exactly what I need.

"You're stalling."

"You're prying."

"Who is he?"

I freeze. I knew she'd get there; she always asks that even if there isn't anyone I'm interested in. Except this time there is.

Suddenly, she's requesting a video call. I click accept and her blurry face fills the screen until the Wi-Fi settles.

"I knew it!" she exclaims. Her long blonde hair is in a messy bun on top of her head and she's cozy on her couch with one of her favorite matching pajama sets. "All the deets. Now." Her wine sloshes in the glass as she gets comfortable for story time.

"He's a writer."

"Obv."

I roll my eyes, my face warming.

"What's his name?" She places her wine on the end table beside her.

"Elijah Evergreen."

Suddenly, she jumps off the couch. "No fucking way."

I slouch down on the bed as she paces.

"You're talking about *the* Elijah Evergreen. Romance writer living in Lake Juniper?"

"I guess so?" Truth is, his bio in the author PDF didn't say where he's from, and we haven't discussed it.

Even if I could have a relationship (I can't) this job would make it pretty complicated to have a partner. When I accepted the job, I acknowledged that and hadn't anticipated meeting anyone. Honestly, it was an upside. I'm here to increase my skill, enhance my resume, and save money on rent so my salary can make payments to the devil.

Before she sits back down, she walks over to her bookshelf. "He's incredibly talented, Austin. Actually, you should read one of his books."

She flips the camera to show me she has physical copies of his entire collection. I had no idea. Honestly, I've admired her display from afar, because it's organized beautifully, but I don't know the names of authors.

"I can lend you them! You've been wanting to get into reading and now you've met him. It might keep you interested."

"Already have."

The camera flips back and Liza's face drops at my confession. I laugh. "Which one?"

"*Don't Forget to Breathe.*"

"Jesus Christ, start off intense, why don't you. Are you able to look him in the face? That one fucked with my head."

"Definitely had trouble with whether it was okay to be turned on."

She throws her head back, laughing. "Yes, yes, I can see that. And you desperately need to get laid." Suddenly, her eyes grow wide. "Ooh! You should see what he's doing over Christmas. Have some hot holiday sex."

"Okay, bye Liza."

"What! No. I'm sorry, I'll be good."

I shake my head, laughing. "I'm off to read another book of his. Goodnight."

She grins, and I can't stop my blush. "Oh, you're smitten. I won't keep you from your new hobby." She winks, and I roll my eyes. "Night!"

Once my phone clears her call, I immediately download the first book in the Hemlock Lake series. I settle back against the pillows with rejuvenated energy.

Within the first chapter, it's obvious the person who wrote this book is not the person who wrote the last. Literally, yes, but there's a drastic difference in tone. Of course, this book came out seven years ago and is subject to being weaker, but it isn't weaker. It's incredible. Much better than most of the cheesy romance movies I consume.

The heartthrob has me yearning for love, wishing I grew up in a small town instead of the inner city I'm from. It has me swooning in a way the other book didn't. This one has sweet, romantic moments where right before they are too spicy, the chapter ends. His other book actually had me wanting to take notes of what to add to the bedroom. I want a combination of both. The sweet, real love of this book with the steaminess of the other. And maybe that's what Elijah is struggling with. How to combine both. It's possible he's not aware he can have both without emotional abuse.

The thought of abuse has me placing my phone down, pausing for a moment. If that book *is* autobiographical, if he was emotionally abused in a past relationship, it isn't him getting *over* critical reviews. It's proving to him real love does and can exist. He's deserving of it simply because he exists and *not* because of anything he does for the other person.

I click out of the phone app and place two separate curbside pickups for tomorrow; the only type of order I can do to make sure I'm back in time. One for food and one to swoon.

Chapter Eight
Elijah

"I can't do this," I say.

"You can't do this?" He scoffs as he closes the distance, hovering over me. "You think anyone else would ever look twice at you?" His hand grips my chin, rotating it left and right before laughing. "Consider yourself lucky that I do."

"You t-treat me like shit." I swallow the tears.

He corners me against the wall. "You're the piece of shit, Eli. Don't get it twisted. What you write in those stupid little books of yours is a lie. Fairy tales don't exist." He presses his pelvis against mine. He's already hard. He always is after a series of ripping me apart. "Do you want to be alone, fucking yourself for the rest of your life?"

"N-no," I whisper.

"Then shut up and remember your place. What we have is good. The best you'll ever get." His lips brush my ear. "You know how good your orgasms are with me, baby," he breathes, his hand coming between us, cupping my dick. "I promise I'll reward you later if you just shut that dirty little mouth of yours."

His lips crash onto mine, gripping my hair, and I betray myself with a moan, sinking into his touch.

I wake, drenched in sweat. It's been a while since my brain twisted memories into nightmares. Mentioning the breakup to Austin, no matter the lack of detail, must have triggered me.

I begrudgingly pick up my phone, click on my notes app, and open a note detailing what to do for nightmares. When I first left my ex James, I would get panic attacks, and to try to curb those attacks, my therapist and I created lists of what to do when my mind works against me. I have different levels, like for a minor disruption, it's grabbing a cup of coffee; how I met Austin. The major disruptions are nightmares, and I even have a catastrophic list: coming face to face with James. Thankfully, I haven't needed the latter.

Major Disruptions
(ex. nightmares)

1. Take a shower.
2. Cancel all plans (except therapy). If there is something crucial, evaluate it based on our stepped system.
3. Text Jade that you've had nightmares (even if no therapy).
4. Treat yourself to something low energy. (Check low energy list.)
5. Allow your brain to operate as it needs. Evaluate percentage. You've already accomplished 4 things today. Don't force yourself to do anything.
6. If you don't have therapy and you cannot make it through these steps, text "Nightmare 911" to Jade.

My eyes are blurry by the time I'm done reading. Despite

having healed so much over the past eleven months, moments like these feel as if I haven't progressed at all.

I can do this. I can make it through all five steps. And I have therapy soon. Easy peasy.

I work on autopilot. Forcing myself out of bed, dragging my feet against the carpet. I shock myself with a frigid shower before allowing myself the comfort of heat. I cleanse not only the sweat from my body but also some stress. I am making it through step one.

I grab my emergency comfort pajamas. Dark gray jersey knit joggers with a matching hoodie. I try to reduce when I wear these, as I have a tendency to keep them on for days. Latching onto the comfort; afraid of change.

Once dressed, I climb onto the dry part of the bed, moving the comforter so my sweat can air out.

Step two is simple. I have no plans to cancel. I haven't attended the sessions.

Step three heightens my anxiety. It makes me feel weak that I'm still not fucking over the asshole. I should be better. I should move on. I should be able to enjoy the feelings of happiness Austin's provided this week without overthinking it and falling into a terror of *what ifs* each night.

Because what if I'm a naïve piece of shit, falling for his confident ways? The way the curl of his finger calms me is the most terrifying thing. The simplest gesture has my heartbeat slowing, breath exhaling. If something so simple could flip my world, what happens if I let him in? Catastrophic blues.

I shake my body, grabbing my phone. I groan when I remember I haven't logged into the Wi-Fi. I trudge toward the desk and retrieve the information. Back in the bed's comfort, I allow my phone to load up, tapping it incessantly. I'm not prepared for the bombardment of messages when the Wi-Fi connects. Mostly from Jemma, my mom, and my assistant.

Thankfully, I silenced app notifications. There is no way I could handle those.

I ignore the messages, find Jade's thread, and shoot off a message without thinking about it. Jade knows how I am on my bad days.

Next up is treating myself to something low energy. Often, that's coffee delivered to my door, whether through a service or texting Jemma: SOS. The resort pamphlet tells me they operate through an app as well as a telephone. It's my lucky socially anxious day. I refuse to call the kitchen, because what if Austin picks up? And what if he demands to know what's wrong? It's already thirty minutes later than I've been coming in.

I follow the directions for downloading the app, place my order, and request they knock on the door and leave it outside.

When my mind gets this way, the less interaction possible, the better.

While I wait for my order, I grab my computer and charger, preparing to have therapy in bed. I need the comfort the bed wraps me in instead of the cold wooden chair at the desk.

My latte arrives a few minutes before therapy. It's in a ceramic mug with a paper lid covering the liquid. A folded note is on the tray with my name. Once back inside, I open the note, my eyes flashing to Austin's name.

My breath catches. *Of course he saw my order.*

"I hope you're in a good writing groove! Good luck!" He's drawn a heart and written his name.

Oh. Right. I could just be inspired. Not having a breakdown.

I breathe out. There's no reason for him to be concerned. I'm in the clear.

I take a few sips of coffee so I don't spill it over the edge, then bring it and the note back to my bed. The coffee has his hint of cinnamon, and I can't help but analyze the heart as I wait for my therapist to log into our session.

It could be nothing. A heart is a common way to end a message without meaning someone professing their love.

"My, my, Elijah. Is that a smile I see?"

I steady the coffee so it doesn't spill as Jade's voice comes through the laptop. Looking at the screen, she's in her usual office; wood-paneled walls with her diplomas hung up behind her. She looks stunning with her auburn hair-blown curls.

I put the note down, straightening my face. I'm not here to discuss Austin.

"Good morning, Jade."

She gives me a cheeky smirk, and my storm cloud reappears. The note was a moment of temporary peace.

Austin's presence is peace.

"Good morning, Elijah. You seem like you might be a bit at war with yourself."

My eyes flicker to her. I suppose I might be.

"I think it's time we work on getting you to forgive yourself for loving James. Not all men are James. You deserve love. You deserve happiness. You're allowed to be vulnerable and put yourself out there. And I'll be here, every step of the way."

Because my therapist is good at what she does, she weaseled Austin's name out of my mouth. Questioning the emotions and fears surrounding opening myself. We dissected the nightmares, too, which have been no different from the nightmares in the past. But forgiving myself is new. Something I don't think I've been ready to think about.

Forgiveness is terrifying because it feels like I'm allowing myself to fall into manipulation once again. I'd be tearing down my walls of protection to give over my heart.

Jade says it's all linked with my writing. Until I forgive myself, negative reviews are going to feel like a personal attack because I'm allowing myself to be shot. Because I believe the words written. I've worked through thinking I'm a worthless piece of shit. But the words about how foolish my character was. How dumb they were to stay. How it was the character's fault for finding the piece of scum. I do believe I was foolish and dumb. And while James was introduced to me through a friend of a friend, I allowed myself to fall for him and I forgave all his red flags.

I tried to write immediately after therapy. Even just a free write, but her words tangled into my thoughts, stifling the process further. Instead, I open the web browser to search for proof that I know what I am doing. I don't need to read reviews, but the year-to-date sales might cheer me up. I am successfully supporting myself through writing. *That is a fact.* I am not a bad writer.

I pause at my December sales so far. We have two and a half weeks left and I've already hit my sales goal. By triple. *What the fuck.*

I check my emails; I have one from my assistant sent early this morning.

I've had a PA for a few years now. She's responsible for my social media, ads, and setting up events. After hiring her, I would still check social media here and there, for an ego boost, but with *Don't Forget to Breathe*, I placed boundaries after I had a panic attack; the first in months after working through them. Now, I only see the big positives. My assistant knows everything. She knew everything with James before Jemma did because it was affecting my job, and essentially hers. Because of this, I trust her to filter the content I see. It's still a quick click away from a rabbit hole of negativity, but it's a start, and it's worked well so far.

The moment I click on her email, though, it's clear today

is different. Usually, her emails are straight forward. This one has caps and exclamation marks.

Fear settles in my stomach. I should click out. I'm not in the right place to handle any news, regardless of good or bad. My eye catches "viral" and I can't stop my eyes from taking in the rest of the email.

My book has gone viral.

I sit up, my hands shaking. I know what that means. My series has had its moments with viral videos. But my own fanbase is uncertain of this book content. Having it be exposed to anyone in the world? Whoever randomly comes across whatever video or post is circulating?

Fuck. Fuck. Fuck.

My heart races. A text from my assistant comes through. I haven't turned my phone off yet. I should have. She sent two texts while I was in therapy. And Jemma's sent five to her already thirty messages since I've been gone. She knows I won't answer this week; they are just her random thoughts to keep me in the loop on her life.

I need to shut off my phone, disconnect the Wi-Fi, rip the Wi-Fi password up, and leave this goddamn room. Go walk into the forest. Escape all of this. Shove my goddamn face in some snow for self-regulation.

But I'm frozen in place aside from my shaking fingertips that have me typing in Goodreads, searching for *Don't Forget to Breathe.* I can't watch the four links provided by my assistant. They are all TikToks. BookTok has been so beneficial to my novels, but when it gets exposed to other people's pages, and other platforms, the comments can be harsh. So much so, my assistant hasn't sent me a TikTok since the end of October.

My hands grip the laptop. 4.35 stars on Goodreads. My rating has gone up from 4.15 stars. *It's about fucking time.* I take a deep breath, feeling the slightest lift of my lip. Eagerly, I allow myself to scroll down to the reviews.

F this book. i'll never wrap my head around why people continue to swoon over characters who treat them like dogshit.

i'm convinced anyone who gives this 5 stars didnt read the same book. This is the most unrealistic garbage ive ever read.

why would the mc sleep with someone who treated him that bad? DNF.

I only stop reading when my vision becomes too blurry. Slamming my laptop shut, I push it underneath my sheets. Sinking further into the bed, I turn my back to the offensive hunk of metal and shut my eyes.

I should have never written it. It was advice from my therapist to write everything down, ideally releasing the emotion, but I couldn't do that in a journaling way. That felt too real at the time; I had to act it all out with my characters.

The only false things about the book are the characters' names, where they live, and what they do. Everything else is autobiographical. I didn't intend to publish it, but I had a schedule of release dates I didn't want to ruin. So after my beta team read it and praised it, I went for it. Now all I want to do is take it down and rip it to shreds. But that won't erase the words ingrained in my mind.

There's a faint knock on my door. I don't know whether it's in my nightmares. I can't seem to decipher between realities with my soaked pillow and pounding headache.

"Elijah?" A new onset of tears brim my lids at Austin's voice. "I brought you dinner."

Fuck. We had dinner plans. Romance 101 is to show up for the actual date.

Was it even a date?

Or was it pity?

"We don't have to eat together, but I got nervous when I didn't see you all day. I wanted to make sure you had something, and that you are okay."

Austin is real; his kindness exists.

Austin is just trying to get laid. He'll flip the moment he comes.

I clench my eyes shut, feeling the fresh tears coat the dried ones.

"Maintenance is going to open the door. Please yell if you don't want me to come in."

A few moments of silence pass before the door clicks open. Something delicious drifts through the air, causing my stomach to growl. The last time I ate was yesterday's dinner.

"It's my grandmother's recipe," he says, and I hear something clang onto the desk in the room.

What could I have possibly done to have him trusting me? I can't even trust myself.

I choke on a sob, cursing myself for making a noise. I partially hoped he would leave if I was silent. Instead, his footsteps round the bed.

"Oh Elijah," he breathes, kneeling in front of me. "What's wrong? Is it the reviews?"

I open my eyes, creasing my brows. I can barely focus on his face so close to my own, but how would he know about them?

"When I didn't see you all day, I had a feeling it wasn't because you were inspired, so I checked social media. I'm sure it doesn't help, but there are twice as many phenomenal reviews as there are bad ones."

I rarely see those. That was my intention earlier, but I fell down the rabbit hole. Filtering to the one and two stars, reading them over and over again.

"Do you want to talk?" he asks, and I shut my eyes again. I don't even know if words exist. "Can I get you anything?"

I need to not feel like my career is in crisis because I haven't written anything substantial in months. Everything I've tried to write hasn't been happy and loving; except for these new characters I thought of yesterday, but the story isn't there yet. It's all choppy and lacks emotion.

"May I hold you? Sometimes we just need a hug." My eyes open at his words, connecting with his glossy eyes. I had forgotten how much I craved human contact until he hugged me yesterday. Jemma gives amazing hugs, but Austin's felt different—purposeful.

I nod, and before I can figure out how to maneuver my body, he's climbing on the bed behind me. I turn, ready to sit up and more so cuddle with him, shoulder to shoulder, but he lays down, wrapping his arms around me, positioning my head against his chest.

Another wave of tears ripple through my body. Austin's arms tighten as my body shakes.

"It's okay. Get it all out." One of his hands trails up and down my back, soothing my tense muscles.

After an intense sex session with James, we would lie in bed cuddling and he'd regulate my body. We used to cuddle all the time after sex, and now looking back, it seems he used it as a form of manipulation. Keep me hooked by overwhelming my senses and regulating me back.

This embrace is monumentally different. I've never experienced this. James was my first relationship. Prior to him, I only had a few one-night stands. I had a high bar; no date was ever good enough to bring home. James had lied his way through my walls.

It's natural with Austin. It should feel strange to have his arms around me, comforting me. Sobbing in front of anyone isn't something I do. This all just has to be from a severe lack of intimacy.

"Would you like me to talk about something to get you out of your head? Or is the silence helpful? I don't know what's beneficial for you," Austin asks once my body settles again.

"You c-can talk." My voice cracks from the phlegm.

"Should I talk about something random or about my experience reading the famous Elijah Evergreen novels? I don't know if you've heard about him, but whoa, have I been swooned."

I blink, leaning back in his arms to glimpse at his face. *Okay, now that's weird.* His lips are mere millimeters from my own, and it suddenly feels way more intimate. His arms loosen, as if he recognizes the same thing, but he doesn't remove contact with me as I shift back a little. I focus on his words, trying to ignore the swell in my heart.

"You've read my books?" I'm not sure whether I should feel flattered or hurt that he lied about knowing who I was.

His eyes dart between mine; he's intentional with his words, thinking before he speaks. I appreciate that. "I looked you up the night after we hung out for the first time. I stayed up all night reading. And then purchased another book. I have to admit I don't read often, but whoa, am I hooked."

I've never laid in the arms of someone who's read my work. Who has complimented my writing. It's a goddamn dream to have a partner I can share my books with.

"What have you read?" I ask softly.

"*Don't Forget to Breathe*, and then . . . "

I don't hear the rest of his sentence as I shove myself out of his arms and sit, pulling the comforter up to my chest, unintentionally burying Austin in the process.

I know the book is public. Fucking goddamn viral. I *know* I can't keep anyone from reading it, and if I didn't want anyone to know the story, I should have kept it a secret. I fucking handed Austin the bait, and he ran with it. I can't blame him for that. He's interested, so he learns more about me.

Most haven't deduced the book is autobiographical. I've forbidden my family from reading it. They don't know the real James, but they'd be able to recognize me in the main character. And while my social media often isn't personal, I sometimes get the urge to share about my life. I've noticed it helps keep my readers engaged. They want more about my personal life, and giving it in spurts helps keep the momentum, but no one ever saw a picture of James. Well, aside from maybe in a group photo, when we were just friends. The post never mentioned we were dating, as he hated to be shown, and I respected that. Readers often ask if I'm dating anyone or if I have a lucky someone I swoon over like in my writing, but I've shared nothing with them.

"You don't have to tell me," Austin starts, sitting up against the headboard next to me. I wish he'd stop and not ask the single thing I know he knows. I can lie. He doesn't need to know the truth. I don't owe this stranger a thing.

He made you his grandmother's recipe.

Fucking hell.

"But was that book based on personal experience?"

I glance over at him, and then across the room to where there are two tin-covered plates and wrapped silverware on the desk. He said we didn't have to eat together, but he had planned for us to. For some reason, he decided to make his grandmother's recipe for me. He worked through his fear, and now he's questioning if I can with mine.

"You made your grandmother's recipe?" I ask to confirm. If I change the subject, we don't have to talk about me. He should be congratulated on his strength.

A smile beams on his face. "I felt inspired to take the risk, and I'm really glad I did."

"You wanted to plan this entire dinner. Is this how you pictured it?"

He laughs, shaking his head. "Nah, the decorations are in the kitchen storage, but being here doesn't take away from the meal."

A part of me questions what the night might have looked like if I joined him at the right time. Was it a date? Or two friends eating together?

"Can we eat now?"

"Of course," he says, immediately hopping off the bed. When he lifts the tin lids, steam pours out of them. "Fantastic. My heated plates worked well. This should be the perfect temperature. So this is my grandmother's lasagna. While lasagna is already incredible, she seasoned the pasta, cheese, and meat all individually, and then made a homemade tomato sauce. Sometimes, I've eaten the entire pan because I couldn't stop myself. With that said, this is just a portion; the rest is hidden in the kitchen fridge."

His joy is infectious, and I find myself smiling, sitting up further in bed, already feeling a little lighter. Austin hands me a warm plate, and as my nostrils inhale the scent, my stomach lets out a loud gargle. I'm starving and might need that second portion.

Austin grabs his own plate, then climbs back into bed beside me. The pasta melts in my mouth, and I can't hold in the soft moan that escapes. Not only am I finally feeding myself, but this surpasses what he's cooked here.

I look over at Austin's rosy face and it clicks. He was acting strange yesterday, after he had spent the entire night reading the heated sex scenes in my book. The positive reviews I have seen are fans telling me how they loved my spicier writing and would love more of it. I love reading steamy romances, and it's part of my struggle now too. I want to connect the sweet and spicy in my romances, but whenever I've tried, my mind pulls from my manipulated experiences.

I think I enjoy knowing Austin has read the scenes.

"This is . . . wow," I say for lack of better words. "How do you feel having made it again?" I take another large bite, trying to balance between scarfing it down and actually tasting every flavor.

"Pretty good. Honestly, I was distracted because I was worried about you. It tastes just like I remember, though. I was so focused on wanting to feed you, I sorta forgot what I was doing. I don't know if I feel satisfied that I made it again, but it makes me happy to see you enjoy it and I love bringing a smile to your face."

"Why me?" I ask, staring down at the food. "Why do you trust me?" I haven't been the best person this week.

"I follow my gut on a lot of things, and my gut tells me it was the right thing to do."

Silence falls between us. I'm not sure what I'm supposed to do with that information. We have two days left, then we will go our separate ways. Whatever this is will be a distraction if it continues past this retreat. It already has been a distraction.

A distraction from you staring aimlessly at your computer.

We both finish our food, and my stomach screams for more, but I need to digest first. I'm feeling a little more human, and I'm sick of being in this bed.

"I don't want to be forward," Austin starts.

"Let's go do something," I finish.

Austin grins, taking my empty plate. "Wanna have some wine and go in the hot tub? It should be dead at this hour."

I don't know what time it is, but I know I won't sleep. And if I force myself to, I'll wake up with the same nightmares and anxieties. I don't understand it, but Austin calms my heart rate, and the silence with him doesn't feel suffocating.

It is only nine thirty by the time we make it to the hot tub. Writers are still moseying around throughout the resort. Most with a beverage and their laptop in the dim light of the fireplace in the den by the large window. I should really spend more time there. It has such a stunning view in the daytime.

None of the hot tubs are occupied, which I'm thankful for. I never packed a bathing suit, leaving me in only my boxer briefs.

"Do you often enjoy the hot tub here?" I ask as Austin uncorks a bottle of red wine we grabbed from the bar on our way outside.

"Only once here, but the friends I stay with have one. On long nights from the other restaurant I worked at, I would relax my muscles in the hot tub. It kept me sane for as long as it could."

He pours us both a generous helping and places the glasses on the lips of the hot tub, where they belong. Suddenly, this feels very intimate. I've never been in a hot tub with just one other person before. Usually it's with a group of friends after a day of snowboarding.

Austin shakes off his resort robe, exposing his bare chest. He isn't toned or golden in the middle of winter, and it settles any anxieties I have over focusing on my writing more than caring about many "packs" I have on my stomach. My eyes immediately dash to the small patch of hair leading into his bathing suit. My face warms, and the robe burns on my skin, despite the below freezing temperatures. He hangs his robe up on one of the few hooks provided for each tub before letting out a shiver and climbing in.

I take advantage of his back to me and slip off the robe, hanging it next to his. I quickly climb in, trying to cover that I'm in my underwear. It'll cling obnoxiously to me when I get out, but ideally the wine will take care of those anxieties. And with that, I take a nice gulp of the wine, settling against the jets.

Austin leans his head against the neck rest, gazing up at the sky, and I follow his actions. It's absolutely stunning out here. My backyard is pretty grand, but it's easy to forget to admire how small we are in the universe. There's only minimal light out here, mainly provided by the tub's inner lights and the string lights intertwined with the vine on the privacy walls; enough for us to see who we are with, but the rest of the outdoors is pitch black. Only illuminated by the stars and crescent moon.

"Do you believe another world out there exists?" he questions, reaching for his glass. I look over at him; his cheeks are rosy with the warmth and water trickles from his neck down to above his pecs before they disappear in the water. He's already used his hands to slick his hair back.

I have to admit, he's attractive. There's no ignoring that fact, but I don't know what to do in these situations. With my one-night stands, I never initiated them. I don't know how to ask someone on a date or when it's appropriate.

"I think so." I remember to answer. "I think it's ignorant to believe we're the only ones. The universe is larger than we could ever fathom."

"When I remember how small we are compared to it all, it helps minimize the hardest parts of my life. Which feels silly in itself because even though we're small, we're still living in a world that makes it feel like our problems are large. And we shouldn't ignore what hurts us. But I don't know. It's comforting in a way?"

"Maybe because we might not be the only ones experiencing the pain?"

His eyes connect with mine, and a smile graces his face. He looks so relaxed and in his element here. As if it's easy for him to get up each morning and exist in this world. But maybe it isn't.

"It's possible," he says softly. "Our experiences are rarely unique, which can be comforting and minimizing, all in the same."

"It's wild how we want to feel special in moments of heartache, like we're the only ones who ever experienced the pain, but if we were, people wouldn't be able to help us through it."

His hand finds mine underneath the water, curling our index fingers, as if anything more might make it too intimate, like we haven't already cuddled in bed. But maybe that's categorized differently, and if so, if that was a comfort cuddle to wish away my sadness, I can only imagine what an embrace may feel like when he's in love.

Stop.

"I think we all just want to be seen for a moment in all the chaos," he whispers, and if my heart wasn't pounding before, it is now.

The temperature of the hot tub increases, and in an effort to not lose his touch, I lift my other hand out of the water, thankful for the instant cooling effect of the winter air.

Abort.

I grab my wine glass, taking a sip to silence my anxieties.

"Elijah?" he whispers, and my breathing stops. My eyes focus on his darkened hazel eyes. I'm terrified what might escape his lips. His fingers interlace mine, and subconsciously, I hold his tight. My heartbeat is in my ears. "I see you. How Jake treats Evan in your book? That isn't love. That isn't okay or normal. You are worthy of so much more."

Abort. Abort.

I can barely breathe as my lungs constrict. "You don't know that," I whisper. "You don't even know me."

His foot nudges mine as he clasps his other hand overtop

our interlaced fingers. "I know you've been beating yourself up over a review. I know you're dedicated to your work so much that you booked an elite resort and have barely participated in the planned activities. I know you've written so many romance novels that readers love, and that doesn't come from nowhere. And tonight, you allowed yourself to be vulnerable in front of me. These are not qualities of an asshole or a jerk. These are qualities of someone empathic. And you know the scariest but most telling sign that you aren't a bad person? You wrote Jake exactly how I'm sure he was, which might not seem like a big thing, but you wrote this after the fact, right?"

I nod. I have another sip, my grip tight on the glass.

Abort. Abort. Abort.

"There were times when I fell for Jake, too. You wrote his sweet manipulative abuse so well. If you wanted to hurt someone, you would have made the readers hate him from the beginning, but even then, you were protecting him in a sense while also protecting yourself. And maybe that's why these reviews are so scary. Of course they feel personal. Maybe they make you feel silly for not recognizing who Jake was from the beginning, but maybe it's possible a portion of you also misses him."

I down the rest of the glass. That went from zero to one hundred, way too fast. None of what he says is new information to me. This retreat is proof enough that readers have fallen for Jake. My friends who don't know James' truth fell for his character. Jemma nearly got sucked in, too. Would've if she hadn't gotten therapy for her own narcissist ex. I've talked about all this in therapy too. Jade's read the novel to help me heal.

"I just want you to know," he continues, "you are worthy of love and care. You don't have to prove yourself to be deserving. You just are deserving."

I stand, letting go of his hand, taking a moment to breathe

as the cool air wafts over my wet skin. This is all a lot, and it's too warm, and I'm too sober, and my emotional exhaustion is seeping in at record timing. I lean toward Austin, and his gaze burns into me as I reach for the bottle of wine. I refill my glass, giving him a top off too, before settling back in my position.

"I like your boxer briefs," he says, and I choke on my wine as I sit down. "Also, I think you should write more spicy books. You're amazing at them," he says before hiding behind his wine glass with a large gulp.

I can't help but laugh. My first glass of wine is infiltrating my bloodstream. Sex with James was the only time we were on level ground. And honestly, the least traumatizing portion of that relationship.

"My series is relatively light, but my standalone books are pretty heated."

"Which do you prefer to write?" he asks, and his hand is somehow interlaced with mine again.

"Honestly?" I ask, and he nods, his eyes bright as he smirks. All I can think about is what he might have looked like in his room, reading my novel. It should scare me; make me uncomfortable knowing how detailed and *real* those scenes were. But I'm turned on. This man has been pursuing me, reading my novels, making the connection to my real life, and he's still sitting beside me, in a hot tub, with a thin piece of fabric hiding himself. I float closer, squeezing his hand, and take a large gulp of wine. "My inspiration depends on when I'm getting laid."

Austin's breath hitches; his fingers disconnect from mine and immediately graze my waistband. His palm reaches the small of my back, gliding me toward him. In one fluid motion, I'm straddling him, our wine glasses on the ledge. He cups my neck, angling my face to hover so close to his, I can almost taste the wine on his lips.

"What scenes did you like the most?" I whisper, smiling

when I feel him twitch below me. I settle further in his lap, and his head falls back to the cushion.

"Everything," he breathes, "but particularly the moments of Evan being edged to near oblivion. I've always fantasized about doing that with someone."

I grasp his neck, crashing my lips onto his, thrusting my pelvis forward. One of the only times I felt loved by James was when he edged me, because he took the time and effort to care for me.

Austin's hands rest above my ass, angling me so my dick rubs against his stomach; the pure friction of my boxers has me rock hard. He's poking up between my ass, and we need to get ourselves out of this hot tub. But I'm so afraid to disconnect our lips. What if the spark disappears? What if it's wine-filled lust? What if—

"Let's go back to my room," Austin whispers in my ear before nipping my lobe. The sensation has me grasping his neck, letting out a low moan.

We jump out, and Austin grabs us towels. There's nothing hidden about how I'm feeling as my briefs cling to me. Austin's abstract bathing suit has the audacity to shield him more. His eyes are transfixed on my boxers. In a moment of boldness, I throw my robe on, barely tying it, before taking my boxers off, dangling them on my finger.

Austin's eyes don't leave my body as he grabs his own robe, repeating my actions. He steps in close, grasping my ass with his free hand, pressing his hips up against mine. "Let's go," he whispers.

Suddenly, he's holding the wine and our glasses and I race off after him, inside, where thankfully most people have retreated to their rooms. We head down a hallway opposite from the guest rooms the writers are staying in. When he opens his door, the room is identical to mine, an unmade king-sized bed in the middle of the room.

He's pouring more wine, handing me my glass, and I question whether this is smart. Whether it's just the alcohol talking or if this is what I need, something to get me out of my head. I haven't slept with anyone since James. No one-night stands, even though I've thought about them. Even made a goddamn Grindr before deleting it; I wasn't ready to make that step. After this morning, I'm confident I'm still not ready to start a relationship.

Austin steps closer to me; the hand that isn't holding his wine caresses my cheek, causing my eyes to drop to his. "What's on your mind?"

"I want . . . I don't . . . fuck," I groan, walking over to the bed and sitting on it. My robe is nearly untied and I want that to cause excitement. Austin's robe is hanging by a thread, but as he walks over to me, he wraps it tight.

"I need you to tell me what you want. I'm okay with anything. Do you want to drink more and have sex, no strings, no nonsense? Do you want to just make out and maybe feel each other up? Would you like to talk? Or do you want to forget this happened, you'll go back to your room and I'll greet you with a latte in the morning?"

I take a sip of wine. "I'm afraid," I whisper. I'm on a rocky surface of tipsy where I'll either orgasm or fall into a pity party.

Austin kneels in front of me, his mouth dangerously close to my hardening cock. His free hand caresses my bare knee.

"What if I focus on you? Remind you what it feels like to be cared for? I have no condoms, so we won't go all the way. But let me give you an orgasm that has you momentarily out of your body. No reciprocations needed on my end. If I come, cool. If not, no worries. I would love for you to just lay back and relax."

"W-why would you do that?" That sounds like a fucking dream, and dreams aren't real.

"Because one of my favorite things about sex is pleasuring the other person, and I'm very attracted to you, and since I've read your book, I've imagined what this might be like, and with your consent, I'd love to give you an orgasm."

"O-okay. Y-yes," I breathe. I gulp the rest of my wine before handing the glass to Austin. No one has outright said they've wanted to give me an orgasm. I'd be a goddamn fool to say no.

Chapter Nine
Austin

I never expected to be so lucky to kneel before him, the musk of him mixed with chlorine, greeting my nostrils. I place his wine glass on the desk behind me, taking a few small sips of mine, and then go back to my kneeled position. This time with my hands on his thighs, which are ever-so-eager to move his robe a fraction of an inch to expose him. How anyone could ever treat this man with any harm is beyond me.

Somehow, he's has gotten under my skin in the best way and I need to figure out how to keep him in my life. Time was a sloth without him today. I almost offered to deliver his coffee, the only thing he ordered through room service, but I figured he'd be in for lunch, maybe even a snack. Just in case, I took my breaks in the dining room, consumed by the first book in his series. As the day dragged on, I decided to still make my grandmother's recipe. Knowing I'd find a way to see him. And find him I did.

My hands untie the loose knot of his robe, brushing gently across his belly. The minimal skin contact has him breathing in. This is going to be incredible.

Running my fingers over the belt, I look up at him. His

eyes are soft and his shoulders relax. I have a thought; another fantasy. "Would you want to be blindfolded?" I ask, taking the belt and gently stroking the end along his bare thigh.

"In the future, yes," he breathes, "but right now, I need it safe."

"Of course," I rush out. *In the future.* My god he has me rock hard. "Please tell me if you ever want to stop."

He nods and then shrugs the robe off his shoulders, taking his arms out and letting it fall back against the bed. Suddenly, I'm face to face with the most beautiful dick I've ever seen. My hand reaches out greedily, feeling the girth in my palm. He flinches with my sudden movement, but I slow myself, softly dragging my fingers up and down his length. He did not give himself justice in the fictional version of him.

I'm not usually one who likes to be fucked, but if I'm ever lucky enough to get the opportunity with him, I would.

"Move up on the bed and lay down," I say. There is zero chance I'll be able to take him all in comfortably with my knees on the floor. I'm going to want to come and have the friction of the bed.

He does as I say, propping my pillows up so he can look down at me. He has a dazed smile with his hands behind his head. God, this man is a saint. He barely has any chest hair, just his happy trail, similar to myself, and the man trims—all my favorite features. Enough hair to inhale his scent and get lost in him. It's always my mission for my lips to touch the base.

I drop mine and Elijah's robes on the floor before climbing up, hovering over him. I connect our lips once more in a brief kiss, loving the way his scruff tickles my skin, then trail my lips down his neck, dipping my tongue over his collarbone as I kiss my way to his perky nipples. It's always a surprise whether a man will have any sensation there; his chest rises the moment my tongue touches his nipple.

"My weakness," he says. Music to my ears.

I twirl my tongue around his left nipple before heading to the right to do the same. As I lick, my fingers twist his left slightly, causing him to thrust upward. I straddle him, brushing our growing dicks together, holding him steady. A moan escapes his lips, and I'm not sure either of us will withstand edging tonight. I'm too eager to blow his mind.

I go back and forth between his nipples, giving them equal love. As I trail my hand between us, taking him in my hand again. And just like that, he's rock hard. I smile against his chest, flicking and biting his nipple as I stroke him. I play with the extra skin of his uncircumcised dick, salivating at the idea of him being in my mouth. I wait, though, until he's writhing under me, trying to thrust up as I go to town on his other nipple before I travel south. My tongue dances around his pubes, actively avoiding his leaking dick, despite my own begging for it. I massage myself against the mattress, licking up and around his balls. Elijah's hand grips my hair as I take one of his balls in my mouth and I moan, grounding down onto the mattress.

We're both so fucking sensitive, it's incredible. I want to come with him right now, but I'm scared it might never happen again. This intensity doesn't exist between people without a connection.

I lick my way to the entrance of his ass, something I'd love to devour one day.

"Holy fuck, Austin," he groans, yanking my hair; I might bust.

I kiss my way up to his dick, directing it into my mouth. I'm not even halfway down before he's yanking my head off of him.

"I need a . . . fuck, I'm going to come too fast."

I grin at him, moving up so I straddle his stomach, flopping my dick straight out on his chest.

"Can I, uh, taste you?" he asks, his hand grazing my hard on. His eyes are hungry and my brain malfunctions, hovering over him so fucking fast I nearly choke him with my dick. He takes me easily, but I don't have a moment to question my average-sized dick because I hit the back of his throat, and he sucks. I grip the headboard with one hand, shoving my other in my mouth to avoid screaming. Fucking hell, this man is a beast. His lips easily rest around my base, his tongue licking my vein, and I all but cry tears of ecstasy.

"I'm going to come," I breathe. He doubles down, sucking harder. His one hand twists my nipple as the other finds my asshole, and I come so fucking hard, I nearly black out. I steady myself on the headboard as he milks me dry. I've never been with anyone who keeps me in their mouth, licking and sucking until I shrivel back up. I'm nearly ready to fall asleep, ideally with him in my arms, but he taps himself against my back, and it reinvigorates me.

I devour his lips, tasting myself on them. And if that isn't the sexiest thing, then I'm not sure what is. I reintroduce my lips to his dick, this time pulling out all the stops. He can't give me a better orgasm than I do for him. That wasn't the deal. I prime my throat, taking him in inch by inch before reaching his base. Once I've worked through my gag reflex, as he's the biggest I've ever been with, I add my finger, twisting his nipple. I take a moment to coat my other fingers with saliva before sucking him back in, and I use those to tease his entrance. I barely penetrate, but every time I tease him, he jerks, hitting the back of my throat, causing tears to brim. His hands grip my hair again, gently maneuvering my head to take more of him.

"I'm gonna—" he says, and with two deep sucks, he fills my mouth. I give him the same courtesy of sucking him until he's overly sensitive. The way his body writhes in pleasure almost has me hard again. As I'm about to wipe my mouth when I pull away, he yanks me up his body, kissing my lips. Elijah lies me on the bed before he breaks the kiss, resting his head on my chest.

I want to say everything and nothing at all. It's been a long while since I've felt this at peace. There's a renewed energy vibrating around me. I'm exhausted, but I want to spend the rest of the night talking.

Just as I'm about to say something, he curls further into me and his breathing settles. I give him a few moments to get into a solid sleep before I situate us better. I shimmy out from underneath him, grabbing a blanket from the closet. I pick my phone up from the desk and then lay the blanket over top of him, leaving some extra for me. Once I'm in a good position, I pull him back against me. He groans a little before settling again.

My alarm is set for five hours from now, and instead of sleeping, I dive right back into one of his worlds.

My alarm startles me. Instead of an exhausted groan, I find myself smiling as I turn it off. I curl toward Elijah, my body hitting a pillow. My stomach plummets when I open my eyes. Sitting up, I see only one robe on the ground.

Fuck.

I hope last night wasn't too much. That his sober state isn't panicking about what he did. What we did. What *I* did. I wanna run to his room and check to make sure he's okay, but I had set my alarm for the latest possible time I could get up, and while I don't want to wash the smell of him off me, I must shower. Crossing my fingers that I'm overreacting, I force myself out of bed and start my day.

After four shaken espresso shots on ice, a breakfast shift, and cleaning the kitchen, I finally have a moment to search for Elijah. He never came to breakfast, nor did he order room service. I take a bold chance of making him a coffee and heading straight to his room. I sulk away when he doesn't answer the door. It's possible he doesn't want to see me. Today, I'd respect his space by not calling maintenance. Just in case, I search the other main rooms, but they are all empty.

I go back to my room and put my jacket, hat, and gloves on to take myself for a walk. It's possible he's outside, but it isn't likely. It's pretty fucking cold. A storm is coming through later this afternoon. I take the long way to my destination, dipping my head into my favorite spot, before walking to the hot tubs.

I would give anything to re-experience last night, not for the first time, but for the future of times. To take that enigma of a man out on a date, cook meals for him, make love to him, hear him moan beneath me.

Impossible. You don't deserve Elijah.

I round the corner, coming across the hot tubs, and find him sitting at a nearby table, furiously typing. The tips of his ears are red and his face looks frozen, but he's typing and that's huge.

The hole in my stomach starts to disappear. He wasn't intentionally ignoring me this morning. He was inspired. *My inspiration depends on when I'm getting laid.* The memory of his words has me smiling. His coffee is lukewarm by now, but anything is warmer than this temperature. I walk over slowly, trying to reduce the crunch of the snow beneath my feet.

I set the coffee down on the table. His fingers stop and he looks up at me. A mixture of emotion crosses his face, but I place a finger over my lips and scurry away. I don't want to pull him from the one thing he's been trying to do this entire trip, but I also don't want to waste his coffee.

I grin the entire way back to my room, allowing myself to

bask in the memories of last night, knowing Elijah's okay. What perfection.

I grab my phone, flopping back onto my bed, inhaling the stale scent of him. I FaceTime Liza.

"Well, well, what do I owe the pleasure, bestie?" She takes off her work headphones, walking away from her desk.

"I'm fucked," I blurt, then laugh at my bluntness. Those weren't the words I anticipated saying.

"Hmm, more like you and Elijah fucked." She winks.

"Just blow jobs." I sigh, but I can't hide the smile on my face. "I don't know what to do. It was so fucking good, Liza."

"So, you ask him out. Properly. Outside of work."

"You know I can't do that."

She cracks a seltzer can while side-eyeing me. "What Liza do you want? The one who tells it to you straight or who pretends she doesn't know anything?"

I don't know why I called. I should have anticipated this conversation. It's always the same if I'm semi-attracted to someone. She tells me to go for it. I say I can't. She tells me to kick my mom out of my life, then I can date. I tell her that's not possible. It's a cycle that'll forever keep me alone.

"It's a nice feeling is all," I mumble.

"Of course it is, and you can feel that all the time if you allow yourself to date someone." I open my mouth, and she interrupts me. "I know," she drags out. "What if you have a casual holiday rendezvous? You get accommodation and sex, he gets sex and maybe inspiration for a book, done deal. Everyone wins."

"And our feelings?"

"It has an expiration date. You go back to the resort and he carries on with his life. You never have to see one another again."

"That sounds like a novel idea."

Chapter Ten
Elijah

"Am I your muse?" Austin whispers in my ear.

Shivers rush down my spine. I stop typing as his fingers trail along my collarbone before he sits to my left, giving me a bright smile.

"Maybe," I whisper, suddenly so nervous. I narrow in on the cursor in my document; this time it's fourteen pages in.

I didn't have any other choice but to curb my hunger and show up for lunch. I have been up since four and writing ever since. I could have ordered room service, but that's now associated with a breakdown and I didn't want him thinking I was overthinking things.

To be honest, I am overthinking absolutely everything. However, it's coming out through written word, which is enough to keep me from spiraling.

Austin's right. He has weaseled his way into my psyche, becoming my muse. The fact that today is the last day of the retreat is utterly terrifying in that regard.

Austin's foot taps mine underneath the table, and I look at him. His hazel eyes gleam and his smile sends flutters through me. In another life, I would ask him on a date. But Austin deserves more than my half-assed self and last night was all it would ever be. A perfect time and place.

Every time I had a one-night stand, I went out with the intention to forget my loneliness. Last night was no different. I used Austin to forget James. That isn't fair to him.

"Elijah." His soft words cloak the daggers rising in me. He reaches his hand out, covering my hands as I twist my ring repeatedly. "Would you like to talk, or would you rather be left to write?"

I've written a stronger version of myself in this new book. I pretend I'm him; a bit more bold with Austin. I want it to work out for him. "I don't regret last night," I force out. He deserves the truth.

He squeezes my hands; his eyes gleam. "Last night was phenomenal."

I breathe out tension I had been ignoring. *Phenomenal.* That's a strong adjective. It replaces my cyclical question: *what if things were awful?* Even the memory of him unraveling at the seams couldn't convince my brain.

"How is your writing going?"

A smile usually reserved for Jemma comes through. One filled with so much unmasked joy. He doesn't miss it; his own smile lifts.

He sees me, and that's all I wanted from James.

"Well then, why don't I make you another coffee, one that's steaming hot this time, and you can continue being brilliant?"

Him bringing coffee to me this morning, even though it was cold, made its way into my book outline. He had wanted to talk more; I could feel the vibration coursing through him, but he respected my space. Noticed my progress and stepped back.

Similar to now. Writing is important. He recognizes that. Has supported that this whole week.

"That would be great," I confirm, my smile masks without consent. I need him to walk away before my mind spirals and he picks up the pieces.

I don't want him to start associating me with melancholy.

There was a time when James wanted to know about my writing. Not intricate details. But he asked about my progress on our first few dates. Showing me he thought my craft mattered. And I can't honestly pinpoint when that disappeared.

Austin picks up my empty dish as he stands. He leans down once more. "You've got this," he whispers. He presses a kiss to my temple, then walks away.

I open my document dedicated to the written descriptions of how Austin has made me feel. Scrolling down, I start a new paragraph. Describing the way his soft lips ignited a fire through my veins.

My fingers ache from typing. I ended at twenty-five pages. It's the second-best feeling in the entire world, right behind the way Austin's lips felt around my dick last night.

The rest of the day I had spent writing up until the community dinner forced me to step away. I mean, literally. I stayed in the dining hall until I had a tap on my shoulder from Jan, asking me to join the last dinner. Once I settled into the meal after my jarring interruption, I actually quite enjoyed myself. Turns out, I don't hate talking about writing when I'm confident about my writing. Though, it's rather uncomfortable to know how many people realized I wasn't writing all week, and then questioned me about my ferocious writing today.

After dinner, I join everyone in the den for a nightcap of hot chocolate by the fire, but only because it's Austin's hot chocolate recipe. All I really want to do is spend the remaining time with him. I don't know where we go from here. If there is a *we* in any form of the word. My body craves being close to him, yet my mind wants to run as fast as it can.

The reality is there is no *we* after this. I'm not ready to date. I compare the nice things Austin has done to how James was in the beginning. It all started out perfectly.

Austin connects his eyes with mine across the room. I swear his eyes glimmer just for me. I've been watching him this entire time. He's able to make everyone smile, and even laugh. He speaks as if he's had plenty of conversations with them prior, and I suppose maybe he has. I've been so invested in my own problems I haven't seen anyone else's experience here.

Was I just a challenge?

I rid the thought as soon as it hits me, but it continues to nag. Everyone was thrilled to be here, but I was apprehensive. Did everyone else warm up to his personality and I was just the one who wouldn't smile? Did it hurt his ego that his charm wasn't working, so he had to dig deeper?

The line for the hot chocolate dwindles. It's getting harder to fight the thoughts with how well he lights up the room. People are admiring his hot chocolate, talking excitedly to each other, and including him in the conversation. I'm sitting on the outside. Though, it's nothing new. I don't know how to interject myself into these situations. And I sure as hell don't have the confidence to push away the negativity that's nestled its way into my mind. Minimizing my experience with Austin.

Suddenly, the line is gone. He announces there's plenty more and people can help themselves from the carafes. Austin pours two more mugs and lifts them up. Looking right at me, he winks.

And just like that, the negative thoughts get pushed down as a wave of calm travels through me. I'm on a two-person sofa. Thankfully, no one has joined me. It was my hope I'd be able to sit with him once he was done.

He walks over, never once losing eye contact. His smile grows as he nears and dare I say I feel *giddy*. He sits down next to me, handing over a mug. "I assume you like full mugs of hot chocolate too?" He grins, taking a sip of his drink and leaning back into his corner.

"I do." I chuckle before I try his recipe. *Cinnamon.* His secret touch to my lattes was his recipe for hot chocolate. I gaze over at him. "This is incredible. Thank you for effectively ruining my latte experiences everywhere else."

"Well, I can't have you forgetting me, now can I?" He winks, and blood travels south.

The thought of forgetting him feels like a punch to the gut. He's reinvigorated my spirits. I could never forget that. "I won't forget this." I muffle my words with my mug.

I might just want him in my life for this recipe.

"Me either." His hand rests on the seam of the couch between us. I curl my index finger around his. "So, tell me, Elijah Evergreen, where are you off to next?"

The difference in tone startles me, but I don't let go of his finger. Instead, I position myself to keep contact comfortably.

"I'm heading to my childhood home for Christmas in a couple of days. Christmas is a big deal in my family, so it's a week-long event."

His eyes go wide. "For real?"

"Oh yeah." I laugh, a sense of happiness coursing through my veins. It's a nice change from the apprehension I have been feeling. It's the first Christmas without James, and my parents don't know what he did.

"Tell me about it." He's beaming, and I don't want to wipe the smile off his face.

"We go to a Christmas tree farm and pick out two Christmas trees."

"Two?" he interrupts, leaning forward, eyes like a kid on Christmas.

"Two." I chuckle. "My mom is very serious about Christmas. We decorate together, we carol, we have a Christmas movie day. Then there's a massive family dinner with extended family. Somehow, my two sisters and I have all been able to work this event into our life as we've gotten older, no matter the job we have. Obviously, mine is easier, but my sisters and their husbands take vacation time each year, and schools are closed, so their kids are off too, which means my entire family is under one roof, as they often sleepover, and it really feels like Christmas as a kid again."

When I say it all out loud, it sounds fucking amazing. And it should be. It used to be. Until James wouldn't come and would give me shit about spending time there, having me hanging on his every word with the hope of not fucking up too badly.

"Gosh. That sounds amazing. Can I pretend to be your boyfriend?"

"You'd be a hell of a lot better than James was. That's for sure." I look at Austin and he's no longer smiling. I don't know why I just said that. I pull my hand into my lap. It's true, but it's too honest. I'm showing too much emotion over something so silly.

"I'm sorry," I whisper.

Austin sits closer to me, and I'm suddenly very aware of everyone in the room. I want to go somewhere else, but the two of us leaving together would look suspicious. There are already a few writers who have eyed us recently. Austin hasn't hidden his advances.

My private life has always been separate from my work life. They are intermixing out of my control.

"Hey, Elijah's brain, can you please stop overthinking for a moment?"

My eyes dart to Austin; he's only inches from my face. We aren't touching, but the force field between us feels like we are. Pressuring the connection. My hand twitches to touch his, but I shove it between my legs, tensing them to keep my hands and legs from shaking.

This is all too much.

His hand rests on my thigh; the outside world disappears. The wave of relief that flushes my system nearly brings tears to my eyes.

"Answer me honestly. No overthinking." His words are soft and direct. I can do that.

I nod.

"Have I inspired your writing?"

"Yes."

"Do you like hanging out with me?"

"Yes."

"Would you be interested in being my friend?"

I glance up at him and he has a cheeky smile. This feels like an elementary school conversation. I wish conversations were always like this.

"Yes."

"May I propose a crazy idea? All I ask is you hear me out before responding."

I lift my brow, creating a bit of space between us so I can look directly at him. The cautious spontaneity in me is intrigued. Questions can be terrifying sometimes though, because what if someone asks you something you'd like to refuse but you're pushed against a corner with no way out?

"What if I do join you for Christmas?" I open my mouth to interject, but he presses a fingertip to my lips and I forget what I was going to say. All I can think about is where else that finger has touched me. "I've really enjoyed getting to know you and I'm not ready to say goodbye, but also my accommodation has fallen through, so I've been looking for a place to stay. I've never experienced a proper Christmas before. It's always been my dream. And this is going to be your first Christmas without James, which if I know any family, they always ask if you've moved on or what happened and it just makes things messy. Showing up with me, you can avoid the negative questions. While I haven't really experienced Christmas, I have watched a hell of a lot of Christmas movies, which means I'd be the perfect boyfriend to showcase. And while you haven't shared much with me, I know through your character how you felt with James. It breaks my heart knowing how you were treated and how you don't believe in love right now, and I really would love to show you how you should be treated and cared for. Bonus points, you continue to be inspired to write."

He stops speaking, and my mind is in overdrive. I feel as if I downed a glass of wine on an empty stomach. What the hell is he spewing?

My mind tries to catch up in an appropriate amount of time with the onset of information. How did it go from one-word answers to an entirely thought out idea of crashing my holiday?

Well, he wouldn't crash it. He'd be a blessing really, but my mom has strict rules about bringing people to Christmas and I already fucked up with James, so I can't bring someone I just met. My mom would likely cut me out the holidays in the future for ruining her memories. And then there's the whole: what the hell do I do if Austin turns out to be a manipulative, abusive asshole?

"I-I'm not ready to d-date," I force out.

"Oh, no!" His volume is loud, startling me. He slinks back just slightly. "Sorry. I mean, no, I'm not trying to date you. Hell, I can't be in a relationship right now, anyway. I meant to say fake boyfriend. We set a timeframe and ground rules. We enjoy each other's company a bit more. I show you trust and respect in a relationship, and then we go our separate ways. No broken hearts. I walk away with accommodation and the experience of Christmas I've always wanted, and you walk away hopefully more healed to start a new relationship and inspiration to keep writing."

I blink. I mean, for cautious spontaneity, this would be it. I'd be in my childhood home, protected by my family, if things went south. I'd get to continue writing this novel about Austin by learning more about him. A fear of mine has been whether I'd be able to continue the book without him. And I can't deny my heart wants to experience more from him.

"What about your family?" I ask. I barely see the shift on his face, but it's there. His happy-go-lucky exterior has cracks in it.

"We aren't on speaking terms."

I honestly couldn't imagine. Even though I haven't been truthful to my family about James, it doesn't mean they aren't in my life. Or that we don't have a good relationship. My family is way too much, but I love them to death.

"My mom has a strict six-month rule." He smiles and I don't understand what's happy about that. "In order to come to Christmas, the couple must have dated for at least six months. Christmas is what my mother lives for and she takes it very seriously. There's no way my mom would believe you're my serious partner."

His smile grows as his hand travels up my thigh. "Why? Because we have such awful chemistry?"

My ditch awakens at the memory. It's not a lack of chemistry in the bedroom that's the problem.

"I'm awful at acting. I've never been able to lie to my mom."

"So she knows the truth about your ex?"

"No, but—"

"Then you've done a fantastic job. Is it that you don't like me? And that's why it would be hard? Feel free to say so. I don't want to pressure you into anything. Otherwise, you can tell your family you kept me a secret because you wanted to make sure we were serious. You didn't want to break their heart again."

It's a good lie. Potentially plausible. I don't want to say goodbye to him, but the way I felt last night terrifies me. The way his goddamn hand can center my body is downright frightening.

"I know nothing about you," I say softly, running out of excuses.

"On the contrary, you know my dick quite well," he whispers, and suddenly the fire in the room scorches my skin. "What would you like to know?" He interlaces our fingers, resting our hands on my thigh. The heat between our palms ignites a shiver.

"What town do you live in?" I ask.

"St Peya. You?" An hour south of me.

"Lake Juniper."

His eyes light up, and it has me questioning how far he is in the first book of my Hemlock Lake series. It's heavily based on the village of Lake Juniper. "Oh nice, so you're right on the crest of this mountain range. I've heard Lake Juniper is beautiful, one of the top places in the state to visit."

"It is. It's quaint and friendly. One of those towns you can't believe actually exists."

"Sounds as friendly as Hemlock Falls." I breathe in at his words; his thumb caressing my hand. "I'm almost done with book one."

I always imagined it would be a wonderful feeling to have my partner read my books. Admiring my craft. Be excited about it. I never anticipated what it might feel like to have the person I'm crushing on read my books. It's a whole new turn on.

I don't want to spend Christmas alone. I've always wanted

to experience Christmas with someone who loved the holiday just as much as me.

How pathetic is it if it's fake, though? Could I really fool my family?

Do I want to fool them?

"Elijah?" Austin's brows furrow with a tilt of his head. "Do you feel pressured? I don't want to pressure you."

I shake my head instantly. "My mom is really intense with Christmas. I'm nervous it'll be overwhelming."

"Pfft," he laughs. "I've worked in restaurants on holidays for years. I almost guarantee I've been more overwhelmed there than I'd be with your mom." His free hand cups my cheeks; fireworks burst through my nerves. "What are you afraid of?"

When the charade is over, who's going to mend my broken heart?

Chapter Eleven

Elijah

"Eli!" my best friend's voice booms over the espresso machines in Isabella's Coffee; the shop in Lake Juniper.

Heads turn my way as I walk toward the register. I wave to the other regulars I see. I come here at least three times a week to write and visit Jemma. It keeps me from becoming antisocial. I almost feel as if I've been cheating on this shop by enjoying Austin's lattes. To be honest, I'm nervous to go back to my usual and lose Austin's hot chocolate recipe.

"I'm so excited to hear all about your retreat! Let me make your drink, and I'll take a break." Jemma starts preparing my beverage in a ceramic mug while Kerrington taps my order into the iPad.

"How's it going?" Kerrington greets. He's a bit younger than me and Jemma, but he's a part of our crew when we hang out in groups.

We banter while I pay and wait for my beverage, then Jemma's coming around the counter with her apron off and both our drinks. We make our way across the cafe to my favorite table in the corner. It's right beside a window that overlooks a garden; no matter the time of year, plants are always in full bloom. I've tested out a majority of the seats, and this one is my favorite. I prefer the chair with the wall behind me, so I can oversee the entire cafe and no one can come up behind me.

Jemma and I met right here, too. I came across Lake Juniper in my early twenties by accident. My car broke down and Lake Juniper had the closest auto body shop. Instantly, the town welcomed me with open arms. I was brought to the village diner to eat and relax, then when my car needed a part ordered, they set me up in the local inn. By the time I left, I knew nearly all the businesses and had started drafting the Hemlock Lake series. My goal was to end up back here someday.

When I met James, his job was in Cyan City, an hour away from Lake Juniper. I loved writing in Isabella's Coffee, so when I found out one opened in Lake Juniper; it was the best of both worlds. About a year and a half ago, Jemma started working here. She delivered my coffee, and we became instant friends, or more so trauma bonded. That is, until she started therapy and set me up with a therapist, then we became life-long, healthier friends. She helped me leave James and hooked me up with a real estate agent to purchase a home in Lake Juniper.

"Okay, tell me all about the retreat at that gorgeous resort!" Jemma exclaims, wrapping her hands around her ceramic mug after we sit. "Was it inspiring? Were you able to write? Do you think it might be worth spending the money to stay there? Simon and I were talking about it." Simon is her fiancé and one of my closest friends.

I laugh as I take a sip of my coffee, thankful that while it tastes different, it isn't worse or better than what Austin made me.

My original plan was to drive straight to Jemma's,

knowing she would want to know all about the retreat. I had a ton of unread messages from her. The closer I got to the village, though, the more I questioned what the hell I had just experienced. Some weird fever dream. I started panicking about the hell I got my future self into. Jemma doesn't even know Austin exists; the man who flipped my entire world and broke me out of my writing drought. It's honestly a little jarring to sit across from the person who knows my innermost darkest secrets and not have her know about Austin.

I don't know where to start, so I pull my phone out of my pocket, scrolling to the first picture I had taken when I arrived. She'll find out about Austin in a few seconds by finding the photo evidence. Amongst the photos he took of me, there are a few in his bed from the last night. After agreeing to fake dating, we went back to his room to negotiate terms. It ended with us cuddling and taking a few photos. Nothing happened, though; we ended up in separate rooms to sleep.

My legs shake in anticipation; her silence is unnerving as she swipes back and forth a few times.

Jemma places the phone down; the screen black. She locks eyes with me, offering a small smile.

"You look different."

I freeze. I expected an exclamation of excitement.

"I haven't seen an Eli like in those pictures in a while. You seemed at ease."

I snort back a laugh. "Most of those pictures were taken after a few days of still not being able to write."

"Writing isn't everything." Her words fall heavy on my shoulders.

Neither is being in a relationship.

I slide my phone back to me, lifting it to find a picture of me and Austin in his bed. Despite me being taller, his arms are wrapped around me. I can't stop the smile that forms, looking at us together.

"Tell me about him," Jemma says softly.

I glance over the phone at her, and she's sipping her latte. Her eyes sparkle; though her fear is evident. I know she wants to jump for joy; she's been telling me to try to get back out there, but she also saw me at my weakest. She helped rebuild who I am today.

And he's going to help rebuild you further.

"His name is Austin, and he is the head chef at the resort."

She lowers her coffee cup. "He's a chef? God knows you need one."

"Hey!" I exclaim, and she giggles. Her stoic mood is dissipating. I sink in my chair with relief; a natural smile on my face.

"How'd you start hanging out?"

I need to tell her it's fake; that she can't get attached. I'm already walking on the tightrope. But the excitement of talking about someone new is too intoxicating to interrupt.

"He kept trying to talk to me and made me a bet. He said he wanted to take me on a walk and if I didn't have a good time, he'd stop bothering me."

"Were you being your closed off self, not talking to anyone else, just staring at your blank screen?"

I roll my eyes at her because I hate how well she knows me sometimes.

"So you obviously had a good time," she prompts.

I nod. "He knows about the reviews, and the first night after we hung out, he read the book all in one sitting."

Her face becomes stone. Speaking it out loud, it sounds ridiculous that I allowed him into my life so easily. I've asked her to keep things from her fiancé, and in just a week's time, Austin knows my darkest secrets. My walls were never up.

"Fuck, Eli," Jemma breathes. "Did you tell him?"

I shake my head. I guess I have that going for me. I never explicitly told him first.

"He figured it out."

Her eyes bug out. "Damn, he's observant, huh?" She reaches across the table and grabs my hand. It's a gesture she does often, but it feels different now that Austin's done it, too. Similar to her hugs. My brain is starting to compartmentalize the different comforts I'd want in a friend and a partner.

I nod. "It feels strange."

Jemma's hand tightens. A few months before we met, she had gotten out of a manipulative relationship. It's how we connected deeper. She moved back to Lake Juniper, her hometown, and began working here to restart.

The guilt bubbles in my stomach; I can't tell her the truth. I have to tell her he's coming home with me, but not that he's fake. She'll tell me it's an awful idea and that I'll end up heartbroken, even if there's an end date. And I already know that. I've done stupider things for book inspiration. This is all research. With the added bonus of getting my family off my back.

"I'm bringing him home for Christmas," I whisper.

"What?!" she exclaims, and I wince. "Sorry." She returns to a normal volume. "Why? What? I need to meet him!"

"Meet him? No." I laugh, shaking my head.

She lifts our clasped hands. "Remember our pact?"

I roll my eyes, but only because I hate she's staying true to her word. When I finally left James, we made a pact that she would help vet all future partners to make sure I didn't fall into the trap again.

"He's still working. He'll only have a few hours at home before I pick him up."

"Perfect. Sounds like we'll grab takeout, bring it to his house, and have dinner while he repacks."

My mouth drops. We didn't prepare for this. "You're inviting yourself to his place?"

"No, I'm inviting Simon, myself, and you; he'll want to see you."

"He lives with his friend and her husband."

She grins. "The more the merrier, and even better for the pact to see the friends he keeps."

"Jem, this is ridiculous."

She shrugs. "Call him and see how he feels."

I challenge her eye contact until I find Austin's number on my phone. I'm more afraid Austin won't like the idea versus being frustrated with Jemma. I *should* know what friends Austin keeps. I still need to be safe regardless of if this is fake.

Nerves twist in my stomach as the phone rings. It feels like too big of a request from someone I don't know. What if it makes him regret his decision? I never intended to bring someone home from Christmas, but if he backs out now, I'll be disappointed.

"Hey Elijah!" His joy brings a smile to my face. I don't miss the sparkle in Jemma's eyes. She's observant.

"Hey, um," I clear my throat, and my mind, "I have a strange request." Jemma nods her head for me to continue.

"What's up?"

"My best friend would like to meet you. I told her there wasn't time, but she suggested getting takeout for everyone and we'd bring it to your place while you got ready for the trip. I know that's crazy because you'll want any downtime you can get between work and my family, and you only—"

"Elijah?" he says softly, interrupting my spiral. "That sounds perfect. She wants to make sure I'm not your ex. I get it. I think it's sweet. I'm sure my friends will want to meet you too. The three of us are easy eaters, so whatever you guys grab is good for us. It'll be my treat."

"Thank you," I breathe. "It'll be me, my friend Jemma, and her fiancé."

Jemma squeals across from me without even knowing what's happening.

Austin laughs. "Is that her?"

"Yes." I chuckle.

"Does she know it's fake?"

"No."

"Perfect. It'll be like practice. Can you put me on speakerphone?"

Using a speakerphone in a public place is one of my pet peeves, but I do as requested because it'll make Jemma's day. I remove the phone from my ear, placing it between me and Jemma as I press the button. "You're on speaker." Jemma does a happy dance.

"Hi Jemma, I'm Austin." If heart eyes were real, Jemma has them as she gazes at me. "I can't wait to properly meet you. I hope I prove myself to you in person, but I just want you to know that I've grown to care for Elijah and I only want what's best for him. I have no intention of hurting him."

Jemma silently slaps the table. This pact is going to be useless. She's swooning already, and I'm hanging on every word he says.

"Hi Austin, I appreciate that. I promise our interrogation won't be too painful."

He chuckles, and my heart swells. This guy will be the death of me.

"I'm looking forward to it," he says. "Okay, I have to get going. I'll call you when I have service on my drive home and let you know an ETA?"

"Perfect."

"And Elijah?" My heart skips a beat.

"Yeah?"

"I'm glad you called; I missed your voice."

I inhale at his words, tears brimming.

"I'll text you once I'm done working."

I barely whisper goodbye before putting my phone down.

We're fake dating. This is all fake. The intention is for him to show me what love is, but fuck, if it doesn't pull at my heartstrings that he misses something about me.

Chapter Twelve
Austin

We're not even twenty minutes into the drive to Elijah's childhood home, and I want us to pull over so I can kiss his lips. Honestly, I contemplate what actions are acceptable in this arrangement and what crosses the line of selfish urges.

He arrived at Liza's house in hunter green sweatpants that framed his ass and a tight thermal; it nearly had me ravenous, wanting to push him up against the front door and greet him. But the sight of his two friends behind him regulated me, and I went in for a simple kiss.

Now, we have a three-hour drive ahead of us on a nearly pitch-black highway. We could be naughty. There was something about seeing Elijah in a new environment tonight; I'm hyped to see him more in his natural habits. He was so relaxed, casually laughing and rolling his eyes whenever Jemma made a joke. Our friends got along; almost too well. They all joked about how it's about time we both started dating.

Needless to say, I passed Jemma's test. Instead of guilt for lying to her about the situation, my mind keeps begging me to make Elijah a permanent fixture.

I'm fucked.

"Can we go over the plan again?" Elijah asks; his left hand taps the steering wheel, off beat to the BlueTooth audio.

I clear my throat, sit up straight, square my shoulders, and turn toward him as best as I can with my seatbelt. "Elijah Evergreen and Austin Kane have agreed to be fake boyfriends until the afternoon of December 26th," I say in my deepest newscaster voice. "During this time period, Mr. Evergreen has provided Mr. Kane with accommodation and Mr. Kane will provide Mr. Evergreen with the most love-sick inspiration Mr. Evergreen could only dream of for his next best-selling novel. Mr. Kane promises to be the best damn boyfriend Mr. Evergreen has ever had."

He tilts his head back with a laugh. *Nailing it.*

"For all intents and research purposes, Mr. Kane will treat Mr. Evergreen better than a Hallmark movie. According to both men, nothing is off the table. But would Mr. Evergreen like to amend the ground rules?"

"No, Mr. Lawyer, sir." His cheeky grin has my insides warming.

"On December 26th, Mr. Evergreen will drive Mr. Kane back to Liza's house. They will say their goodbyes and they'll both be on their ways. No amendments can be made. Mr. Evergreen and Mr. Kane are respectively not ready to commit." I pause for a moment, feeling the mood shift. "Without further ado, fake dating now commences!" I hit the glove box with my fist like a gavel, and his laughter fills the car.

I need his lips like I need my next breath. The thought startles me, and I lean back in the seat, looking at the highway ahead. I make the executive decision that pulling over to kiss would be selfish. If I can't get through this car ride without wanting to devour him, then I need to slow my roll. In a week's time he'll be gone forever; that needs to be okay.

"Okay, break down your family chaos for me," I say,

changing back to my regular voice. "What's off topic? What quirks am I walking into? Any embarrassing history you'd like to tell me before your mom does?"

"My mom loved James. Reminds me often how she misses him."

And my sex drive is shot.

I reach for his hand on the stick shift, placing my palm overtop. "May I ask why she doesn't know the truth?"

"I don't want her to feel sorry for me and think I'm weak, or to be disappointed that I lied to her face, or feel bad that she didn't recognize what was going on. A slew of things she doesn't need to worry about."

A gut punch to the throat. This isn't about how I feel. This is about making Elijah feel seen and heard. Respected and loved.

"Elijah, you aren't weak." I squeeze his hand.

"I think I mentioned this, but I have two sisters, Emma and Esme." Smooth move, subject changer. "They both live within ten minutes of my parents. Both are married with kids. Thankfully. Otherwise, it would be another thing for my mom to harp on about."

"Would you like children?"

Elijah taps the brakes, and we jolt forward before he recovers. "Do you?" he bounces back.

I hadn't thought about how the question might sound on the receiving end. Suddenly, it feels like if I choose the wrong answer, it might mess this charade up.

Does it matter in the course of our fake dating whether the answer is yes or no?

"If I met a person I trusted entirely—one I could love—I would consider it," I say honestly. My mom fucked me up in more ways than one, but it doesn't mean I haven't thought of starting my own family. Giving a partner and/or a child the life I never had. Hell, I dream big enough for all of us.

"Same," he replies. I don't miss the way my heart slows at this response. "I like my routine now and wouldn't want something to mess it up. Truthfully, I'm not sure it's possible to have a love strong enough with someone that I trusted sharing children with them. I don't think I'd be bad at the parent thing, and my family is wildly supportive, but I also won't regret it if I never do."

I smile and squeeze his hand. The bursts of information from him are rare, but in those moments I know he trusts me. I want to bring out more of that guy. The one who was care-free with Jemma. I want the laughs, smiles, and his look of peace to be all because of me.

I want to love him.

"What is your favorite Christmas tradition?" he asks.

Goddamn whiplash reminding me why I can't fall in love with him. My mother ruins everything and I'd never forgive her if she ruined Elijah. I can't subject him to that hurt. It isn't his battle to fight.

Christmas barely existed to my mom, but Christmas morning at The Diner was my favorite.

"Christmas morning, my mom would always take me and my sister to her favorite diner. We'd order pancakes shaped like reindeer, have the largest mug of hot chocolate, and my grandma would give us special holiday coloring books, just for the two of us. We'd spend hours in the booth together coloring and eating."

Truth is, the person I consider my grandma was the owner of The Diner. She took care of me and my sister, especially on Christmas. She also taught me how to cook. As I got older, I realized our mom left us alone in the booth to hit on sleaze-bags, even on Christmas. Whether it be to get drugs or get laid, I never wanted to know. I made sure to protect my younger sister as much as I could, making sure she always had the sugar coma bliss for longer than me.

My phone buzzes with the daily message from my mom. Her reminders have become more urgent. Demanding I don't fuck up.

Chapter Thirteen
Elijah

The front of the four-bedroom, two bath colonial home is decked out in white twinkling lights lining the eaves. Candles are on each windowsill, where real garland, coated with a dusting of snow and strung with lights, frames the outside of the windows. No doubt my mom was up on a ladder today patting the snow off to make it look more magical. A pair of eastern hemlock trees planted by my parents on their wedding day are lit, too.

"You grew up here?" Austin seems amazed, as if this home is anything more than the average home our parents' generation could afford in our state. He leans closer to the windshield, gazing out as I pull into the driveway next to my dad's pickup truck. We have a two-car garage but my mom's car and her Christmas decorations use it. "It looks beautiful."

"My mom is obsessed with Christmas," I say. Maybe he's referring to the decked out lights on the relatively mellow street. No amount of persuading has gotten our neighbors to go overboard on decorations. It's been a pet peeve of my mom's throughout my entire childhood.

Like a little kid on Christmas morning, Austin's beaming,

and it makes me question what he might want more: showing me love or experiencing an Evergreen Family Christmas.

"I'm so excited!" He practically bounces out of the car to the trunk.

We gather our belongings and head to the door. Despite the array of lights, my mother has left the porch light on.

My childhood home has a rather strange layout from what I'm used to friends having. Through the front door, there's a living room off to the left and a kitchen to the right. Down the hallway, we have all the children's bedrooms and a bathroom before it opens to a large den, with a porch extension and the master bedroom. All one floor. My parents barely had silence when our friends were over, but it was incredibly easy for us to sneak out. Though my parents have admitted they always knew.

Inside, all the Christmas lights are off. My mom waits to add Christmas trees to her decorations, but for the most part, everything else is set up. The transition from children to adulthood was hard on my mom. She used to want to wait to put up all the decorations for when the family could get together, but we could never coordinate more than the week before. She never wanted us to lose the magic of Christmas, but for someone who always decorated on November 1st, waiting until the week before Christmas had been agonizing to her. So the compromise is that all other decorations go up, but we always get the Christmas trees together and decorate them as a family.

I nod down the hallway to Austin, locking the front door, before directing him to my bedroom. My door is the last one on the left before the den. It's already open, my bedside lamp offering a soft glow to the room. I turn on my two standing lamps. My full size bed stops me in my tracks. I'll be sharing a bed with Austin for the next week. Not a queen or a king, a full size, barely big enough for both our bodies.

This is a bad idea. I'm not sure why I agreed to this. It isn't like I just show up to my parents for Christmas Day. No. We are here for the next seven days. In one small room, on one very small bed.

I had lied to my mom shortly after I got home from the retreat. She called me, and I surprised her with the exciting news that I'd be bringing my boyfriend of seven months to Christmas. I added a month for security. However, I hadn't considered the timing; Austin looks like a rebound relationship after my four-year relationship with James. Naturally, my mom rapid-fired questions, keeping me on my toes, like was he a rebound, what did he have that James didn't, why did I keep Austin from her? I'm certain I blacked out because I don't remember what I said back. She somehow agreed, through huffing and puffing about not having enough time to make him a sweater and a Christmas gift. There was no point in telling her it wasn't a big deal. It *is* to her. She's likely made it her entire personality to ensure he'll feel at home.

When I gather my thoughts and toss my bag on the floor, I turn to find Austin looking around.

"This is incredible. Like a time capsule," Austin says, gesturing to the room; though he's transfixed on my bookshelves, fingering the book spines and taking them off the shelf to read the back.

My parents have kept mine and my sisters' rooms relatively intact, aside from what has traveled to our new homes. When I first left, I was trying to find distance, so I only took clothing and my favorite novels. Now, while some of these belongings (particularly my bookshelves) would be nice in my home, I keep them here to reminisce when I come back. A sense of safety when I am overstimulated.

A reason I agreed to Austin being here is because of how he isn't afraid to express himself. He introduced himself to me; he got me out of my head, and now he's walking around like he grew up surrounded by these four walls, too. He even dressed comfortably, not caring to impress. Though he looks amazing. James always showed up dressed to the nines. That is, when he showed up.

"You have a stellar book collection. I really need to amp up my reading game if I'm going to compete with you." He winks, and I sit slowly on my bed, my down comforter fluffing around me.

A book reading challenge sounds like a dream coming from a partner. But that's what this is, right? Him being the ideal boyfriend? Setting me up for success, but probably more like failure if this isn't real? The thing is, I would love a book challenge. I *do* have a stellar book collection. Partially why I don't need these books in my home. I have more than enough in both locations. These books held a purpose for a time and place.

But who is the real Austin, and who is fake boyfriend Austin? Will they ever mingle?

He reaches on the top shelf of my bookcase, showcasing the way his muscles flex in his henley and how his butt clenches ever-so-slightly on his tippy-toes through his sweat-pants. *I should have taken sex off the table.* My mind flashes to the way my hands clenched his ass as I came so hard down his throat. My dick awakens and my asshole throbs, craving the feel of his tongue doing more than just a swipe.

Calm yourself, Elijah.

I blink, glancing at my beige carpet. I was feeling confident and unhinged when we created our boundaries. I wanted the full Austin fake boyfriend mode to inspire me how he sees fit. I didn't want no sex to hinder his performance, especially because I'm trying to write spicier fiction.

Problem is, what's best for writing isn't always best for my heart.

"I uh, I'll take the floor, and you can have the bed," I say, standing up, adjusting my sweats. My extra pillows and blankets are in the closet right beside him.

He swivels, dropping a few centimeters once he's flat-footed again. His hand grazes my wrist as I pass by, stalling my movements. Goosebumps scatter along my skin, and I inhale.

"I don't mind sharing a bed," he says, his hand rests on shoulder. My skin is on fire and I need to abort this situation. "If you don't want to though, I'll take the floor, as this was my idea. But it might be smart for us to share a bed. Does anyone in your family not knock?"

My parents always knock, but depending on tomorrow's meet up schedule for the tree, my nephews and niece might make their appearance here first, and they *never* knock.

"I don't bite." His words are soft as his hand trails up my arm. "Well, not in a bad way," he whispers while his fingers circle around my left nipple, and I hate how I gasp. Despite my shirt, my skin tingles, reminiscing how his teeth grazed them. He drops his hand, curling his fingers around mine. "You tell me what makes you uncomfortable, but my mission here is to show you what care, compassion, and romance is, and I'd love to lie by your side and hold your hand while you fall asleep."

While that sounds lovely, my dick is disappointed at the vanilla suggestion.

"The agreement was showing my parents that you love me."

The "L" word feels strange coming off my tongue, like a weird spark of angst. We aren't in love; we can't be.

He shakes his head, a small laugh escaping. "Our agreement was to remind you what romance is, so it'll help you write again. I'm confident I'll convince your family."

I'm silently grateful for his choice of words. I don't think I knew what I was fully agreeing to. This isn't a charade that ends behind closed doors. A loving, real relationship is twenty-four seven. Acting for my family is only a portion of the gig, and it's a bonus to not look single on Christmas.

"How about you show me where the bathroom is and then we both head to bed?"

I nod, needing a few more moments to process my thoughts. A part of me wants to dive heart first with no fear into this experience. Take all he'll give and throw it into my work. God knows his touch is amazing and I've been craving physical contact. But I don't know how much my patched up heart can survive.

Chapter Fourteen

Elijah

The smell of something incredible wakes me. It isn't the usual cinnamon rolls from a tin, but there's a warm sweetness in the air. The moment I open my eyes, the sounds hit me full force. My entire family is here, acting as if Austin and I aren't still sleeping. It's not the first year I've had to ask them to keep the noise down. Because I work from home, I write when it feels natural. Sometimes that means in the middle of the night. The writing retreat has gotten me more on par with my family's schedules, but transitioning onto my family times for holidays is usually tough.

I turn to apologize to Austin, contemplating dashing down the hall and telling them to shut up, but my eyes dart around the room. He's nowhere to be found.

I see one family Christmas sweater folded perfectly on my desk, but there should be two. They were there last night. Austin promised not to look at it until morning, but I told him that was the dress code for today.

Oh no. My heart rate rises.

"Oh yeah, Elijah keeps telling me about this. He said he'll take me." Austin's voice travels down the hallway.

My blood freezes. *What is he doing?*

No. No. No. No.

I jump off the bed and get dressed as quickly as humanly possible. Just a pair of dark jeans and the red and green striped Christmas sweater with "Evergreen Family" stitched in white felt on the back. The front is a cartoon version of a Christmas tree farm. At least this year the sweater is comfortable. Last year, it was so itchy I developed a rash.

The moment I set eyes on Austin, in my family kitchen, I see him wearing my mother's Mrs. Claus apron, leaning up against the counter next to the stove. I told him not to tell my family he was a chef. I didn't want them to take advantage of him. He didn't listen; instead, he took it a step further, already proving he could cook.

He might just win over my mom. My heartbeat pounds three times in my left ear as the scheme races through my mind.

"Good morning, Elijah!" His eyes shine as he greets me from across the room before he walks toward me. The conversation silences. All eyes turn to me and my family wishes me a good morning. Austin places a hand on my cheek before connecting our lips.

No big deal. Just some morning PDA, something I've never showcased in my entire life.

He grins when he steps back, his hand caressing my cheek as it warms. Everyone's eyes are still on us. I can feel the lasers through Austin's back into my chest, but I'm frozen in place.

How does one show love?

"Homemade cinnamon rolls are almost done," he says, then whispers, "and a fresh pot of coffee, but your parents don't have a frother?"

Am I the guest, or is he?

My fake boyfriend doesn't even know my coffee order

when an espresso machine is unavailable. Scratch that. I don't even know if he drinks coffee.

Yeah, we can lie for a week.

"Elijah, Austin is such a saint!" I hear my mom's voice before she's standing beside us.

Austin's hand drops from my face, quickly grabbing mine to squeeze, before he's back to the oven as the timer goes off.

"He helped himself to the kitchen and started making cinnamon rolls for us," my mom continues. "He was already halfway done when we woke up. They smell phenomenal."

She has no care that he raided her cabinets? While she spews the "make yourself at home," she's never meant it. At least, I don't think she has. She's particular with her home and belongings, everything has a place and she has a plan. What drugs did he place in the coffee to calm my controlling mother?

Austin winks at me before he bends over, pulling the hot dishes out of the oven. I shiver as my body overheats in the cotton sweater. If anyone looks out of place here, it's me.

I make my rounds once my mom rushes to help Austin, greeting my sisters, brother-in-laws, niece and two nephews, before patting my father on the back. I then grab my personalized *Elijah* snowman mug. We all have Christmas themed mugs with our names on them. I pour myself coffee, find my mom's peppermint mocha creamer in the fridge, and add a healthy dollop into the steaming liquid. Austin's eyes zero in on my coffee as I stir it. I don't know whether to be flattered or frustrated. He's so dedicated to being the perfect boyfriend that he's going to create an unattainable expectation for my future prospects.

Austin brings the warm pans to the kitchen table, and it's like my family has never eaten a day in their lives. They collectively moan at the smell; eyes shut momentarily before they look ravenous. My five-year-old nephew barely contains himself.

"Can I get you guys any refills on coffee?" Austin asks, and I dart to his side, wrapping my arm around his waist without thinking.

"You've done more than enough. Please sit," I say. He looks like he's about to challenge me, so I raise my brow and shimmy my hand into the back pocket of his jeans, gently squeezing his butt. A smirk greets me. Before I think twice, I kiss his lips, wanting to gain control.

"Either get me coffee or get a room!" my sister Emma jests. She's two years younger than me, always calling me out.

I pull away. My face is on fire. I don't know who I am right now. *Is it possible we're acting too hard?*

"Thank you. Now go eat." I try to demand, but Austin laughs and heads for the table.

I grab Emma and my father's mugs to refill, catching sight of an *Austin* mug. It's red with snowflakes. It does, in fact, have coffee in it with the slightest bit of creamer. I glance over at my mom. She's already watching me, but her eyes are soft. I mouth, "Thank you," to her and she just smiles.

I refill the mugs in my hands, breathing through the wave of emotions that want to crush me. My mom doesn't deserve to be lied to. About Austin *or* James. I take a deep breath and return to the table, sitting down next to Austin. His hand immediately comes to my thigh, out of view of my family, as if it's the most natural reaction. My stomach twists at the thought.

My fake boyfriend made my family breakfast, already has them swooning, and we've been here for less than twelve hours. He has the family Christmas sweater on underneath the apron he's still wearing, never once questioning the attire. He didn't even wait for me to wake up before leaving the room.

My family devours the cinnamon rolls while mine remains

on my plate. It feels like if I eat this, I'll succumb to the Austin magic too. I'll be way too far in to tell what's real and what isn't. The line is already blurred. This man *will* destroy me.

Just as I'm about to take a bite of the cinnamon roll, Emma says, "So love birds, tell us about how you met. E, I can't believe you've kept him from us for so long!" She smacks my shoulder.

In the "seven months" we've been together, I've visited my family at least seven times. I try to come home once a month, sometimes more depending on what holidays or birthdays happen. The one good thing about my ADHD masking abilities, it's plausible that I could've been in a relationship and hid the entire thing.

"Yes, please share! We love a good love story. It's almost unbelievable he's been able to hide his joy for so long."

Austin's hand squeezes my thigh before my poker face can drop at my mom's words. I focus on him. She has reason to doubt, but I've lied so well about James over the past few years that her reality is skewed, and she doesn't know.

But we never discussed this. Our intention was to take the three-hour car ride to create our love story because we got off track at the resort, but it turns out we went off on tangents in the car, too. When I allowed myself to relax last night, there wasn't a silent moment between us.

"Elijah was a customer at a restaurant I used to be a chef at. I made my favorite recipe of my grandmother's one night, and he loved it so much that he told the waiter, and well, I had to meet him. I'm sensitive about introducing family recipes wherever I work, so it meant a lot that debut night I already had a fan. Turned out to be this incredibly attractive man, eating alone, writing. I interrupted him, asked him on a date, and the rest is history."

My mom watches me; her smile is friendly, but the rejection sensitivity crawling through my neurons convinces me she's looking for any minor crack in my story.

"Wow, you're bold." My older sister, Esme, laughs. "You didn't even talk to him before asking him out?"

"Nah," Austin shrugs. His hand caresses my shoulder, a spark travels down my arm to the tips of my toes. "Anyone who compliments my cooking and has the courage to take themselves out to eat is someone worth getting to know."

Jokes on him. I'd never take myself out to a restaurant alone. A coffee shop, sure, but a restaurant? A fancy-ass restaurant like Austin told me he used to work at? Not a chance at that humiliation. But it makes a hell of a story, and likely ups my brownie points in my sisters' eyes.

"And naturally, Elijah fell head over heels for you because he can't cook for shit, and he had the chef asking him out? Hello, romance novel," Emma says, fanning herself with her hand.

"Hello, husband right here; can we not be in love with the new guy?" Blake, Emma's husband, jokes.

Emma makes googly eyes at her husband and kisses his cheek, while Blake sarcastically rolls his eyes.

"Elijah, how'd your writing retreat go?" my mom asks from across the table, already starting her third cinnamon bun.

I breathe in, trying to not let the stark transition startle me. *Where do the lies overlap?*

While we had spoken on the phone the other day, it quickly transitioned to why would I keep Austin from them. I ended the call before any stories could be told, wanting Austin on the same page.

I take a moment to rip my cinnamon roll apart. Did I go on a writing retreat with my fake boyfriend? Do I want to say how shitty my writing experience was because I'm stunted? How does Austin fit into this actuality?

I'd rather escape to my room now and do some writing, based on the character Austin inspired, instead of answering this question.

"Funny enough," Austin starts. This man is a saint. "I actually work at Enchanted Juniper Resort. I got the job a few months ago, so we were able to spend the week together, which was wonderful."

"Oh, how lovely!" my mom exclaims, but her watchful eyes are still trying to read my soul.

It's nothing. It means nothing. She has no reason to doubt the legitimacy.

"Is that how you found out about the retreat, Eli? I thought it was a bit strange you mentioned wanting to attend one. You never have in the past."

"Uh, yeah," I mumble. "Shortly after Austin got hired, they mentioned a writing retreat. I was able to sign up immediately before it was announced to the public. It was a nice blessing being accepted because Austin's schedule is tough sometimes with working up there." This elaborate lie is falling way too effortlessly off our tongues; a romance that sounds so sweet; a fleeting thought has me wishing it was our love story.

I catch Austin's eyes, and I swear there's a flicker of sadness. He's created his boundary. He can't commit with his schedule.

"Do you stay on site while working?" Esme asks.

"Yeah, two weeks on, one week off. We want to see if Elijah can come up and stay more often, but because it's a relatively new job, I want to get my bearings first before we ask. It's pretty incredible, though. It's my first kitchen I get to run and create the menu for."

Dating Austin and visiting the resort while he works sounds like a dream come true. Unreal, really. There's zero reason why I can't write anywhere I want. We'd never have to be apart.

The thought startles me. Would the resort allow something like that?

I sit back in my chair, allowing my family to grill Austin, grateful to escape into my mind.

What kind of Christmas miracle is this that the chef at the writing retreat found me intriguing enough to speak to *and* happens to not have holiday plans? The latter is a potential red flag I'm ignorantly ignoring until our trip is over. There has to be a flaw in this man, and his instantaneous approach to life has my anxiety quaking. I needed two to five business days to wrap my head around this plan of ours; he asked for a couple of hours to pack.

The conversation shifts to my mom asking Austin if he'd like to help her cook the rest of the week. It's an instant yes. It's hard to imagine Austin is fake in this reality. That he hasn't always been here, sitting at this kitchen table. That he only met my family this morning. He looks so natural, laughing and carrying on. He doesn't just have my family hooked on his food; he has them hooked on him.

He's the jack of all trades, and I barely know how to form a sentence.

Chapter Fifteen

Austin

This family is straight out of my imagination for the perfect Christmas experience. I didn't think it existed. Cheesy Christmas movies have gotten close, but they always lack authenticity. The Evergreen dynamic is what I've always wished for. They love each other, that much is obvious, but their honest banter and fun-loving attitudes are really what draw me in. My like for them has little to do with the fact that they love my cinnamon rolls.

We're at a real Christmas tree farm. I'm talking about a full-blown quintessential Christmas tree farm. We aren't at a grocery store parking lot, convincing the person in charge of the dwindling pine trees to stay open later on Christmas Eve because my mom forgot to get a tree until I threw a tantrum, terrified Santa wouldn't come without one. By my 6th Christmas, she gave up the charade and told me Santa wasn't real. I don't think my sister ever believed.

Sparkling white snow coats the entire farm, with snowmen scattered around the property and trees lined for miles. I'm not even exaggerating. The drive up, there were a few different entrances we could have gone through. Elijah told me they always head to the main entrance because that is where the cafe is for lunch, as well as the sleigh ride and other activities for kids. Getting a Christmas tree is so important to this family that they all do it together, in matching sweaters, despite being adults now.

My younger self used to pray to whomever listened for a Christmas like this. I didn't need the presents. Hell, I didn't even need the Christmas tree farm. I just wanted a *family*.

A golden sun gives us the serotonin to get through the day, and to mask the temperature drop. Hard packed snow crunches beneath our feet.

We're walking down a lane with just his family present as his parents inspect each and every tree. Elijah's niece and nephews dart between the evergreens, playing tag. Everywhere I look, pine trees loom over us, their scent consuming my senses. My body vibrates with excitement.

I interlace my hand with Elijah's, and despite the chill outside, his hand radiates heat. I pause our steps, and he turns toward me, brow lifted slightly. I don't know how I got so lucky he walked into my life.

"Thank you for letting me join you. This," I extend my hand, "this is a Christmas experience I've always wanted to have."

"This one!" Louise, his mother, exclaims. I glance a few trees down. It looks like all the rest, tall, bushy, and full, worlds above the stick tree my mom finally purchased one year. Louise no doubt has a skill-set, though. The kids run over to her in excitement. They can't wait to watch the saw in action.

Looking back at Elijah, he's smiling at me, interlacing our other hands. "It's nice to share this with someone who enjoys it. James came the first Christmas we were together. He was a sweetheart to my family, but whispered complaints to me the entire time."

My mind refocuses. I dedicated myself to showing this

man what love could be. Every so often he lets his guard down and falls into us being together, but then something happens, likely his intrusive thoughts, and he shells up. It might only be the first full day with his parents, but it's a consistent pattern. He likes me, he's attracted to me, all that's evident. And even if he doesn't fall in love with me—no, I can't let him fall in love with me—he needs to know it's okay to take a risk again. To step out of his comfort zone and start again. Not all men are James.

A wicked thought comes to my mind. I might have fantasized about Christmas tree farms throughout my childhood, but those fantasies continued as I grew up, and if this is my moment here, I plan to take full advantage.

"Come with me," I whisper, yanking his hands as I step backward. The tree distracts his family; they all surround it, offering support. It's the perfect time to duck out.

"Where are we going? My dad might need help."

"We'll help in a moment." I dip us between trees opposite of his family until I find one with a thick trunk. I hide us between two trees and push him up against one, placing my leg between his, clasping his cheeks.

"What are we—" he breathes, and I crash my lips onto his, breathing him in. I've been dreaming about taking him ravenously since the night in my resort room. We've only kissed once since then, and that was for show. But this, this right here is what he needs to realize can happen too. Finding moments of sneaking around because you're so in love you need to express it and it can't wait until you're home.

He catches on, his hands tangling in my hair. We don't have much available space with our bulky winter jackets. I don't even feel like I have the power to press myself up against him in a way that would be seductive; though, likely safer to not do so with children around. I shift my lips to his jawline, and as he tilts his head up, I travel to his earlobe, nipping it, captivated by his heavy breathing. I swipe my tongue below his ear before pressing light kisses down his neck. I want this man so badly. To give him everything he wants, even to have the opportunity to swallow him one more time. This idea of mine is awful because it's going to leave me in a fetal position and back to work in a place where we fooled around.

Elijah grips my hair, tugging my head up level to his, connecting our lips once again. The pressure on my head has me devouring his lips, dipping my tongue to dance with his. My hands travel down his coat, reaching beneath the fabric to press my palm against his front. His groan is music to my ears, and I get hard by just feeling the intensity of his breath.

Cheering separates us in an instant. The tree must be successfully cut. I step back from Elijah, needing physical space to cool down. His eyes are dark and hungry for more, but he's fighting for focus in a semi-blissed out state.

Perfection.

"That was—"

"Hot," I confirm. His chuckle and nod combination has my stomach fluttering.

He repositions himself in his jeans before pushing off the tree. "Straight out of a romance novel."

I wink, interlacing our hands, leading us back to his family.

"Eli, there you are!" his dad yells the moment we're back in their lane. Elijah's brother-in-laws both whistle, eliciting smacks from their wives. I steal a glance at Elijah; he's blushing, but there's a pep to his step.

Over the next two hours, the men collect the tree to attach to one car while the rest of the family goes on a sleigh ride with the kids. We then all meet up again to find tree two. This is faster, as I learn this tree doesn't have to be perfect, but it does have to be enormous. This one takes the help of some staff members to carry, but I received the honor of helping saw.

Never in my life have I held a saw. I didn't do it for long, but my inner child checked another thing off his Christmas list.

We eventually all head to the cafe on site, a literal building copy and pasted out of Santa's Christmas village. It's decorated to look like a gingerbread house, thick icing and all. Though, real snow covers portions of the icing. Large candy pieces decorate the front of the building, acting like bushes. Gingerbread statues of a family welcome you up the pathway. I swear I even smell gingerbread.

We step into the cafe; his family has left us behind, already ordering at the register. There's a minimum of three decked out Christmas trees on this level, and a garland-wrapped staircase suggests there might be more on level two. Despite how packed this place is, it's relatively quiet; I can hear the fire crackling across the room. The first portion of the cafe is filled with tables, but at the back of the building, there are bookcases lining the walls, a stunning stone fireplace, and a collection of sofa chairs.

"When I was a teen, I used to live in this cafe," Elijah says. "Writing romances about finding love on this farm. Creating my own Hallmark dream."

I imagine a young Elijah sitting in a sofa chair, furiously typing away on his laptop. Likely hopped up on hormones and unaffected by the heartbreak his future might hold.

The thought of him sharing this experience with anyone but me has my blood boiling. I have zero right to feel any sort of way, but this place is healing my inner child. Selfishly, it wants this place to be our special something.

"James never understood the joy of walking through a tree farm. The crunch of the snow, the smell of the pine. It's funny when I think about it. I was writing these romances, yet I fell for the man who was the complete opposite."

I breathe in and out, regulating my heart rate. My emotions are high strung, flashing from all-time happiness, to jealousy, to hatred for James. I need cool, calm, confident Austin. The version of myself I wish I always was.

"You told me he was a sweetheart to your family," I force through an even tone. "He might have been whispering things he hated, but what he showed was entirely different. You love your family and if he treated them well. Manipulation at its finest."

He snorts, catching me off guard. "Yeah, that's true. He was so bored out of his mind after the first year that I considered myself lucky if he showed up on Christmas Day."

I halt our steps, turning him toward me. "You're telling me your mom loves your ex and he barely even spent Christmas with you guys? How did your mom get to know him enough to want to keep you guys together?"

He shrugs, but his eyes cloud over. I'd love to get him back to that blissful state, but we're starving. The smell of savory foods has my stomach growling.

"We were together for four Christmases. The first year he spent the whole week, the second he spent three days, the third he missed entirely, and the fourth he celebrated Christmas morning. Before every Christmas, he'd call my mom and explain to her why he wouldn't be around. She was wrapped around his finger. A part of why I don't want to be honest. I don't want to ruin those memories for her."

I squeeze his hand, urging him to continue. This may have my insides reeling, but he's opening up and I can't hinder that.

"To make up for Christmas, he'd invite my family to our place for elaborate catered family meals throughout the year. He was phenomenal at acting like the best boyfriend in the world. He preferred to spend time with my family in our home. It was easier for him to be in his element. And my parents didn't care. My sisters often couldn't make it. But my parents enjoyed seeing the life I created, so they'd come down for dinner or the day. If they ever stayed over, James would put them up in a fancy hotel. It was all a perfect setup. The more I think about it, the more it makes me sick."

"Thank you for opening up to me," I say softly, wrapping him in a hug. I press a kiss to his temple and his frame softens in my arms. "Let's eat, and instead you can tell me all about your teenage fairy tales."

He was phenomenal at acting like the best boyfriend in the world. How am I any different?

It's safe to say Elijah's parents live in a replica of the perfect Christmas home in a holiday magazine. A soft glow of white Christmas lights illuminates every room. I swear, they each have their own scents, too, whether pine, sugar cookies, hot cocoa; I just haven't come across the hidden candles yet.

The warmth radiating from the fireplace in the living room wraps me in a hug, reminding me of the Christmases I grew up believing existed. When I was a kid, I thought I was unlucky to not have the experience, but as an adult, I've grown to learn it was no reflection of me. I was just unlucky to be born to a leach.

We're still decked out in family sweaters and drinking spiked eggnog with tequila. I've never had spiked eggnog, especially because it's made with dark liquor, but I always promised myself I would experience it in the right setting and today's that day. Blake is apparently the master bartender, and after confirming if tequila was cool, he concocted the beverage. Honestly, it's quite delightful, and I didn't have to break a promise to myself.

It's baffling to me how welcoming they've all been. I'm a stranger in their home, yet *Evergreen* is stitched on my back as if I've married into the family. Elijah warned me his mom is intense, but not in a strict, overbearing way. Yes, there's been bouts of anxiety about things going a certain way—she seems particular in routine—but it hasn't overshadowed her love for her family.

Louise downs the rest of her eggnog before rolling her eyes and laughing. "Okay, fine. Place the tree wherever."

The room erupts in laughter. Elijah and his father, David, have been moving the tree back and forth, inch by inch, for nearly a half hour because the positioning wasn't the same as last year.

"Just like that?" Esme's eyes have teared up from laughing so hard. I imagine this happens every year; as if it's tradition itself.

"Just like that!" Louise states; a double entendre as David and Elijah step away from the tree, calling it a done deal.

"Decoration time!" Myles, the oldest kid, shouts, and the three kids dive toward the bin of ornaments.

I step away from the new chaos now that the heightened tree debacle has simmered. Despite Louise's perfection, she allows the kids to decorate with mismatched ornaments. Most of which look homemade. She sits on the arm of a sofa chair David is sitting in, and immediately his hand rests on her back. They both glance at each other before watching their grand-children with bright smiles. Elijah's kneeling, helping his niece Lola put ornaments up.

My eyes slip back to Louise and David; she's now in his lap with his arms wrapped around her. She looks at me and her smile grows. I tilt my eggnog toward her before I take a sip to subdue the burn of my eyes.

"Can I do the star?" Lola asks, eyes wide as she asks Elijah for permission.

Elijah looks over at his parents. "Whose turn is it this year?"

"Austin, would you do the honor?" Louise asks, and my breath catches. I've never had a star on my Christmas tree.

The most we had were string lights with half of the bulbs dead.

"Can I help Austin?" Lola still directs her question to Elijah, making my heart seize. She gazes at him as if he created the world.

I swallow my emotions and some eggnog before grinning. "I would absolutely love your help, Lola. May I pick you up so you can reach?"

The light in her eyes as she squeals is nearly too much. It's reminiscent of how my sister used to gaze at me. As if I created the world, and for her, I had. I was her protector. Her warrior. Up until my demons considered her one of their own.

Lola grabs the sparkly golden star and lifts her arms up high. I swoop in for the lift, sitting her on my neck. Her giggles vibrate my shoulders.

"Alright, Lola, you're taller than me, so let me know where to position you. Can you reach here?" I intentionally squat to hear her roar with laughter.

"No, silly!"

"What about here?" I go on my tippy toes, grateful for the tall ceilings so I don't hit her head.

"Too tall!" She laughs.

"Hmm," I murmur, going up and down.

"Here!" she yells as I stand at my normal height. She maneuvers with grunts to place it on top and once she's done, I straighten it.

The family claps once it's complete and I lift Lola off of me. Kneeling in front of her, I offer a high five. "Thank you for the help." I grin.

She launches into me with a hug, ignoring my hand. "Thank you!"

Just as quick as she hugs me, she's grabbing after more ornaments.

My vision blurs. Fragmented memories of twirling my

sister around in our studio apartment flash through my mind. Her giggles. Her happiness. We had nothing, but together we had everything.

I look at Louise once I'm standing again. She nods toward me with a smile and a thumbs up. Elijah comes up behind me, resting his hand on my hip.

"She adores you," he whispers.

I don't know whether he means his niece or his mom, but my processing time has slowed. All I've ever wanted was to be seen; make my mom proud. In less than twenty-four hours, in the simplest gesture, Louise has shown me I belong here.

I excuse myself to the bathroom to catch a breather. With the door closed, I lean my hands on the lip of a sink on the two-sink vanity. I inhale as deep as I can before I blow the air out loud. I had hoped the celebrations would be overwhelmingly happy. And they have been, but the ultra highs scatter my equilibrium.

I splash some water on my face, then wash my hands with the Santa soap dispenser. The towel to dry my hands and face is covered in the phrase, "Ho, Ho, Ho".

On the way back, I see a village between the living room and dining room. It's showcased on a table disguised as a mountainside. I have never seen anything like it.

I venture toward the tiny lit buildings, coasting my fingers along the edge of the table, feeling the hard papier-mâché forming the landscape. In the middle of the table, there is a village center, with a block of shops, then it expands outward to have streets with little people walking and random homes. On the peak of the mountain, snow trails cascade down the left side. Reminiscent of where Elijah and I met.

"Impressive, right?" Elijah rests his hand on the small of my back, and my body instantly relaxes to his touch. His forward movements have been few and far between, but I love each moment his guard is down to make the move. I lean toward him, and his hand wraps around my waist, allowing my head to rest on his chest.

"Stunning. Is this a replica of where you live?" It seems silly, especially because his parents don't live there, but I recognize some of the shops' names.

"Actually," he lets out a laugh, and the vibration from his chest has me sinking further into his touch, "my mom creates each piece by hand. This village is inspired by my town, but more so, is a replica of the village in my book series. She's in love with the series. The little people are a lot of the characters too." He chuckles again, and I damn near buckle at the knees.

"Wow, that's like the best support she could ever give."

I haven't told him yet, but I'm about to start book three of six in his series. Liza gave me book three to read instead of using my phone, just in case I had downtime here. The days Elijah and I had apart, I consumed as much of his writing as I could.

I don't want to leave his hold, but I squat, becoming eye level to admire the artistry. The amount of detail in every single building: the paint, the siding; there are even decorations inside each home, like their own little doll house. I know Elijah doesn't want me to get close to his parents, but I have to fangirl with his mother about this series and her craft. I recognize some of the characters in the little figures she's created, too. To have a mom supportive of my passions would be incredible, but to have one so inspired by my craft that she showcases her love to everyone? That's out of this world.

Right on cue, my phone vibrates in my back pocket. My stomach drops. A quick glance tells me it's the devil herself.

"I'll be right back. I have to take this." I dart down the hall to Elijah's room before I dare to answer.

"Hello," I offer a monotone voice. Shouts of cheers and slurs drown out the bass beat of the music. I can practically smell the rum and cigarette smoke. I press a finger between my brows to regulate the pressure.

I find Elijah's digital clock on his bedside table; it's 4:32 pm. She has one minute.

"When are you coming home?" My mom's nasally voice filters over the noise at Mo's, her favorite bar.

Glancing around the room for some sort of anchor, I zone in on Elijah's picture collage on his wall.

"What do you want?" I try to keep my voice even, my eyes trailing over the middle and high school photos of Elijah. He was adorable. Never the center of the photo, always on the edge, but his grins are so bright in each one, not self-conscious of who saw how happy he was. There are two faces that reappear in nearly every photo, and I store a reminder to ask him about his best friends, and if they are still in his life.

Growing up, I was in some photos with people I hung out with growing up, but they were on their disposal cameras. I never had access to them. For all I know, they cut me out. The kids in the nice part of town wanted nothing to do with me because of my mom and the kids with parents like my mom, all got into drugs by middle school.

"It's your birthday. I'm down at Mo's; everyone wants to celebrate."

4:34 pm. Usually the conversation starts with a happy birthday at 4:33 pm, when I was born. It's one of the things she's always kept track of, only because she tells me my birth is the reason I made her miss one of the biggest drinking competitions Mo's had. She would have won free drinks for a year if I wasn't destroying her body, she always claimed.

I breathe in, tracing Elijah's face on his graduation day. I wasn't able to attend my graduation; I had to work.

I pull the phone from my ear, clearing my throat. "I'm not coming home," I say sternly, straightening my stance.

What are you doing? What about the agreement? Stop in,

drop off the money, then bounce. No more than an hour. But you have to go home.

"You're really going to ditch the people who raised you? Love you? They all want to celebrate."

My breath hitches. Memories of running around Mo's and The Diner across the street as a kid, delivering people drinks and food, hits me like a freight train. I did it for fun, then they hired me the second I was legal and needed a job. They are my family.

"Mom, I'm not ditching you guys. I love you. And them. You know that."

Love them? Austin, what they love most about you is mooching off your mother's tab. If you don't pay, you're scum to them.

"Exactly why—"

"I have other plans," I interrupt, gripping the phone tight as my hands shake. It's not a lie. It's exactly what I wanted from my agreement with Elijah. A reason not to fall back into her life, because I sure as hell am not strong enough on my own.

Her laugh infests my brain. "What's more important than spending time with your mom? The reason you have anything to celebrate."

I glance back at Elijah's graduation photo. My chest constricts; the love is overwhelming. His whole family surrounds him, holding each other tight. Louise is crying, and it's so clear how much his parents loved one another in this photo, and still do. Instead of looking at the camera, they gaze at each other, like they are so fucking proud of him.

A few tears travel down my cheeks. My mom has never been proud of me. I missed so many things as a kid and a teen because I had to protect my sister and I needed to get a job to keep a roof over our head. Everything I've worked toward always went back to them, without as much as a thanks.

"I can't bail you out this time," I say, focusing on the warm brown eyes smiling back at me.

I want Elijah. I want this life. I just need to break this godforsaken suffocating chain.

"We had an agreement. Don't you care whether your sister and I eat?"

A pain shoots through my heart and I close my eyes, more tears roll down my cheeks. My sister was fifteen when I left for college. I couldn't protect her from my mom's lifestyle, but I could make sure she had a home and food. My mom continuously worked that avenue. Guilting me into paying their bills if I got out of town. And as my sister got older, the guilt ran deeper. That it was my responsibility to help my mom because she gave me life. Or how much my sister looked up to me. How badly my sister needed me and if I couldn't be there in person, the way I could show my love was through money. On the very rare occasion I have threatened to stop paying, she threatened to destroy my life. I never questioned her word. Her friends are fucking terrifying and I've seen what happens when you cross them. So, we came to an agreement. If she left me alone, I'd give her and my sister money quarterly. She agreed, and I legally changed my last name to have some control over my new life.

"Consider the agreement off," I say, breathing in. I try to channel my inner Liza, who can be a demon when she needs to be. She's walked me through countless conversations I could have to stand up to my mom. Explaining to me how my sister and my mom are grown ass adults. They are more than capable of providing for themselves.

"You're really going to let your own mother and sister be kicked out of a bar because you don't have the decency to lend us a couple bucks?"

A couple bucks? I nearly scream as my lungs sear at the thought. I grip my free hand on Elijah's chair to keep from falling. A couple bucks wouldn't be a problem. I'd be able to afford a home. I could have a boyfriend. A future family. They wouldn't care about a couple bucks.

They are leaching thousands off of me. Mo's and The Diner are only two places the money goes; unless she lost the apartment.

"You're supposed to treat me on my birthday." My voice strains through the guilt wrapping around my heart.

The Christmas music in the living room increases in volume, followed by the kids laughing and singing to "Jingle Bells". I need to get back out there.

"I gave you life. That's your present. You're lucky you're alive. If you get your ungrateful ass down here, Mo will give you a free drink."

I never asked to be born, but I'll always be paying the cost.

There's a knock on Elijah's door. I quickly wipe the tears off my face before it opens.

"Hey! I don't want to rush you," Elijah starts as he bounds into the room. Excitement radiates from him, and my heart swells at his happiness. I need his presence, and I need to be his pillar of strength. "But we're about to do the Christmas tree light unveiling and it's a whole thing. My mom wants to wait for you to experience it."

"Don't tell me you have a boyfriend." My mom's laughter knocks against the well of my insecurities, demanding for them to overflow.

Elijah's face drops when he settles in the room. His eyes soften; so help me god, I cannot cry in front of this man.

I can't lose him.

I try to tear my eyes away, but his strength keeps me centered on him. I don't want him to see me like this. Be infected by my mother too.

A sob lodges in the back of my throat. I can't breathe as tears escape down my cheeks.

"You're ditching your mother, the woman who gave you life, for some guy?" My mom's voice is thick with emotion. "W-who the hell is dumb enough to be with you?" Her voice cracks.

He starts to cross the room, and I hold up a trembling hand, stalling his steps.

"Are you really going to abandon your mother like this? Austin, baby, am I nothing to you?" she cries out.

I freeze. I can't answer my mom without Elijah questioning my response. And I can't answer Elijah without my mom tearing me and him apart. There's no confirmation that Elijah is talking to me; my mom is assuming, but if I answer, it's confirmed I'm with someone else.

I can't have her break him.

Elijah's movements are slow, but he closes the distance, his palm resting on top of mine over the phone. I have ample time to stop him as he lifts the phone from my ear, but I'm powerless.

"Hello, who is this?" Elijah says.

The blood drains from my face as my worlds collide.

"Excuse me?" Elijah's tone shifts as he speaks, and suddenly, I'm rushing out of the room and down the hall to the bathroom. I gently close the door behind me to not draw attention before hurling in the toilet.

I should have hung up the moment he walked in. Shrugged off that it was just a friend. I could have handled the backlash when I snuck out to see her. But trying to stand up to her? And failing miserably? I am going to be reprimanded.

I vomit again, retching until my stomach acid greets me. A cool towel rests around my neck and the toilet flushes before I look up to find Elijah. He kneels beside me, taking another towel to wipe my mouth.

I'm fucking pathetic. Who am I to try to fool this man into thinking I could show him what love is.

"Happy birthday," he whispers, his fingertips brushing along my temple.

I swallow the lump forming in my throat, but I can't control the tears that fall. Elijah is so goddamn patient. I can't remember the last time someone said happy birthday to me. That wasn't my mom's manipulative disgust, at least. Every job I had, I specifically asked for my birthday to not be recognized, and whenever I became close enough to a friend, I strictly told them I don't celebrate it.

I foolishly convinced myself that because Elijah would only be around for a short period of time, I could get away with him never finding out.

Elijah sits against the wall, pulling my hands to him. I move over and he swiftly has me in his lap, wrapping me in a bear hug.

He isn't walking away.

"We're going to sit here for however long you need. And if you don't want to go out and join my family, we can either go hang out in my room or go do something else."

He structures his breathing for me to mimic, and I allow myself to sink into his embrace.

Chapter Sixteen

Elijah

Austin cried himself to sleep in my arms while we sat in the bathroom. All I could do was replay the last thing his mother said to me before hanging up. *Tell my fucking son to get his ass here. It's his birthday. He should be celebrating with his mother, his family.* I don't think I'll ever get rid of her scratchy voice shooting venom. She had mumbled curses and slurs, and something about money, but I couldn't put the pieces together. All I know is Austin isn't on speaking terms with his family and today's his birthday.

The moment his mom had mentioned it, I knew without a doubt he needed to experience an Evergreen birthday party.

I carry Austin into my bedroom and tuck him in without him startling. I turn his phone off and stuff it into his suitcase, hoping if he doesn't see it immediately, he won't try to search. I want to hide it from him, but I don't have that right.

When I make it back out to the living room, the Christmas tree lights are still respectively off, only string lights illuminate the room. The children are watching *The Grinch* animated movie. Everyone else seems more than happy to rest for a moment. Christmas in my house is a marathon.

"I need you to not ask any questions," I say to my family.

My mom sits up from her position, no doubt panicking. Those aren't exactly the words you want any child of yours to say.

I put my lying cap back on. I hadn't thought about how I'd explain that I just found out when my boyfriend-of-seven-month's birthday is.

"It's Austin's birthday today, and well, would you guys help me celebrate him?"

The mixture of expressions my family shares would be comical if I didn't just see that man puking because of his mother. My mom opens and closes her mouth numerous times, likely trying to word a question that I wouldn't shut her down for. She glances at Emma, who then looks at me.

"First, of course, but what information can you give us that explains the spontaneity?"

Very clever wording. I walk into the living room, taking a seat on the ground. The hardwood starts to regulate my system.

"On our first date, when I asked about his birthday, he kindly asked me not to, so I respected his boundary. I learned it's today for reasons I cannot disclose, but I know he has never truly experienced a birthday celebration." I have a hate love relationship with how easily the lie slips from my lips.

My mom's face drops; she's always been go big or go home. She plans for our birthday parties at least a month in advance. If she's even a day off, she'll start to stress about being out of time.

"How do you know he wants to be celebrated?" Esme asks, and it's a fair question.

I'm not sure. I could cross the boundary and he could decide no accommodation over Christmas is better than being around me. I had crossed multiple boundaries with James. Once because I threw him a surprise Evergreen party. It was before I knew he hated surprises. He played the role, and I learned my lesson in the privacy of our home.

But Austin's different.

You don't know him.

I'm getting to know him.

It doesn't matter that his mom opened the door to his trauma in front of me. I'm confident a person who says, "Tell my fucking son to get his ass here" with the tone she did, doesn't deserve to see her son. The man who experienced a Christmas tree farm today, the light in his eyes at traditions I took advantage of, that man deserves to be celebrated. And he told me he had no contact with his family. There must be a good reason. I have to trust him.

"Trust me," I say, looking each of them directly in the eyes. They all sit up, and the kids are still happily distracted.

"Okay, tell us what to do," my mom says.

Over the next three hours, we get to work. I have no idea how long Austin will be out for, so we have to act quick. My mom tells me plenty of times how I really need to stop stressing her out with all of these new additions to her schedule. Though, it's partially in jest. It hasn't even been a full day here and Austin's already made a positive impression on her. My sisters go to a store for decorations while my brother-in-laws head to the liquor store to concoct an Austin Cocktail. My dad watches the kids and digs out old birthday decorations while my mom and I go to the grocery store.

I decided to throw him a thirtieth birthday party. My sisters and I have already turned thirty, and it's the most fun to plan, so it'll be easy to throw together. I know Austin's thirty-one, only from context and not him directly telling me, but I figure he never had a big thirtieth blow out.

I guess on Austin's food preferences as my mom spitfires questions at me. I nearly shout James' answers. They are right on the tip of my tongue. But I think back to what he baked for the pastry cabinet at the resort and what meals he served at the retreat. They may not be his recipes, but they aren't James'.

My mom and I are waiting for the timer to go off on a three-layer cake we made and my brother-in-laws are concocting something with blue curaçao when my sisters burst through the front door.

"Shh!" my mom instantly shushes them.

"Sorry! Sorry!" Emma giggles. It doesn't sober their excitement, but they lower their voices. "Austin is going to have *the* best birthday."

She turned thirty this past summer, and it was a rager. I'm honestly concerned about what the two of them could have gotten, especially being the last to return.

"We have themed shirts!" Esme grins, and they both toss their bags on the dining room table before Esme dives into one.

Themed shirts are a must in my household. Though, usually, they are handmade.

"You absolutely, without a doubt, cannot see Austin's shirt until it's on his body; do you understand?" Emma narrows her eyes at me as Esme has a pile of shirts in her hand.

"Sure." I laugh.

Esme hands a shirt to Emma, and Emma folds it inside out and sets it aside. Then Esme hands me and my parents shirts. They say, "Dirty Thirty Club" on a beer bottle.

"They aren't perfect, but Austin's makes up for it." Esme and Emma share a look before laughing.

I'm honestly terrified of what they may subject him to. The Austin I know from the retreat would be all into this. The Austin asleep in my bed? He makes me nervous that I made the wrong decision. Everyone deserves to experience an Evergreen birthday party, but it could be too soon. He might need rest to recoup instead of high chaotic energy.

"I don't know whether I should be proud or concerned,"

my father says, snapping me out of my thoughts. He's walking toward the kitchen from the hallway. The space is filling up with dick decorations and innuendo dirty thirty phrases.

"Thank you, Dad!"

My sisters are giggling and I turn to see them hanging something up on the back of the front door. I walk over to analyze and it's a picture of me shirtless on the beach with a printed out cartoon picture of a dick. The picture was taken over the summer by Esme. I had been walking out of the water after swimming with the kids. My hair's slicked back and the setting sun hits the water droplets just perfectly on my skin. My sisters told me it was the perfect photo for a dating site; and it was, if my interest had been to get laid.

"What the hell is this?" I try to be stern, but my voice catches as my cheeks warm.

Emma throws her head back and laughs. "Pin the dick on you! Our family shall not be participating, as that's weird, but this is a solo game for Austin, to see if he has game." She winks, sticking the large dick where it should be on me, and it's all sorts of wrong.

"Emma!" my mom exclaims as she pulls the cake out of the oven. "This is not how we operate an Evergreen birthday party."

Esme, Emma, and I all share a look before roaring with laughter. Thankfully, it helps settle my nerves.

"This is exactly an introduction into who we are," Emma exclaims.

"Mom, you freaking bought me dick pasta for my thirtieth," Esme calls her out, and I remember that. It was almost five years ago; she wanted to remind us she was still cool.

"We're the fun family," my dad chimes in. "Nothing is off limits, despite me being slightly concerned about how many dicks are in my kitchen."

"Oh my god!" I laugh, rubbing the tears from my eyes.

"I'm going to check on Austin. The food should be ready for pickup in five minutes."

My mom salutes, as Emma shouts, "Wait! Put your shirt on." I do as she asks; everyone else has theirs on. Then she tosses me Austin's shirt. "Don't unfold it!" she demands with a smirk.

I walk down the hallway, double checking on the kids in the den. They are set up with unlimited snacks, a fort, and Disney+. It'll be a late night for them, but we'll all want extra sleep in the morning.

When I open my bedroom door, Austin is on the floor, in front of one of my bookshelves, combing through a photo album of mine. I stop in the door frame, not entirely prepared to see him awake. He doesn't jump at my presence, just glances up briefly before looking back at the photos. I close the door behind me and sit next to him, seeing my twelfth birthday party. He must have heard us talking. My mom recreated the den to be the ultimate Avengers headquarters. My birthday is in October, so I always had costume parties. I was already so in love with reading and starting to write that dressing up like someone else was fun. My parents dressed up too; my mom was strict on if you come without a costume, you aren't allowed in, and if a kid couldn't get a costume, she'd make them one.

"Your family is incredible," he says softly, his fingers on a picture of me and my parents.

My dad was Iron Man, my mom was Pepper, and I was Captain America. The shield, an authentic one from Marvel, hangs on a wall in my current home today.

"I hope I'm not overstepping." He tenses at my words, and I connect our fingertips. His tension subsides and I breathe out. I had never calmed James with just one gesture. "But it's in my blood to throw a birthday party once I know it's someone's birthday."

He opens his mouth, and I place a finger on his lips.

"You want to show me how to love again?" I ask. He gazes at me with a nod. There's a pain behind his eyes I haven't seen before, and I desperately want to take it away. "Then let me show you it's okay to be celebrated, and how it's done." His shoulders sink, but the curl of his fingers tighten. "If you haven't noticed, my family goes hardcore for Christmas, but that extends to all holidays."

"I'm sorry for—"

"For absolutely nothing." I hold my gaze steady with his. He needs to hear my words. "You don't have to share anything you're not comfortable with. If you want to talk, we can, whenever, but I am not expecting you to."

He breathes in, holds it, and then exhales. I watch as a shift happens on his face. I know it all too well; the handy mask to hide behind. He's helped me start to remove mine, and I want to do the same for him.

He nods toward my shirt with a soft chuckle. "I appreciate the gesture, but I'm not turning thirty."

"I know, but have you celebrated your thirtieth?"

His mask falters. I need to shift this back to neutral territory.

"It's a rite of passage to hit your thirties. A time to stop giving a fuck about others and live your life comfortably."

He raises his brow. "And wise old thirty-two-year-old, how is not giving a fuck going?"

Touché. He came to play.

I pull the photo album out of his hands, tossing that and his birthday shirt on the floor, before gently laying him on the ground, hovering over him. "Quite brilliantly," I whisper, mere millimeters from his lips. His breath hitches, and I have him right where I want him.

My hands caress up his body. He thrusts toward me, and I release my hands to tickle his pits. He squeals beneath me, writing, and I press my pelvis down into his, holding him steady.

"Okay, okay," he laughs, and my hands surrender flat against his sides. "Let's celebrate my thirtieth."

I smile down at him, trying to figure out the best course of action. Whether it is important to keep it go, go, go, so his negative thoughts can't enter or if he might need a moment to come to terms with what's happening.

"My mom is picking up dinner right now, which means you can't go into the kitchen until she's back because she'll be devastated she missed your reaction. You have two choices: shower and reset or we hang out here until I receive confirmation we're good."

A sly grin appears on his face as his hands grip my hips. "How long do we have?"

"Maybe twenty minutes."

Austin's eyes dart to the clock quickly before he leans up on his elbows. "Lemme brush my teeth, and then maybe one of our lessons can be how to love the birthday boy?" His hand grasps my shirt and my dick awakens. "Do I get one of these?"

I nod, forcing myself to shuffle off of him to hand over the white shirt. "I don't know what it says, though."

He unfolds it and immediately starts laughing. I try to come around and read the words, but he holds the shirt against him. "Nope. Not yet. First, who got this?"

"My sisters. Be prepared for a potentially raunchy party. This isn't a let's have a polite dinner because we're with family."

"Oh, I hope not; otherwise, I'll be incorrectly dressed. Correction to my birthday wish. I'm going to brush my teeth, and when I get back, I want you sitting on the bed pantless."

I swallow as my dick grows, pressing tightly against my jeans. "I thought I was—"

"Oh, you will," he whispers, pressing a kiss against my cheek before he dashes out of the room.

I have never done anything sexual underneath my parents' roof, at least with anyone else. Sure, I masturbated a ton as a teen, but I never brought anyone home. Not that I ever felt like I couldn't, but it felt strange with my parents down the hall. On the rare occasion James was here, he'd try to force me, but instead of saying yes, I'd suggest an even better time at home, making him wait. He'd agree, and I'd endure the consequences when we got home.

But now, Austin doesn't have me second-guessing it at all. I comply, pants off, sitting at the edge of the bed. I should be the one giving him a blow job; it is his birthday, but maybe that can be rearranged for later. When the door opens, I have a momentary fear that it's one of my sisters, but Austin walks in with his new shirt on.

My god, Esme and Emma. His shirt says, "I lick the salt, swallow the tequila, and suck the lime." The "I lick, swallow, and suck" are bolded. *Naturally.*

"I'm so sorry," I rush, my cheeks blushing. I can't imagine being asked to wear a shirt like that around a family I didn't know.

"What are you sorry for?" He smirks, crossing the room.

My dick stands at attention, despite my embarrassment, twitching as his eyes narrow in on it.

"The shirt is truthful." His voice is seductive, crawling beneath my skin. He drops to his knees, wrapping his left hand around my dick, the right trailing over my balls. I squirm, gripping the comforter beneath me.

"I love to lick." He licks my length, coating it with his spit. "I am a master sucker." He devours me in one go, my length hitting the back of his throat. He sucks in, creating pressure before twirling his tongue around, licking my base. His hands disappear to his pants, but his mouth controls my dick. His head bobs up and down. Each time I hit his throat, he sucks in deep, lighting all my nerve endings on fire. His mouth is incredible. Once his pants are down, one hand pumps himself and the other grips the bulb of my cock, so his tongue can flick and circle around my tip. His fingers pinch my foreskin up and over my tip before exposing my nerves, kissing and sucking the veins.

Austin stops momentarily, making eye contact with me. He's horny, and I wish I could push him over and fuck him. But it isn't his birthday wish at the moment and we don't have enough time. A quick look at the clocks says we'll be interrupted any minute.

With his eyes on me, he traces my dick over his lips, applying my pre-cum like lipstick and my god, if it isn't the hottest thing he's done. His tongue swipes over the creamy liquid, receiving every last drop. I lean over, lifting his chin to meet me, tasting myself on his lips. He opens his mouth, his tongue transfers some to me and I all but blow my load, but I can't until his mouth devours me again.

"Make me come." My voice is rough, and he groans, pressing his head against my stomach, swallowing me as deep as he can. I'm so far down his throat that if I reach out to caress his neck, I'd feel my tip. My eyes roll to the back of my head at the thought. With an inhale, he buried his nose in my pubes. His cheeks hollow with a suck and my hot load shoots out, the force causing him to dig his fingers into my legs to steady his mouth. I fall back on the bed, thrusting up as he milks me dry.

"My fucking god, Austin," I breathe. My nerves are shot, but the thought of his mouth leaving my dick weighs me down. I don't ever want to lose this.

"And I swallow," he whispers.

Before I can react, he's hovering over my face, the tip of his dick asking for entrance. I comply, his girth filling me up. He mouth fucks me, only slowing the moment I gag, but I clutch my hands on his ass, pushing him down, sucking in, allowing his cum to coat my throat. I swallow him, sucking until he softens. He's perfect.

Austin removes himself from my mouth, and a part of me disappears.

"That was," he breathes, slinking down the bed to snuggle against me, "amazing."

"You're amazing," I say before my thoughts get in my way. His tightened hold tells me he needed to hear that. It's possible we aren't so different; both of us needing strength and guidance from the other.

"Dinner is ready!" I hear my mom yell. Something I had given her permission to do, confident that I would have been able to talk Austin into the party.

On cue, Austin's stomach growls. He laughs against my neck, nuzzling closer to press a kiss on my skin.

He's so vastly different from my ex. The confidence is there, but it isn't cockiness. He's playful and so unserious at times. He's bold. I could learn way more about how he presents himself instead of just how to love. I imagine loving Austin isn't all that hard. Maybe love shouldn't be hard. I surely don't showcase that it is in my novels.

We force ourselves up, wiping any remaining stickiness with an old T-shirt and some saliva. I open my closet, revealing a floor-length mirror so we can both ensure we're presentable. Our flushed cheeks might give it away, but it's on par for the theme.

I slam my bedroom door shut behind us, another sign for my family to be ready. We enter the kitchen, hand in hand. My family is decked out in party hats as they shout, "Happy Birthday!"

Austin's clasp tightens, and I tense. This might be too much. I don't know why he chose to keep his birthday out of our plan. It's possible I should have been more sensitive to that. James always told me I was too sensitive in the wrong areas. Sensitive with my emotions, but I never took other people's thoughts into consideration. Like how he hated surprises. James hated feeling out of control. He had said if I would have respected him by asking if I could throw him a party, he'd have continued to celebrate with my family. Instead, I had ruined all chances of him attending any Evergreen birthday; especially my own.

"—dirty thirty is way more fun to shop for." I only hear the last of Emma's statement before she's grabbing Austin's arm, pulling him away from me. "Let me give you a tour."

He has a smile on his face. It seems genuine. There isn't an undertone of anger or frustration.

Not all men are James.

My mom pulls me into a side hug. "I'm very proud of you," she says quietly. I sink into her hug as the guilt of my lies sizzle in my stomach.

"First," Emma says, "we have the blue margarita. It's essential to have the blue liquor that feels like you shouldn't drink it after thirty, but it's incredible. Margaritas, well, they are always a good idea, and tequila, because of your shirt." She winks as she hands him a drink.

He immediately sips it, and his eyes brighten. It pushes a portion of fear back into its hiding spot.

"This is delightful, thank you," he says.

Emma beams, as Blake shouts, "That was our idea!" He and Timothy fist pump.

Austin chuckles, placing his drink down, before he goes to hand Blake and Timothy theirs.

"Wait, wait! Our tour isn't done; we can cheer afterward," Emma exclaims.

Austin's eyes find mine; he's amused by the seriousness. His eyes flicker to my mom, who is still hugging me, and my heart clenches. He follows my sister a few feet to the kitchen island, where there are five trays of food, all still covered.

"Then we have dinner; orgasmic Italian."

I snort as Austin's eyes widen. We are not a normal family, and maybe I should have warned him about how debaucherous it could get.

"Emma!" my father reprimands.

"Father, I do believe you've described it exactly that way."

My dad reddens, and Austin lets out a chuckle. A few more sips of that blue drink and he'll be right at home.

"Then we have a lovely three-layer cake that Elijah and our mom made. I don't know what flavor, but all my mom's cakes are heavenly. Just hope Elijah's only job was to stir."

"Hey!" I shout.

The cake is finished with buttercream frosting, but there's a drawing I can't decipher on it.

"Dear, you suck at baking," my mom says, rubbing my back, "but we love you all the same."

"Is this your doing?" Austin asks. I walk over to the cake, seeing a dick drawn on top in red gel icing.

"Absolutely not!" I pout, crossing my arms. "I was trying to be romantic by making a cake."

Austin's eyes soften, and Esme chimes in, "Yeah, and it ruined our theme. That's my drawing."

Austin's laugh is unmasked. Loud and carefree. I want to savor that sound. A wave of loneliness washes over me; suddenly I'm desperate to not share him. My family doesn't know there's an expiration date on us, but my heart does.

"Now for my favorite activity," Emma continues, pulling Austin over to the front door. His eyes immediately widen and his cheeks turn cherry red. "Pin the dick on Elijah!"

"Ohhh-kay," I say, walking over to Austin and guiding him back to the drinks. The feeling of his skin beneath my palms settles my mind. His skin is my magic cure; it's intoxicating. "Let's allow him to process how bizarre our family is first."

"I have never come across a family so open like this," Austin says. "It's hysterical."

"I don't know where we went wrong," my dad jokes, walking over to the counter and grabbing a drink. "Louise and I are as innocent as they come."

Everyone, except for Austin and my dad, breaks out in laughter. My mom has tears in her eyes, and my dad can no longer hold it in, chuckling himself.

"My parents used to travel the country in an RV before they had kids. Smoking weed, eating shrooms, having three and foursomes. They settled themselves with kids, but not their minds or their stories," I explain.

"Y'all would find out about the world, anyway. Might as well come from us," my dad says.

"I think that makes sense," Austin says. "Better to not be too strict and know what your kids are experiencing instead of them hiding it."

Austin leans against my chest, continuing to face my family as if it's the most natural display of affection. I drape my arms around him, and he tilts his head to rest under my chin. When I exhale, he sinks deeper into my hold. He makes me feel like I'm floating.

"Turns out our kids have barely scratched the surface of what Louise and I experienced." My dad caresses his jaw, pretending to think. "Though that's likely better."

My parents have some wild stories. The newest stories they've shared over the past couple of years have been ones where my parents could have gotten in serious trouble from being in the wrong place at the wrong time.

"Okay, okay. We aren't scaring Austin away. Let's sit down and eat before everything gets cold," my mom says.

"I don't want to interrupt, but it doesn't seem like your

tree is lit yet. Would you guys like to do what your tradition is?" Austin asks.

My heart warms at his memory. I didn't think he processed what I had said to him when he was on the phone.

I glance over at my mom and her eyes shine. She clasps her hands and nods. He's won her over.

We don't disrupt the kids as it's almost nine. They are a bit too young for the tradition, anyway, but they'll be excited when they wake up. We all grab a margarita before heading into the living room, circling around the tree.

"Okay, Austin. You don't have to take part, but each year we go around and talk about one thing we loved about our year and one thing we hope we can continue or work on for the next year. Then we light the tree," my mom says.

"I'll participate," he says.

My heart skips a beat. James never joined whenever my mom offered an out.

My mom's taken aback. Her smile falters before she grins so wide I'm confident her cheeks are going to ache in the morning. She may have liked James, but I'm not sure if her smile was ever so grand.

I'm never going to survive once she learns this is all fake.

I realize I'm holding Austin's hand when he squeezes our fingers slightly. Being with him is natural, and I don't know what any of it means. Does it feel easy because he's good as a fake boyfriend and his task is successful? Or are our bodies magnetic? Always drawn to one another.

My mom begins. "My favorite part of this year is seeing my Elijah so at peace. I've missed your smile, sweetheart."

Austin's hand moves to my back, steadying my body at her words. I blink away the instant tears. That was unexpected. I thought my acting had been good. I thought my fake smiles over this year were as genuine as they could be. Obviously, I was allowed to be heartbroken over a four-year relationship, but because I only saw my family once or twice a month, I tried my hardest to not bring them down.

Austin traces a heart on my back; I gasp with his touch; the dam is about to break. I can't keep lying. I want to confess. I want to tell my mom about James. I want to tell Austin exactly how I feel. I want to explain how fucking terrified I am to start a relationship, but how I think I'm more frightened of living without him. I want to explain to my family that our relationship is fake, but goddamnit, the chemistry between us is electric.

There is absolutely no way he could fake that.

"My favorite thing about this year"—Austin's voice startles me, and I look down at him as he speaks to my family—"was getting the job at the resort. Being head of a kitchen is where I belong. What I'd love to work on for next year?" he questions, then our eyes connect.

It feels like we're the only two in the room with his intense gaze. He's trying to communicate something my family won't hear. My insecurities resurface, keeping me from hoping he wants something real.

"I'd love to keep working on us," he says.

My heart soars before it sobers. That's exactly what my family would expect to hear. If Austin didn't mention me in his wishes for Christmas, when I'm brand new in his year, my family would get suspicious. Even my heart twinges at the thought that I wasn't his favorite part of this year, even though that's plausible. I've only been in his life for less than two weeks. That's nothing compared to his career.

If I'm honest, my favorite thing about this year has been meeting him. Attending the retreat flipped my world upside down. But if he isn't looking for anything past this, that's too forward to say. And I don't want the best thing that's happened to me to have been a guy.

I take a page out of his book. "My favorite thing was

publishing the first book in my second series." I feel like a drastically different person than when I first drafted the book. It was right when I got a therapist and we crafted a plan on how to leave James. Somehow, my mind was still able to write a romance. No one criticized that book for lacking chemistry when my home life was atrocious.

"And I'd love to keep working on us too," I tell Austin, using his exact words so there is no miscommunication when it all breaks apart. I can't be accused of expressing myself too intensely.

Austin leans his head on my shoulder when Esme and her husband go.

Once everyone has gone, we all count down from five and my dad flips the switch at zero. We all act our part of the oohing and ahhing.

"Wow," Austin breathes.

My mom suggests we all go eat, but Austin remains frozen, admiring the tree.

"This sure as hell beats my scrappy ass tree growing up." He laughs, but I can't miss the sadness in his tone.

I want to say something. Want to comfort him in some way, but before my brain catches up, he's standing in front of me, cupping my cheeks.

"I meant every word," he whispers, sealing it with a kiss.

Austin leaves me stranded in the living room with my heart in a puddle.

Means that he wants to work on us? A stupid little laugh escapes my lips as excitement bubbles within me.

When I join the family, they are taking the foil lids off the still steaming food. There's penne alla vodka, zuppa di pesces, chicken marsala, fried calamari, and bread rolls. Way too much food for all of us to finish, but it'll be a lovely lunch. The drinks don't pair well with the meal, but it's a solid effort on everyone's end.

The conversation around the table is basic. My family is well aware of not asking questions, though I'm sure they are curious to know about his other birthdays and why it might have been so important to go all out on this one. I'm itching for those answers, too, but it's up to Austin to talk about them. I can't demand to know anything without the actual title of boyfriend, and even then, he's subject to his privacy.

Once stuffed and boozed up on our second drink, my sisters decide that "Pin the dick on Elijah" is not just an Austin game, but actually a family game. My parents opt to clean the dishes instead. Each person must be spun in a circle five times before they are straightened and told to walk with their blindfold.

Something about Austin wearing a blindfold and holding a paper dick has me imagining what I might do to him in the privacy of my own bedroom. I rarely had control in the bedroom, but it's something I've always wanted and I might be able to ask for with Austin. There are quite a few things I'd like to try with him the next time he's off.

The thought startles me, and I back myself away from the game. He's in good hands as I create space. I take the moment to refill our drinks. We shouldn't have another drink, as he's teetering with family issues and I'm on a balance of professing love for a man who is a mystery. But what's a dirty thirty without being foolish?

"If I ask a question, will you be honest?" My mom scares the living shit out of me, and I spill blue curaçao on the front of my white shirt. "I'm sorry." She chuckles, placing her hand on my back.

I hate when she does this. It isn't the first time she's asked this question and snuck up on me the minute I'm alone. Most of my life, I was honest. The last time she did this was Easter; the first time I saw her after James and I broke up. She had pestered me when the break up happened, wanting to come visit, but she respected my space. On Easter, I straight up lied to her, telling her it was an amicable breakup, because I couldn't get into everything at Easter with our extended family. I wanted to protect her. She didn't need her memories tarnished. He never hurt her.

But now she's cornered me while I'm intoxicated, holding the biggest secrets of my life. Some aren't even mine.

"Depends on the question," I say, focusing on the drinks in front of me.

"I did it!" I hear Austin yell, and my sisters cheer, saying something about how spot on he was. I'm not surprised. I wish I was over there whispering some sort of innuendo in his ear instead of here with my mom.

"When did you meet Austin?"

Fuck.

I look toward Austin. He's now wearing a crown with a cut out of a dick attached to it. *Of course, they got a crown for the winner.* He's beaming so fucking bright as Emma gushes to him about her thirtieth. Blake chimes in, fact-checking her story. She likes to exaggerate.

I focus back on continuing to pour mine and Austin's beverages while I think. I'm at a loss. On one hand, it makes no difference to Austin whether my parents know or not. He wanted accommodation and a Christmas, and he's receiving even more than that. We could come clean, continue the holiday as friends, and still go on our merry way on the 26th.

"He's infatuated with you," my mom offers. She knows something. "And I'm certain you've never felt this way about someone before. Not even James. But I don't buy that you met seven months ago. There is no way you could have hidden this happiness from us over the past few months."

My dad comes up behind my mom as I look at them. The dishes are now complete.

When I'm ready to confess, she'll be amazed at how much

I have been able to hide. But she's right; Austin has a way of lowering my defenses, and it's likely I wouldn't have been able to keep the mask around my parents.

Even if I was ready to be honest, it would involve telling my mom the truth about James, and that story is far longer than this birthday party. We don't need any more intense conversations happening today.

"I can't talk to you about this right now," I say, and I hate the way her face drops. "I need to. Soon. And please force me to before I head home. You both deserve that. But right now, Austin's happiness is too important, and I can't dive into my baggage."

My mom nods, but the conversation isn't complete. She watches him for a moment, and I follow her gaze. Somehow between Austin winning and now, he started learning a dance with Emma. Austin turns the wrong way, catching Emma's foot, and they both tumble to the ground laughing.

"Is he worth my heart getting attached?" she asks, catching me entirely off guard.

With one more gaze at Austin, I wrap my mom in a hug. More so to heal the ache in my heart. "I hope so, Mom," I whisper. "I really do."

She hugs me tight as I swallow the overwhelm of emotion. Readying myself to be on Cloud 9 for the birthday king.

Chapter Seventeen
Austin

I feel like death with the bittersweet desire of not wanting to die. I never broke my promise of drinking dark liquor, but I always promised myself I wouldn't get drunk. I wouldn't, under any circumstances, turn out like my mother. *Like my sister.* The few times I have been drunk were at college when the new environment and pressures became too much. I didn't know who I was, who I wanted to be, but I learned real fast I couldn't be my past.

Elijah warned me tequila shots with Emma weren't a good idea. I remember him guiding me away from them, but Emma and I were having so much fun together. She's the sister I wish mine was. She joked I *had* to do tequila shots because my shirt said so. By that portion of the night, I couldn't disappoint my shirt. Or her. Or be the downer and come across as ungrateful. His family is unmatched. I want to be like them. I want to fit in.

I deserve this. At least that's what I kept telling myself. That I should be able to live my life how I want; it's not my fault my mom's an addict.

Getting drunk once doesn't make me an alcoholic. That

thought alone had me walking away from Elijah and toward Emma's cheers. Downing not just one, but three shots of tequila.

I don't remember anything after that. Definitely not how I made it back into my fake boyfriend's childhood bed. Elijah's not even beside me. It's the start of day two, and I'm already no better than my mother. Because I always had to clean up after her, I studied etiquette books at the library growing up, wanting to impress others. Show them I'm more than where I came from.

In a single night, I forgot all the rules.

My heart stops. *I hope I didn't tell our secret.*

I have to go. Catch a cab to my hometown, let my mom rip me to shreds. Give up the goddamn act and fall where I'm meant to. At least there I know what type of disappointment I am. The idea of looking any Evergreen in the face today has me wishing I could vanish.

They are too good. They are carefree, loving, and hysterical. While they aren't perfect, it's the ideal family I always wished for. All I want is to get to know them better and figure out a way to solidify Elijah as mine. But I caught the way Elijah and his mom were looking at me last night while I played the game with his siblings. Elijah looked spooked and his mom was straight-faced. I don't know what they were talking about, but it had to do with me.

The bedroom door opens and I shift my eyes, too nervous to turn my head. I need some ibuprofen and a nice greasy burger. It might do the trick. Though I haven't been hungover since I was twenty.

Elijah smiles when he recognizes my eyes are open, and it all but brings tears to my own. *Why is he happy?*

His hands hold a cloudy glass of water and when he sits on the bed, he showcases the holy grail: ibuprofen.

"I have some Liquid IV for you," he whispers. "Take these, drink all of this, and my dad is making burgers."

My brows furrow as my eyes shift to his clock. It's a little after nine, and the light seeping through the curtain tells me it isn't nine at night.

"My dad has been hungover way too many times to count. He's got all the tricks. Try to get up slowly. I promise this will help."

I do as he asks, moving like a sloth to keep my head from slashing in half. "I'm sorry," I whisper, taking the drink and medicine. He sits next to me, leaning up against the headboard, his shoulder brushing alongside mine.

I want to lean into it. Allow his strength to hold me up. But I can't. I can't bring him into my darkness. I sacrifice my energy to create a few inches of space.

"For what? Getting drunk?" He tries to connect our eyes, but I focus on tossing the medicine down my throat instead. "Austin, it was your birthday party *and* thirty themed. If you didn't get trashed, my family might consider it an insult to their party planning."

An insult? I hesitantly glance over at him. Our upbringings couldn't be more different, but my mom would consider it an insult, too.

"Plus, my sister is mostly to blame. She's feeling like absolute shit at the moment, so you're no worse off. She won't be semi-coherent until she eats a burger. Then we'll likely be couch potatoes the rest of the day."

I should have told them no. That I don't celebrate. Don't waste time on me. I could have told Elijah in my semi-coherent state when he first wished me a happy birthday. But now, the whole day is ruined because alcohol got in the way.

"Your mom has plans, though," I say pathetically.

Elijah's hand rests on my cheek, turning my face toward him. "This day is *always* a rest day. Getting the tree and decorations can be a lot. It isn't the first time we've woken up hungover, so it's always a holiday movie day. This isn't your fault."

I lift my electrolyte water to avoid looking into his eyes and he lets go of my chin. I drink the rest of it, allowing my brain to process his words. I don't have the energy to not believe him. He takes the empty glass, setting it on his nightstand.

"Thank you," I whisper.

"What for?" He interlaces our fingers.

I meant every word. I squeeze his hand. I want to be the guy who meant what I said last night. I want to work on us in the new year.

"Taking care of me. Throwing an amazing party. Getting Italian food, god—" I pause, thinking about how much more wrecked I'd be if we didn't carb load last night. "That was a good call."

"Oh yes." He chuckles. His lips press against my temple, momentarily pausing the pounding. "We never have an Evergreen party without carbs. It's simply irresponsible."

I need this. I don't know how to walk away from it. I didn't realize how lonely I was before Elijah walked into my dining hall, but he opened the door I had securely shut. I don't know if I can go back to life before him. Living on my married friends' property. Shielding myself from physical touch. Working for someone else's life. Drowning my bank account.

"What can I do for you?" Elijah's soft words enter the cracks of my barriers.

I slide underneath the covers and face the wall. I curl my legs up to my chest, inhaling as silent tears drip from my eyes.

I can't have this. If I don't visit my mom, she'll do damage. I have a resume now. I have trusted people in my field who can vouch for me. But I don't know what she's capable of. I can't have Elijah attached to whatever wrecking ball she throws. If only for the reason he has a public name. He's already having trouble with reviews saying negative things about him. He doesn't need the scumbags of my hometown spreading shit.

It could all be an empty threat. My mom could fuck off and go find someone else to fund her life. But I'm terrified of taking that leap. Because what if it isn't? What if I lose everything I've ever fought for?

What if I hurt Elijah?

His arms wrap around me in an instant, molding his body against mine, chest on my back. A sob lodges in my throat. He gently kisses my temple down to my jaw line, nuzzling my head up so he can reach my neck. His scruff tickles as he trails down toward my collarbone before he repeats the process back up. His fingertips stroke my arm, sending shivers down my spine in the best way possible. He's awakening my nerve endings. My intrusive thoughts pause, anticipating his next move.

His hand comes around my front, reaching up to caress my chin, but it pauses as his fingers hit tears. "Oh, Austin," he breathes. My body is weightless as he turns me toward him. Our faces align, and it's like he's staring directly into my soul. I want to shrivel up and rewind the last twenty-four hours. Press decline on my mom's phone call. It'd be easier than explaining my past. His hand presses against the small of my back, holding me close to him.

Our mouths connect in a salty, lazy kiss. His tongue teases my lips, but it's clear this is not advancing. He's trying to show me he cares, and the thought alone breaks my heart.

"Can I tell you a secret?" Elijah whispers against my lips. His words have me shivering into him. The pressure of his hand increases, like he can't fathom any space between us.

Desperate for the truth, I kiss him in response, encouraging him to continue.

"I'm falling for you."

My blood runs cold. His breath burns on my skin, his hands searing into my back. I clench my eyes shut. Flashbacks of arguments with my ex bombard my mind. We had planned a trip for our one-year anniversary. We were going cross-country, hitting all the major stops. Barely any money had been put out for it yet, but it was in a joint savings account. My mom was in a rough place that year. Not only was I supposed to pay my dues before the trip, but she got assaulted and guilt tripped me into paying her hospital bills. I drained not only my checking and savings accounts, but I gave her the few thousand we had in our joint account.

In one stupid act, I was kicked out of my apartment, lost my boyfriend, and didn't even receive a thanks from my mom. Though, she let me sleep on her couch—that I paid for—until Liza rescued me from there, giving me a place to stay. That was Liza's first time saving me.

"I don't understand what happened yesterday, but I'm here to listen. I *want* to listen. You don't have to be the strong, confident Austin if that is just a mask. I'm interested in getting to know the real you, all the mess that might entail."

My head screams at me to push him away. His hand applies pressure to my back and my stomach turns, but my heart softens. I don't know which way is up.

I'm good at being a friend and a partner. I have strengths I bring that surmount my weaknesses. I know I'm a kick-ass chef and fucking incredible in bed. I *know* I need to separate from my family. Logically, I can't keep doing this. It's not just hurting me. Elijah's in it now. He's gotten a small preview; his writing mind likely has created an elaborate story already. He's invested.

What if I don't have the strength to walk away? What if someone else leaves me because I run our income dry?

"I l-like you," I whisper, my voice clogged with mucus. My shirt is soaked with tears, as I'm certain this pillow is, too.

His body tenses against mine. "But . . ."

I lean back and our eyes connect. I've manipulated him. I knew what I was doing. I'm no better than his ex. I took his vulnerability and ran with it. Molding it to fit my selfish plans. I'm a great caretaker. I was born to be one. I knew he'd fall for me because of how he acted at the resort. He trusted me, and I'm going to leave him to pick up his shattered pieces. In no world can you show someone what love is and then walk away without doing irreparable damage. Creating expectations too high for the average person to reach. I wanted to give him a fairytale. Love that exists in his novels because, for a moment in time, people don't have real-life problems to deal with.

I'm already going to hurt him. Being honest is the least I can do.

"I can't love you. I'm living a double life. One that's striving for more, but I'll always be tethered to my past. If I didn't pass out from being wasted last night, I would have taken a cab to go to my mom once everyone fell asleep."

I watch his body deflate, *feel* it against me. Something flashes in his eyes and he breathes in. He removes his arms from me, sitting up in his bed.

Tears blur my eyes at the emptiness.

"You told me you weren't on speaking terms with your family."

Tears stream down my face at his guarded tone. He has every right to be angry.

"I'm not," I whisper. "Well, except for two weeks every quarter."

His eyes narrow. "You give her money every quarter?"

The air is stripped from my lungs. I was hoping she hadn't mentioned money. Just that it was my birthday.

"Why does she have a hold on you, Austin? Why is she asking for money?"

I turn toward the wall. Curling into myself. I can't have

this conversation while he judges me. His frustrated tone is more than enough.

"She's my mom. She needs me."

"No, she doesn't." I flinch at his tone. "She was so disrespectful about you on the phone. She had you in tears *on your birthday*. You didn't ask to be born. Your mother brought you into this world, and it is not your responsibility to take care of her. It's her responsibility to take care of you."

"You don't understand. She doesn't have anyone else."

"Does she always speak to you like that?"

I press my hands against my eyelids, trying to stop the waterfall. I can't let my body shake. He doesn't need to watch the hyperventilating sob take over my body.

"Are you paying her bar tab?"

The pounding in my head increases. I grip my scalp to relieve the pressure.

"You do not owe her a single dime of your hard-earned money unless she lent you a loan, but I'm certain that isn't the situation here. Is this why you don't have an apartment or home? Can you only afford a week here and there of rent because the rest is drained through your mom's life choices?"

A soft tap on the door has us both jumping. "Breakfast is ready," his father says through the door.

"Austin," his hand rests on my shoulder, "were you just using me?"

The question hits me like a freight train. I can't breathe. I desperately gasp for air as the sob I've been holding in begs to be released. A piercing throb sores through my head.

"Please get out," I whisper, shrugging off his hand. I shove my head underneath the pillow, as if I have any fucking right to stay in this bed and take up space.

"Austin—"

"Out!" I scream through thick mucus.

I hear a muffled sigh before feeling the shift of the bed as he gets off. The moment the door clicks shut, I choke out a sob, wincing as a throb explodes in my head, spotting my vision.

I need to get out of here. We don't live in the same town, we won't cross paths. It's likely he'll never come to the resort again, with it being too close to his home to pay for an escape. I could disappear like we had never happened. Keep my head down, pay my dues, continue on alone.

But I'm lying if I say I'm not falling for him. Like he hasn't consumed my every thought. As if I haven't pictured what a future could be. He upended my life, giving me not one but two of the best orgasms I've ever experienced. Gave me the confidence that I could provide something for someone else.

The door opens and I tense. I'm going to get kicked to the curb. It's time to go find my mom. Disappointment floods my system, mixed with the scent of a greasy burger and bacon. My stomach rumbles. It's a cruel joke to kick me out with that heavenly scent.

"Hi, dear," his mother says gently, and it expels another set of tears. The bed shifts as she sits on it. "I'm going to leave this breakfast here. Please try to eat something."

Why is there still kindness in her voice? As if I didn't just break her son's heart.

I turn around. If she doesn't think I'm the biggest asshole on the planet, I can't be one directly to her face. She's welcomed me so generously.

"Elijah said you weren't up for company, but may I say something?"

Her tone is sickly sweet. The idea of what she has to say makes me nauseous. If she tells me I'm a disappointment, instead of outright kicking me out, that'll be worse.

"I don't know your story with my son, but I have never seen him happier. You two have a spark that feels so rare nowadays. There's a reason he felt so adamant about throwing you a party, and I can create my own story about why you've never celebrated a birthday. These aren't my stories to pry for if you don't want me to know. But please know we care for you and we hope you stick around. You fit in naturally with our family. If you need an ear, I'm here. I've experienced a lot more than my relatively sheltered son. And if you want, our conversations can be private until he needs to know."

She reaches her hand out and I'm quick to grasp it like a lifeline. Her eyes grow glassy as she squeezes my hand tight.

"In case no one has told you recently, you deserve the world. Don't let anyone tell you differently."

With that, she leans over and presses a kiss to my forehead. When she closes the door behind her, I gasp for air as my body convulses, no longer able to contain the pain. My mom's never kissed me.

Chapter Eighteen

Elijah

I don't know how to take care of someone in a precarious situation. In fact, it's one of the things that James used to harp on me for. I'm a bad caretaker. Yes, I clean and order takeout, and take care of the house things, but when it comes to other's emotions, I don't know how to support them. For my novels, it's different. My characters often have minor problems. If they have complex situations, it's easier to handle because they are fictional and I can control the situation. *Don't Forget to Breathe* has the most intense emotions, and the only reason I could write that well was because I wrote verbatim what I remembered.

I'm awkward around things I don't understand, and not being loved by a mother is something I can barely imagine. I want to understand, though.

When I left my bedroom this morning, I was riled up from my conversation, or lack thereof, with Austin. Before I left, I grabbed my laptop bag and told my parents he didn't want company, then stormed out of the house. It wasn't the most mature way to handle the situation, but he's in better hands with my parents. I don't need to scare Austin away with rash thoughts when my emotions are unstable. So I drove to the cafe at the Christmas tree farm, which is where I always end up when I'm back home and need to write.

Often when I'm in these situations, I grab my laptop, create two characters, and try to work it out between them. For me, written word is always easier than speaking. That's the only reason my novel about James came to be. I tried going back to the beginning of our relationship to see what went wrong. My book ended up being over 300,000 words. I severely edited it down to roughly 100,000. But when I finished, I could breathe again. I was out of the relationship and the words were therapeutic.

By the time the cafe closes at six, I'm barely at a break-through for how to solve the situation with Austin. Though, I've written a ton for the novel inspired by him. I may not know how to support Austin, but I do know this man has me feeling things I never felt with James, giving me the start of my own fairy tale romance. I need to figure out a way to not push him away because I don't know how to speak cautiously.

My mom had texted me shortly after I left with an update. My sisters' families all went home; movies would happen another time, and Austin was okay. She gave him food and was keeping an eye on him. She encouraged me to recharge and they'd be home whenever I was ready to come back. Regard-less of if I am ready, I have to come clean tonight.

When I get back home, the house is quiet and dark. Walking down the hallway, I viciously twist the ring on my finger, wishing there was a holiday distraction. A way we could all mask and go on our merry way. It always worked with James; it had become my specialty. But everything is over-whelming and I can't focus on what has priority.

How am I supposed to come clean about years of lies?

How do I take care of Austin?

How do I get over my trauma to give him what he deserves?

He lied to you. You deserve better than him.

I take a deep breath.

Austin may have lied, but I want to believe it was to protect himself. It wasn't meant to harm me. Not like James.

Austin needs help. He needs me. And in return, I have to be calm and patient. When I was under James' spell, the only way Jemma or my therapist could help me take the steps to leave was with patience. Understanding that I would fall back plenty of times before getting out entirely.

I inhale again, hand on my doorknob. I can do this. I push the door open with an exhale.

My stomach drops; my vision blurs. I grip the doorknob to steady my knees. He isn't here. I pushed him too far this morning. I wasn't patient. I was angry and frustrated about a life I'm privileged enough to not understand.

I'm so goddamn stupid. He brushed cobwebs off my happiness and he broke through my writing block. So much so, I was resentful that the cafe closed, forcing me to stop writing and face reality.

This man selflessly turned my world around and all I could do was judge him.

Fuck.

I need to ask my parents what happened. They were supposed to be taking care of him.

You should have been there.

I drop my laptop bag on my desk, tripping as I do so. *His bag.* My shoulders ease as I sink to the floor. He didn't run away.

Pressing my fingers against my wet eyelids, I breathe in, swallowing the overwhelm of emotions lodged in my throat. I can't . . . I can't do this if it isn't real. He's been stitching up my broken heart, and I'll be damned if I allow him to tear it apart. His loss will be too grand to recover.

I race to the den, only slowing when I hear the television. *Be calm.*

As I round the doorway, I spot my parents cuddled on the far end of the L-shaped couch. Curled in the corner, wrapped in a blanket, is Austin. He's awake, focused on the television, watching some true crime show. His eyes are puffy. He looks utterly exhausted, resting his head on the couch. Suddenly, my fears are replaced with the need to protect him. It doesn't matter how I feel about any of this. He needs me.

I tiptoe in, only giving my parents' brief glances and a wave, and sit down next to Austin. In an instant, his head is in my lap and he reaches for my hand to clasp against his chest. I hold back my tears. I never thought I could feel such intense emotion about someone. I truly believed what I experienced with James was the most I had to offer, but Austin's proving I had only scratched the surface of my emotional well; it's utterly terrifying.

We watch the rest of the show and as soon as the credits roll, my parents shut the TV off and shift toward us.

My heart rate increases just by their presence. They aren't stern or angry, or even seemingly upset. I don't even know what the conversation will be, but the air is thick; it's like I'm in trouble.

Is it possible all my lies have caught up with me?

I glance down at Austin, wondering whether he gave away any secrets. All he does is squeeze my hand, but that could mean he's apologizing for saying too much or he's giving me the courage to brave this conversation.

"I know it's been a long day," my mom starts, "but I'd like to take the opportunity, while it's just the four of us, to have some conversations. Tomorrow till Christmas, the house will be full, and I think it'll be better if we're all on the same page."

My stomach sinks. Austin squirms in my arms.

Are they kicking him out?

Instead of sliding away, he sits up on the cushion to face my parents.

"Okay," I say softly. Austin interlaces our hands, placing them between his chest and lifted knees. I love that even under my parents' gazes, he doesn't feel the need to have perfect posture. He has made himself at home.

"First," my mom says and my lungs constrict, "we will not be disappointed or upset with you, Elijah, and second, we care for you, Austin. We would love the opportunity to get to know you better."

I look at Austin. His eyes are unreadable. Just glossy, like they were this morning when I left him. What happened while I was gone?

My stomach churns with a gargle. I'm starving, but I won't be eating anytime soon.

"When did you and Austin meet?" my dad asks, and I tense at him taking over the conversation.

My parents aren't mean. I'm not frightened of them by any means, but when they want answers, they know how to get them. They barely ever raise their voice with me and my sisters. However, when they stare us down, straight-faced with a nudge sharper than usual, me and my sisters always sit at attention. There will be no more lies once I leave this room. The thought alone frees a portion of myself I haven't been able to work through in therapy.

I have to be honest.

I think back to the exact date I met Austin. They didn't address him with this question. It isn't his battle to fight.

"Technically, twelve days ago, when he took my order at the retreat. Ten since we've become friends."

Austin leans his head against my shoulder. That timeline

isn't even scientifically long enough to develop a habit. Though, I've always defied the neurotypical lifestyle.

My parents are fantastic with their poker faces and it irritates the hell out of me.

"So you met him at the writing retreat? While he was working?" My mom's voice is even, but it irks my RSD. I know exactly how ridiculous this all is.

I want to defend it. Come up with reasons left and right to prove it all makes sense. Chemistry isn't always explainable.

"Yes," Austin interrupts my thoughts. "He caught my eye the moment I saw him, and then one day he wasn't taking a break and seemed stressed, so I interrupted him with lunch and we hung out." I look over at him, and he smiles. "And we realized we have a pretty incredible connection."

I see the twitch in my mom's lip. She wants to smile; she *does* like him, I just didn't introduce him properly and she means business for breaking her rule.

"Please explain to me your thought process," my mom says. "We have a six-month rule, and you lied to me. Not to mention, you both seem like you're together, but you say he's a friend? Are you trying to deceive us?" The hurt in my mother's voice comes through, and tears brim my eyes. It's so multi-layered. "Have we ever made you feel like it isn't okay to come to Christmas alone? To be honest with us?"

Guilt settles in my stomach. She hasn't explicitly stated it isn't okay to be alone. But sometimes my brain can't remember that. Morphing questions or concerns of hers into faults of my own.

Austin lifts his head, stroking my cheek, turning my chin to look at him. "I'm right here," he whispers. "I'm sorry about what happened before, and I can explain, but I think it's time to tell your parents about James."

"James?" My eyes dart to my mom. Her poker face is gone

as her brows narrow. "Elijah, what the hell is going on? How long have you been lying to us?"

A shooting pain crosses my chest as my throat aches, thick with emotion. Tension nestles between my brows. I can't run from this.

I don't know when I became the person who lied. I hated deception as a kid—still do—but I think I've justified it to spare people's feelings.

Austin gives me the gentlest of pecks on my cheek. "I'm not going anywhere."

We didn't rehearse this scenario.

Inhaling, I don't even know where to begin. I catch sight of my parents' interlaced hands; my mother's fingertips are red from her death grip on my father. It's all or nothing now; she will lose her cool if she finds out I've lied past tonight.

I exhale. "Did you read *Don't Forget To Breathe*?"

Bless her patience as she exhales. "No, you told me not to, and I respected that."

I nod, and semi curse myself for telling her that. A part of me had hoped she would have read it and slipped up one day. It would have been the perfect time to add information to her knowledge instead of starting from scratch. Though, I'm grateful I am spared the embarrassment of the sex scenes.

"The book is about my relationship with James," I say slowly. I hold up my hand when she opens her mouth to speak. "James wasn't the boyfriend anyone thought he was—" I inhale, blinking back the tears. I never said the words out loud. I've heard them; my therapist has told me so, but me saying the words solidifies them as the truth. "He was abusive."

My dad shifts in his position as my mom gasps. Austin wraps his arms around me, rubbing my arm with his hand.

"W-what do you mean by that?" my mom whispers.

I knew the question would come over this past year. I tried

figuring out what I'd say to her, how I'd explain the depth of his destruction, but I never found the words.

"He manipulated me, and everyone around him. In the beginning, he had me hooked, head over heels for him. I truly thought he could be the one. But it shifted so slowly that it took me years to realize how he destroyed my self worth and brainwashed me. He continuously told me I wasn't good enough, but then would praise the hell out of me when he wanted sex. Sex was consensual. He controlled who I saw, where I went. I could never do household chores correctly, or well, much of anything to his standard.

"He constantly reminded me of how shit of a boyfriend I was. That I didn't know how to be in a relationship. That no one would read my books because I didn't know what I was talking about. When we first got together, I was barely making money with my writing, so once my books took off, he never knew. He didn't follow up with researching me. So thankfully, I was able to deceive him slightly. But I had another job while we were together, and he took all those paychecks. I didn't dare spend a dime of what I made from my books, because he would have taken everything. He'd constantly humiliate me in front of my friends when he would allow me to see them. But it was so nuanced that my friends barely picked up on the signs. He had them swayed. Near the end, I started getting help. I was becoming confident in my plan to leave, but I wasn't good at hiding it. He knew he was losing control, so he tried a new tactic. He'd lock me in our guest room, leaving me in total isolation until I was convinced I would have nothing without him."

Austin squeezes me. I left that portion out of the book, because while I was getting stronger, those were some of the worst days I experienced. Depending how badly I spoke back to him, depended on how long I was in there. The last time was up to five days.

My parents get off the couch and come toward me, sitting as close as humanly possible, as if being surrounded by bodies is enough to show me I'm loved.

"How did you get out?" my dad asks. There are tears in both of my parents' eyes, and a damp spot on my shirt from Austin. My mom reaches for my free hand, caressing my palm.

"Do you guys remember Jemma, my friend from the coffee shop?" They both nod. "A few months before I left, Jemma started to recognize what was happening. Her job has a mental health program and she introduced me to a therapist. One day, I missed my session and my therapist called the police for a wellness check. She notified them of the situation and they came with a warrant to search the house. They found him at home and I was in the guest room. They arrested him and an ambulance brought me to the hospital for an evaluation, but I was fine. He hadn't touched me. James was put up on bail and he paid it, but I got a restraining order. I moved in with Jemma until I could find a house in Lake Juniper. I believe James has moved. I was seeing a therapist twice a week, but now I'm down to once a week."

"Why didn't you tell us? I understand while you were with him," she shudders, "gosh, he was under our roof and had us so entranced. When he'd come here, were those moments good for you?"

I shake my head. "Not usually. Sometimes he was okay behind closed doors when we were here, but without fail, he was ten times worse when we got home. Honestly, when he didn't show up here, I could breathe better. But he had tracking on my phone and car, and I had to be in constant communication with him when I was away from him. I almost told you guys a few times, but I was terrified he had a bug somewhere. If I was being tracked so intensely, who's to say he wasn't listening?"

I pause, taking a moment to breathe in and out. I feel like

I'm having an out-of-body experience. Numb to the words coming out of my mouth.

"We are sorry we didn't notice, E. We discussed your irritable moods sometimes when you came home but you were working another job while still writing and gaining your readership. We really wrote it off to you overworking yourself," my dad explains.

I guess my mask wasn't entirely foolproof.

"That's what most people thought."

"You even had us convinced that you weren't making money from your books. But we knew you had to be lying when you bought your home," my mom says.

"I had to tell everyone I wasn't making money, because what if someone had let it slip, you know?"

The disappointment of losing so much while with James settles over me like a heavy cloud. As a teen, I always dreamed about what it would be like to live off my writing, how I might celebrate when I made a lot of money.

Yes, I purchased a house. I even had a housewarming party with my family and some friends. But it wasn't in the moment. It wasn't a celebration when my book series first went viral. Instead of running into James' arms to show him, he criticized how I missed a spot mopping the floor and had me start the entire house all over again.

Even now, despite him not being in my life, I can't enjoy the success *Don't Forget to Breathe* has had because it's riddled with him. I haven't even looked at the email from my assistant since it had me spiraling at the resort.

"The benefit of not spending a dime while with James was that I had a down payment for a home. The purchase didn't eat into my current income. But I'm doing good, and my books just keep growing. In the past year, I was able to focus more on marketing the series. I'm close to six figures."

A collective gasp from them has me feeling warm and

light. The year isn't over yet, and we haven't gotten through winter break, so I don't know my year-end total, but I'm nearing $95,000 this year. In November, I was at $86,000. While my book with my ex doesn't have the review count the others do, I had enough readership prior to it coming out that release day was my most successful one yet. Add in another book, and if I continue my new series, I don't think it's unreasonable to hit and maintain $100,000. If anything, it's the fire under my ass I need.

"Wow. We're so proud of you, Elijah." My mom smiles with tears in her eyes, squeezing my hands tight.

"We love you," my dad says, clasping his hand on top of mine and my mom's. "We're so sorry you've been carrying this."

I look between both of my parents; I don't have a good reason for not telling them. It all feels silly now, not feeling like I could trust the two people who have been the most honest with me my entire life.

"I kept it from you guys because I didn't want you to think less of me. Sometimes it all feels ridiculous. Like I'm being dramatic and I made it all up. My therapist explained that's because of how he manipulated me, which is why it took so long to recognize what was happening. Other days, the feelings are so intense, it's like I've taken steps back. I had been lying to you both for years by the time things ended. It felt easier to pretend things separated peacefully. Especially because he was always so good to you guys. I didn't want to ruin your memories of him."

"Elijah—" my mom chokes out, "it isn't your job to protect our feelings. It doesn't matter how he treated us, and that goes for anyone in your life. If someone hurts you, we are on your side. We want to know. I'm so sorry if we didn't make that more clear growing up." My mom wipes tears from her eyes as my dad tightens his hold around her.

"Hey," Austin says, and I glance over at him. He squeezes my shoulder, his expression earnest. "I don't believe for one second you made any of that up, even the book."

My heart swells; like it might burst from the overwhelming feeling of admitting my lies and still being loved and supported.

I don't deserve this.

"Have you read it?" my mom asks, her eyes on Austin. I'm curious if she'll read it now. For how passionate she has been over my other novels, I'm impressed she had the restraint. And her proof with her reaction right now, she didn't deserve to be lied to, especially with the respect she gave me.

"I did the week we met. It helped me understand him a bit more, and what started this whole ploy. I wanted to show Elijah what love was, how he should be treated, and I needed a place to stay over Christmas, so I . . . well, I invited myself. I know you have rules, but I'm so grateful I'm here."

My parents both smile. "I don't know what you both think is real or fake, but you've done a great job in front of us showing Elijah he's loved," my dad says.

Austin curls into me, as if he's embarrassed, and I gaze down into his eyes. I'm not so sure we know what's real or fake, either.

"Okay, we're going to head to bed," my mom says, squeezing my hand. "We love you so much. Thank you for telling us about James. If you ever want to talk more, you know we're always here. You'll try to keep us in the loop in the future?"

I nod, giving them a small smile. I appreciate the "try." Much more attainable. "I love you both."

"And Austin?" my mom continues. He sits up a little, and my mom smiles. "You're more than welcome here, okay?" He nods, gripping my arm. "Thank you for caring about my son.

It doesn't matter how long you've known him; we can feel and see your intentions are real."

"Thank you," Austin whispers, with tears brimming. Something happened between them today, but I'm not sure either of us have the energy to dive into that tonight.

My mom kisses us both on the head and my dad says goodnight before they disappear. Austin rubs away his tears when I turn to him.

"I know we have to talk," I start. I love that I can read him so easily. His eyes droop with exhaustion. "But how about we call a truce tonight? Let's go to bed and cuddle for a bit?"

His shoulders relax, and he nods.

We stand and lean on one another to walk out of the room. Both tired and unsteady, but the giggle that tickles my neck has my heart swelling. I kiss his cheek and he leans his head against my shoulder as we walk down the hall and into my bedroom. This feels natural. I gently guide him on my bed, hovering over him when he sits. He's already in sweats, so I'm the only one who has to get changed. I brush my lips against his; the electricity between us has my toes curling and his fingers pressing the back of my neck, forcing our lips together.

I unbutton my jeans, tugging them off before I straddle him. My intentions aren't sex, I truly want to cuddle, but maybe some innocent heat-of-the-moment kissing isn't such a bad thing. He mimics my thoughts as I flip onto my back. Straddling me, he sits down on my hardening dick, presenting me with a dazzling smile.

My dick pokes him, begging for a way out of my boxers. I love the way his sweatpants shrink around his thick member. I'd love to go all the way, feel the pressure of him filling me up; have him cum on my chest. The thought alone has me moaning; Austin smirks.

"Want to fill me in on your fantasies?" He grounds down, the friction on my dick has me gripping his thighs. A motion of trying to stop his movements but also keep them steady. At this rate, I'll orgasm from his dry humping.

"Not yet." I grin, and his smile is devilish.

Austin leans down, nipping my neck. With each bite, his tongue slides across the tender skin, all before he sucks. This damn man is going to have me blushing in front of my family tomorrow.

Grasping his hair, I yank him away. "If you're gonna suck, suck my dick."

The fire in his eyes has me thrusting up. "Fuck, Elijah," he breathes. Austin's hands are magic, sliding my boxers off so effortlessly. My dick is in his mouth, immediately hitting the back of his throat. This man, my god, he feels so good.

"I w-want to, my god, Austin." He sucks in, and I clench the bed sheets. "I need you in my mouth." If anything, to shut myself up from moaning too loud. I've never 69'd before. James didn't care to pleasure me at the same time, but I was always fascinated by it.

Austin swivels his body so fucking fast, never leaving my dick. He nearly knees my stomach. I clasp his hips, digging my nails into his skin as I position him. His dick swats me in the face, leaving a trail of pre-cum on my cheek. A shiver runs through me at Austin's breathy laugh, hitting my tip. I take him in my mouth, and with just a shift of my neck, he slides in, curving down my throat. I want a lifetime of nuzzling in his musk. The vibration of his moans has me seconds from coming. I focus my efforts on moving his hips up and down, slowly, allowing me to coat him in my saliva. He tastes amazing, and I can't wait to feel his hot liquid down my throat.

Cool air hits my dick as he licks the tip. "Elijah," he moans. "Fuck!" He tightens his grip on me before swallowing me whole, grinding his hips down. I breathe through the gag. His pace quickens with his hips thrusting. Suddenly, his hot cum shoots down my throat, and I coat the back of his.

We both suck one another through the aftermath, then reluctantly part.

Austin curls into my arms, pulling the blanket over us once we've cleaned up and replaced our boxers.

I want this man in my life, in my bed, in my home, and it scares the living shit out of me.

"I know we probably have plans tomorrow with your family, but can we do something together in the morning?" Austin asks.

"I think tomorrow is our movie and baking day, so nothing terribly pressing."

I can almost feel his eyes bulge as he huffs. "Baking is pressing. I want to bake with your family."

I laugh, leaning up on my elbows. He lies on his back as I look down at him. "I thought you wanted to hang out?"

"I do!" He chuckles. "But is it possible to do all of the above?"

"Do you have anything in mind you want to do?"

He shakes his head. "I want to spend time with you, and just you. Not with writing distractions or family around."

I glance at the clock. It's just after ten. "Let's grab breakfast at my favorite diner, then we can be back mid-morning when the kids come over and you can be the star baker."

He grins widely. I think this might be the first year I actively pay attention to baking. In past years, I wrote while the baking happened, waiting around for the movies to start. But this year, the star of my novel will be in front of me, potentially with flour all over his face.

Chapter Nineteen

Austin

We walk hand in hand down Elijah's street as the sun rises. A fresh dusting of snow overnight coated the tree branches to create that perfect winter silence. I inhale the crisp, fresh air and exhale until my lungs are empty.

Before I met Elijah, I had a meticulous routine and what I considered stone boundaries. After my ex, I needed to find a way to maintain stability in my life while keeping up with my mother's agreement. That's when I swore off anything more than one-night stands. I came to the understanding that I lived to work for my mom and any money or energy I had after could go to friends. To fill the void of loneliness, similar to growing up, I consumed romance after romance movie. Dreaming one day, I'd have my own prince charming. It was only ever a fairytale, though.

Then Elijah waltzed into my life, jumbling my routine, finding cracks within my walls. Now, my existence between both of my worlds has me spiraling.

How can I open myself up to Elijah, get him to understand my life without him thinking I'm an idiot or just plain ignorant? His family loves him so deeply. He can't possibly understand the death grip my mother has on me. How I have a game plan of the latest time I can leave the Evergreen household to meet my mom and be back on Christmas morning before anyone knows. In the past, I have paid her tab on my birthday. As it was easier to get time away from any restaurant I was working at. But my agreement is no later than Christmas morning, so my mom can have Christmas dinner at The Diner. If she doesn't pay her tab, she's kicked out. I know it shouldn't be my problem, but she gave me life, and with that life, I have the opportunity to grow something with Elijah.

Not if he doesn't want you paying your mom.

We turn the corner, off his street, and there's a diner in the distance. A few couples and one family are walking toward the diner too. There hasn't been a car in sight, just neighborhood customers.

Together, we're still silent when we walk indoors. I wonder what's on his mind, or if he's picked up that I might have needed the quiet escape.

The smell of bacon and freshly baked bread consumes me and my stomach growls. A woman, nearly a splitting image of Elijah's dad, but more feminine, greets us with a smile.

"Elijah, my love, come here!" she says, pulling him into a hug. His cheeks redden, but he embraces her; his shoulders relaxing as she rubs his back. "I've missed you. How are you?" The woman pulls away enough to look him in the eyes, but her hands hold his arms.

Elijah smiles easily. They both have the same smile, thin lipped on top, a bit more plump on the bottom, with a curl of a smirk.

"Hi, Aunt Jude, I'm great. This is my boyfriend, Austin. "

My heart skips. Not to toot my own horn, but I think his smile increases at the label. When I woke up this morning, I wasn't sure whether we were continuing the charade. It's part of what I wanted to talk with him about. The healthy side of me truly hopes this is a confirmation of the real thing.

"Boyfriend! Oh, how lovely." She moves to me, pulling me into a quick hug, before glancing me up and down. "What a handsome fella. How are you, dear? I'm Elijah's aunt, and this is my diner."

"I'm good!" I say, letting out a breathy laugh. I feel trapped in all the love oozing around me.

Is anyone in Elijah's family mean? Rude? Neglectful?

"You?"

"Just marvelous that you both are here! Come, come. Let's get you the best seat."

She isn't joking about the best seat. She travels us through the already packed country-esque diner to the back, seating us in a booth with a private window. The back of their property has two frozen ponds and a plethora of pine trees. There's a person ice fishing on one of the ponds. It seems peaceful down there; like you might be the only one in the world.

We're left with thick menus, and I don't even know where to begin. The diner I went to with my mom was very basic, aside from holidays when they'd go all out. This place has skillets of eggs, hash, and bacon, a variety of pancakes and waffles, breakfast wraps, and sandwiches. Even an entire section of smoothie and smoothie bowls. I can't keep my mind from hoping that this is one of many times we'll be visiting.

The back of the menu has an array of espresso-based beverages. My heart is so happy I could cry, and I might at some point with my confused emotions.

Aside from Elijah pointing out his top picks on the menu, we haven't spoken a word. The longer the silence continues, the more my nerves eat away. He called me his boyfriend. He didn't have to continue the lie. His aunt could just believe we're friends.

All I know is that I need to get my shit together. I'm the

one who is supposed to show him love and take care of him on this trip, and I've been shit at it.

We each order lattes, his with hot chocolate and mine regular, and two different skillets. It hits me that we're in a new environment with food and I wonder if he's the person who allows his partner to try his food. I love getting a taste of everything; I'm usually awful at choosing one item because I'm always creating dishes in my head to try. It's gotten worse since my job at the resort, knowing I get full reign once the new year starts. I want people to crave my dishes and think about them long after they leave the resort. Booking again just to experience my food once more. It's a tall order, but one I guarantee I can accomplish.

"So, this is my aunt's diner. She's owned it for nearly thirty years. She lives right next door. This diner, those ponds, and her home are all owned by her and her husband. That's him down there fishing. They'll both be at dinner tomorrow. My uncle's an accountant. He doesn't work directly with my aunt, but helps her with the books, making a pretty perfect team." I'm growing to love Elijah's onset of information after periods of silence. No questions were asked, yet I got a family history I don't need, but I appreciate it all the same.

"I love it." I smile, gazing out at the pond again. There are a couple of deer hovering between a few trees, keeping their eyes on his uncle.

His foot taps mine beneath the booth. He reaches his hand across the table, and I grab it, squeezing a little.

"Tell me what's on your mind. I think it's more than wanting some space," Elijah says, caressing his thumb across mine.

I study him. His brown eyes are warm, yet concerned. His brows knit; he knows the conversation that needs to happen. I don't want to lose those delicious lips of his or his silky hair that I can knot my fingers in. Or the feel of his scruff on my neck or creating friction at my base. He's wearing a flannel; his collar popped slightly, on purpose, because my mouth got a little happy, loving on his neck. Just the thought of last night has me repositioning myself.

"Austin, I want to understand you and where you come from. I have no intention of walking away."

My eyes glance to his face again. I watch as he lifts my hand and kisses it. This could be my future. Casually grabbing breakfast at a diner together before we take on the day. It should be simple. The hardest part should be confessing how much he's invaded my heart.

He deserves my honesty. Even if it terrifies me. Liza is the only person who knows everything. Only because she had to help me through my weakest points. Elijah unintentionally got himself involved and instead of demanding answers, he threw me a rager.

"What would you like to know?" I ask softly. Maybe if he directs the questioning, the answers will be easier.

"Are you really from St. Peya?"

My stomach plummets at the question. He thinks I've lied about everything.

I take the rolled silverware on the table, unwrapping it in my hands to alter my focus. "No. I've lived in St. Peya for years because that's where Liza and I settled, but I grew up in the inner city of Cyan City."

His eyes don't pity me. He's focused, intent on receiving information. But his hand twists the ring on his finger.

"Why did you tell me you had no contact with them?"

"Because I do, except one to two weeks before every payment is due. Otherwise, my mom isn't supposed to reach out to me."

"I don't understand."

I sigh. It isn't directed toward him, but I don't think he'll ever truly understand. "You and I grew up very differently. You were raised in a beautiful multi-room home on a quiet street with lovely parents. I grew up in a studio apartment in low-income housing with my mom and younger sister. Our complex wasn't quiet."

Elijah leans back in the booth, focusing on his hands.

"I raised my sister. She's three years younger. I was her caretaker and her protector while our mom was gone half the time. The only good thing she did was not bring home whatever she did. The other half, I grew up in the local bar or diner. Those were the good days. The days where I didn't have to find food. But they were also the days where I actively had to shield my sister from seeing the lifestyle my mom had. She's an addict, in all the sense of the word. As I got older, her habits increased, and we nearly got evicted." I pause as our food gets delivered. Our conversation doesn't need to get back to his aunt. The food smells so delightful. I wish we were past this conversation so we could enjoy some light-hearted banter.

"From age twelve, I searched for cash paying jobs to keep our place. At fourteen, I worked at The Diner on payroll, then other cash jobs here and there to not let the government know. Every dime I made went into my mother's pockets. It was never enough. The more I worked, the less I could physically look after my sister. Instead, my mom brought her into the lifestyle. She was drinking by the time she was thirteen."

"Fuck," he breathes, fork midway to his mouth. His eyes shift to mine, but I look at the nick on the wooden table, massaging it with my finger.

"It all happened so quickly. I had failed my sister, but I didn't know how to help her and not fail myself. There was no path in my head that I could foresee to protect us both. All I could do was keep a roof over our heads, keep my sister fed, and get a scholarship. And I fucking did it. I got a full ride to university. But I couldn't leave my sister without helping. So I agreed to keep paying everything in exchange for being able to leave. I give them money four times a year; it's their responsibility to prioritize where it goes. Whenever I try to get out of the agreement, my mom guilts me. Whether it's something with my sister or her or losing the house or needing money to eat. She's got a chokehold on me. I'm very much aware of that. But my guilt for letting my sister get sucked into that lifestyle is too strong. At this point, it's become routine. I'm set in my ways. I'm working less now for more money, so it's all fine."

"Austin," Elijah sighs, placing his palm open on the table. I reluctantly put my hand in his and he interlaces our fingers. "It isn't your fault your sister is an addict. She isn't your responsibility. It's your mom's fault."

I wish I could believe his words, just like I wish I could believe Liza, but like it or not, they both come from two-parent households. They never had to wonder whether they'd have three meals a day.

"Someone has to take care of her." I shrug, taking my first bite of food. I'm done with the conversation. He has the information he needs. It is what is. He can't say I never told him.

"And who is taking care of you?"

His words slice through me, my bite of food solidifying in my esophagus.

"This is delicious," I say once I successfully swallow. To break the serious tension between us, I scoop up a bite of his skillet. I swallow it before his mind processes the shift of mood.

He lets out a chuckle. "Did you just steal my food?"

I grin, rubbing my stomach. "Yes, sir. Good choice." And it was. I need to add a skillet dish to my menu, for sure.

His fork steals a bit of mine, his eyes mischievous as if he's onto something. What he doesn't know is it's always been a dream of mine to have a partner where we can order different things and combine our meals.

Elijah's face becomes serious after he swallows, squeezing our still-interlaced fingers. "I hear you and I see you. And I want to support you. I'd like for you to tell me how best to do that. I'm not good at this, and I feel like I failed you yesterday."

Tears brim my eyes, and I focus heavily on the seasoned hash in the skillet. I honestly don't know what I need. I need to not give my mom money. I need to be strong enough to separate myself. I need to understand that my only responsibility is myself. But I can't ask a partner to put up that boundary for me. That isn't fair to them.

"Do you like me?" I whisper.

He brings our hands up to his lips again, pressing a kiss to the back of my hand. "I'm well past like, Austin. I'm fucking terrified," he breathes.

The tears fall at his words; I understand completely. He's quick to slide into my booth. He wraps his arms around me, kissing the top of my head.

"I'm falling for you too, Elijah," I whisper. He tightens his hold. "All I want from you is to be with you. But I . . . I'm afraid to let you into that life. If my mom has threatened to make my life hell, I don't want you to be involved."

Elijah's hand cups my cheek, lifting my face to his. "My life has already been pretty hellish. I think I can take on a bit more with you by my side."

My fingers brush his scruff, watching as his eyes soften. I don't want to break him further. He deserves so much more than I can give him.

"I can't promise you I won't fall into her trap. It's thirty-one years of damage. I've been trying to end things for years now."

"And I can't promise that I'm not going to be haunted by my past." Elijah leans his forehead against mine. "I don't know much about our future, but I know the way I feel is what I've written in my books before. Whether that gets us through the hardships, only time will tell. But I've never felt this way before."

"Who's the one teaching who how to love?" I laugh through another onset of tears.

Elijah grasps my neck, connecting our lips. I inhale and sink into the kiss. My defenses are crumbling, and for once, I don't want to rebuild them.

"Austin?"

"Yes, I'll be your boyfriend," I whisper, sealing it with a kiss.

"Hey," Elijah says, yanking my hand before I open the front door to his home. After the intense conversation, we ate a phenomenal breakfast, side-by-side, then decided to walk the long way home, admiring the Christmas decorations in the neighborhood.

"Yeah?" I look back at him, wondering if he's nervous about breaking this bubble of newly found bliss. Our conversation was crucial, but I feel at ease. There's a lot more to unpack for both of us as time goes on, but I feel safe exactly where we are. Doesn't he?

"Just one more moment," he whispers, closing the space between us, backing me up against the siding of the house.

I can hear the children laughing inside. His niece and nephews are ready to bake. I'm eager to get myself into the kitchen. Nothing better than baking with kids who are so excited and have zero standards. It helps balance out my perfect-to-code, sanitized kitchen.

"I need one more lesson on love before I go write." Elijah's mouth hovers over my lips.

The joy flooding my bloodstream at the connection between me and his writing is unmatched. I close the gap, and his body presses into mine, grasping my neck with one hand and cupping my cheek with the other. I wish he wasn't wearing an adorable knitted cap so I could tangle my hand in his hair, but that might lead to a public quickie, and we don't need that. But I do need him in me the moment we are no longer under his parents' roof. I don't think we've been waiting for that, we've just naturally gone straight to blow jobs, but if we are taking this seriously and I will see him after this trip, then I think that is exactly what I'd like for Christmas.

I pull back, panting with the thoughts in my mind. He's looking at me like he wants to devour me. And suddenly, I'm waiting for the ball to drop. The moment he doesn't find me desirable. The moment his family doesn't care for me.

What will shift as we drive away from here?

"Hey," Elijah whispers, cupping my cheeks. "What's going on in that mind of yours?"

"I'm s-scared," I breathe. It takes a moment for his mind to register my words, but his embrace tightens, and I rest my head on his shoulder.

"I'm scared too."

"I'm a fool to believe that I could have taught you how to love."

His chest rumbles with a soft laugh. "Austin, you've allowed me to believe again. It's the most thrilling yet terrifying feeling."

I lean my head against the house, connecting my eyes with his. I've never fallen so fast. Never felt like I might not be able to breathe if I don't have my eyes set on him. Like his kisses are water and I'm dehydrated. Like knowing he's mine would guarantee no tough day is bad, and that's the greatest gift. A goddamn Christmas miracle.

"Where's Austin?" I hear Lola ask from inside the house. The noises have gotten louder, like his mom opened the windows.

"And now I'm chopped liver," Elijah teases with a grin, stepping away from me.

The immediate space has me gasping for air. It'll be a good distraction to bake, to separate myself from this cascading waterfall of emotions. The kitchen will center me.

I take the opportunity to open the front door, walking in first.

"Austin!" the kids exclaim the moment they see me. They've all got mini aprons on, the baking supplies are organized on the counter, and the warmth of the house tells me the double ovens in the kitchen are already preheated.

"Are you going to help us bake? Your cinnamon rolls were soooo good," the oldest boy, Myles, says.

"Of course!" I naturally match his energy. There's nothing better than a child's compliment. "Just need an apron, then tell me what we're baking."

Lola runs over to me, nearly tripping on the ties of an apron, and hands it to me.

"Oh, thank you!" I glance back at Elijah, and he's beaming.

Little hands drag me to the kitchen, where Louise and Oliver, the middle of the three, are. Oliver gives me a wave, leaning his head on Louise's shoulder. Suddenly, I'm thrown into the beautiful madness.

We're making an array of cookies, some for the extended family Christmas dinner tomorrow and some for the local hospital. Elijah's family carols on Christmas Eve. I've never experienced such a packed amount of family events, but it's also exactly what made-for-TV Christmas movies showcase.

When the first set of cookies are in the oven, me and the children are already covered in flour, and Elijah is typing away on his laptop at the kitchen table. He looks so focused, as if the commotion of us hasn't caused him any distractions.

He suddenly looks up, his eyes intense on me before he scans my appearance. His face softens, and he winks before diving back into writing. So help me god if this man is writing me into his book. The thought of being a character, in hopefully a spicy novel of his, has my body warming and my dick swelling.

"Did you guys have a good talk this morning?" I jump at Louise's words. Her hand on my shoulder steadies me and she gives a cheeky smile.

Does she know I was imagining making love to her son, because . . . *fuck, I need to refocus.*

"We did." I nod, offering a smile.

"So, are you two officially together or are you two still pretending?"

I look back to Elijah before taking in the entire scene. His father and his siblings are in the living room, all in conversation about something. The TV is on, but I don't think they are watching it. The kids sit on the island stools, sneaking chocolate chip morsels and giggling. And Elijah's mom gazes at me, like she has all the love in the world to give.

"We're officially boyfriends." I grin. Elijah glances up, his eyes gleam like he can't believe this bubble of happiness exists either.

His mom pulls me into a hug. She's warm, and the hug is so inviting. I find myself sinking in. "Welcome to the family, Austin. We're so happy you're here."

I tighten my grip, trying to swallow back the tears. Her hands trail up and down my back, not helping my situation.

"Don't ever hesitate to reach out if you need anything or just want to talk, okay?"

I step away from her embrace, and her gentle eyes tell me she knows *something*, but I'm confident Elijah won't tell her anything. I never discussed my family situation when she offered me an ear and a place to escape.

I nod. "Thank you. I appreciate it. I'm just gonna use the restroom, and then I'll be back to bake."

"Of course," she says, before walking over and tickling the kids, "catching them" for eating the sweets.

I squeeze Elijah's shoulder as a reassurance that all is well. Before I go to the bathroom, I find my phone buried at the bottom of my bag. It still has battery life, though relatively low from the amount of calls it's received. I needed this phone to ground me. To bring me back down from this fucking fairy tale. All this love is suffocating. I don't know if I'm cut out for it.

I listen to my mom's voicemails in the bathroom. Each one is progressively worse as she gets more drunk. My sister chimed in yesterday, according to my phone log, telling me lies about how much our mom did for us and how much she needs me. She's somehow skewed all my hard work in her mind to think that our mom did it. It's been a while since she tried wedging herself in the middle, but maybe it's because I'm trying to put the boundary up. There's a day and a half until Christmas. I technically still have time to pay the tab.

A knock on the door has me flushing the toilet and washing my hands, hiding my phone in my back pocket. When I open the door, Elijah's standing there.

"Do you want to talk? How bad were the voicemails?"

I furrow my brows, playing dumb.

"I saw you walk into my bedroom, and then to the bathroom. I'm great at sneaking around; you can't fool me." His hand hesitantly touches my shoulder. If I'm not mistaken, there's fear in his eyes.

"What do you need?" His confidence grows with his hands cupping my cheeks.

I stare at him, feeling the weight of my mom's demands in my pocket. I could be back by tonight if I left now. A text vibrating in my pocket confirms they haven't given up.

"Are you going to run?" he asks, brushing his thumbs across my skin.

I'm frozen. My words have vanished. I have one of two choices. I go without looking back, losing more than money this time around, or I ask for help. Neither are ideal. The little boy in me reminds me how my mother is family and family means we drop everything to help. But thirty-one-year-old me knows a true family wouldn't leech off me.

"I want to," I whisper. I don't lose eye contact with him. Trying to show I'm confident in my decision, even though the thought of running has me nauseous. He expected my answer, though. He isn't surprised or disappointed. His eyes don't shift. He doubles down on being my focus, stepping an inch closer so I can feel his heat. It's like he's trying to short circuit the signals in my mind.

"May I say something potentially out of line?"

All I can do is nod, because if I'm about to walk out on him, the least he can do is feel like he made a difference. He steps forward, pressing me up against the door. My body relaxes against the wood. I'm not stable; if he lets go of my cheeks, I might collapse.

"Do you believe you're helping your family when you give them money?" I inhale, opening my mouth, but his finger silences me. "Yes or no."

"Yes," I breathe out.

"Do you realize that you're enabling them?"

I want to argue with him. Tell him he has absolutely no

idea what he's talking about. He knows a portion of the story and now he's coming in with assumptions.

"Your mom isn't taking your money to get her life together. She's taking your money to put into her addiction. She's given you years of proof that she has zero intention of changing. The only way she might change is if you stop giving her the money."

My legs shake, and his reaction is immediate, steadying my shoulders. This is too much. What if . . . what if I trust him . . . what if it fails . . .

Then I'll lose him *and* my family.

"You get to decide. I won't tell you not to go. I don't want you to resent me. But if you need me to make sure you don't leave, force you to stay until you see it yourself, then I can do that too."

My phone vibrates again. This time it's a call. Elijah's eyes shift, darkening. We stand in silence, listening to the rhythm until it shuts off.

I lean forward, resting my head on Elijah's shoulder. He closes the space, embracing me. I'm utterly exhausted. I want my actions to speak for themselves. Have him decide what he believes I'm saying.

"I need you to say the words, Austin. Tell me you want my help; if that's what you're asking for. I know it's scary. I've said those exact words before. I promise you, though, letting the words out gives a sense of freedom."

I lean back enough to connect our lips. He understands the assignment. His fingers crawl up my neck, brushing my cheeks, and tangling in my hair. His lips are my strength, refueling me. I don't want to be someone who needs a person to lean on to. I want to have my own strength, but maybe a little support isn't the worst thing.

His tongue teases, dancing with my own, before his lips

retreat, exploring my skin to the dip of my neck, his teeth nibbling my earlobe.

"I n-need your h-help." I sigh, leaning my head against the door, giving him more space to roam.

"I'm so proud of you," he whispers in my ear.

My body collapses against his. All I've ever wanted was to make someone proud.

Chapter Twenty

Elijah

I have always wished to share this holiday week with someone I loved, and it never really caught up to me until last night. After I found Austin hiding in the bathroom listening to his mother's voicemails, I brought him back to my bedroom to cuddle. It didn't last long before the kids yelled for him. Getting back to baking was a good distraction for him. Once all the baking was complete, we started our holiday movie night. In the past, this tradition was always the loneliest for me. While I loved the movies and I looked forward to them every year, I always wanted someone to hold, like my parents and sisters had. Even the kids all snuggled into one another. James did watch the movies with us one year, but he consistently pointed out the plot holes in my ear.

This year, I had the privilege of holding Austin. My heart had already been full, knowing he trusted me enough to keep him safe, and he stayed. But watching the joy and laughter on him was the best movie I could have seen.

Usually, the family dinner is the second hardest event for me. My extended family means well, but I was always questioned about where James was if he wasn't there, and if he was, he'd control the room with his energy, spewing off lies I had to remember. This year, Austin commanded the room in a different way. He wasn't bragging about what he did or what his opinion was of the world; his actions spoke for him. Though, his words did ban me from the kitchen.

My mom recruited him to help with our family dinner, which is one of the highest honors. Instead of my mom telling Austin how Christmas dinner operates, she allowed him to be head chef. He naturally delegated tasks to the family members trusted enough with a spoon. As for me, I dodged questions left and right by my aunts, all while they admired Austin from afar.

I didn't lie when questioned about how we met. I never said specific timelines, but our "meet cute", coined by my younger cousin, had my aunts' swooning.

His laughter cuts off my thoughts. Austin's arm is around my mom's shoulder as she laughs, covering her face with her hand. On the floor in front of them, there is a massive spill of steaming liquid.

My mom's laughing? This is a category 5 disaster for her.

I stand up from the couch, slinking my way to the dining room. My mom is all smiles and cheers until something gets ruined in the kitchen. In the past, she's kicked everyone out of the kitchen while she came up with a silent game plan.

"It's all good. We can improvise," he tells her.

They can *improvise?* My mom is not a nonchalant cook.

"You're right. It's no big deal. We've got plenty of other food," she says, laughing again. Then she shrugs, pulling him in for a hug.

I slide in the archway, leading to the hallway, and hold the frame.

What the hell is happening?

"Thank you for keeping me calm this season," my mom says.

"My pleasure." He gives her a squeeze before she lets go, and my mom casually goes to grab cleaning supplies.

Every year, there are a strict number of people allowed in the kitchen. A lot of food was usually prepared throughout the week too, as my mom trusted no one. If dinner happened under her roof, she said she was always responsible for any mistake. And mistakes weren't allowed on the most important dinner of the year—or so she claimed.

And in less than a week's time, Austin single-handedly uprooted her entire system. It is his magic, and it is very attractive.

"Alright, dinner should be ready in less than five minutes!" Austin announces. "Sheila, go round up the family. Mark, make sure everyone has drinks. Lily, go find Elijah and tell him he's no longer banned. I want to make sure everyone is seated before I carve the ham, so it's as warm as possible."

His confidence has me hoping he has the energy to command me in the bedroom tonight.

As my family members leave the kitchen on a mission, I walk in, placing a finger to my lips to make sure Lily, my sixteen-year-old cousin, stays silent. She grins before darting off toward the living room. I sneak up behind Austin, who is turning off stove burners, and rest my hands on his hips. He doesn't jump, instead he leans into my touch.

"Careful, I might fall in love with you," I whisper in his ear.

He swivels in my arms, clasping his hands on the base of my neck. His smile brightens face and his eyes shimmer before he closes the gap between us, sealing the thought with a kiss.

The smiling radiating off Austin throughout dinner is contagious. My cheeks fucking hurt. I love my family and I love Christmas, but there's something about experiencing these memories with another person. Admiring their joy. Having it overflow your cup of happiness.

I already can't wait for next year. It will only be more magical because it'll be our one-year anniversary. Ideally, we'll be oozing with happiness instead of some family drama. And I'll have plenty of time to plan a proper birthday party for him.

The thoughts don't startle me. They filter through my bloodstream, wanting to wrap this man up in my arms, take him home, and show him he's mine, in more ways than one.

There's still so much to figure out, like how the hell are we going to survive being apart when he works at the resort? Our agreement was until December 26th. Once we left my parents, I'd drop him off at Liza's and that was that. We haven't discussed the next steps. The thought of dropping him off at home in two days sounds awful. I want every single minute with him until he has to be back at work on the 27th. I desperately want to bring him to my home and go all the way with him. Solidify our relationship. Remind him how deeply I've grown to care for him before we're forced apart by obligation.

"Earth to Elijah," Austin says, rubbing my thigh. Just this man's hand is going to have me hard under the table.

"Y-yes?" I clear my throat. He eyes me, but nods toward my aunt who owns the diner.

"Are you working on anything new, Elijah? I'm dying to know if there's a sequel to *At First Sight*."

If anything, meeting Austin at the resort has confirmed that there won't be a sequel to Ansel and Arlo's story anytime soon. Finishing his story is more important. But I try to ward off the pressures from work. Maybe Austin going back to the resort won't be such a bad thing. My entire month has shifted, all for the better, but it's time to refocus my efforts. Can I find my way back to Ansel and Arlo's characters? Continue the series? Figure out what their love was? I haven't decided if my story of Austin will remain private, but if it does, I need to work on something new for my readers. The last thing I want is for them to lose interest.

"I want to," I say, trying to focus on the family members listening. A few other conversations are happening around the table, but my aunt is an avid reader of mine. "I've been a bit distracted, but once the holiday is over, I'm sure I'll be back in the game."

"Oh good. It was such a great start. I was surprised by your last book. It was very well written, but I hope the main character finds his happy ending."

I catch my mom's eyes; my aunt didn't listen to me. I'm surprised by how my stomach doesn't drop or how my anxiety remains leveled. I look at Austin and he's grinning. I interlace our hands underneath the table.

"Yeah," I tell my aunt, "I'm confident he's found his happy ending."

"Gosh, I've always wondered what caroling might be like. I did it as a child for some school function, but families who still carol? That's adorable."

I don't know whether to be flattered by Austin's words or not. He keeps bouncing on the balls of his toes, running through his sheet music in prep.

The good thing about my family caroling is we don't go door to door outside. We go room to room in the local hospital my mom used to work in. She had coordinated events like this for upping morale in specific units. Our family were the first volunteers when my sisters and I were kids, but it soon picked up, and now we are joined by a few different families.

I always tried my hardest to love caroling. It isn't that I hate us lightening the mood and making people smile. I absolutely love that my family has the ability to do it. It's the actual portion of singing, being around hours of tone deaf family members, including myself, and getting secondhand embarrassment from that. The only portion I actually enjoy is where we are now. The children's cancer unit. Not only are we there to carol, but Santa does a special visit, giving the kids their Christmas presents early. It's an entire skit to help make the children believe they are important. Each child has his undivided attention, as he asks what they want and then produces that gift instantaneously. It's all a big set up; the parents usually provide the gift they know their kid wants, but seeing it in real time feels magical; as if Santa might really exist. The children in my family still believe in Santa. They are so amazed by his presence. Instead of rushing to get home in case Santa misses their house, they are always reminded of what great hearts they have. That no matter the time, Santa won't forget them.

Austin interlaces our fingers, and I zone in on my family gathering around, facing toward the children sitting so nicely, waiting for our performance. As we start our first song, I admire Austin as he puts everything he has into singing. Glancing every so often to his sheet music, his mouth is animated, his eyes crinkle, and his body inhales and exhales energetically. It's evident he's the missing piece of my family, and I'm possibly the black sheep. He was born for this.

After our five-song performance, closing out on "Rudolph, the Red-Nosed Reindeer", Santa makes his appearance with a hearty "Ho, Ho, Ho." The children all squeal, gathering around him, my niece and nephews rush up as well.

"Thank you for bringing magic back into Christmas for me," Austin says. His lips brush my cheek. "All this," he gestures around the room, "everything your family does, it's all I ever dreamed of. It's what I would want to create if I had kids."

I look down at him, resting my hands on his hips. I honestly hadn't thought of my own family in so long. Before James, I toyed with the idea of whether I wanted children. It only made sense with my family, but I knew it'd be harder for me and I had to ensure I had the right partner.

The day James and I got serious, he said he never wanted kids and, just like that, it was off the table. Thankfully, too. The last thing the world needs is more James' running around.

I think ahead to what a future might look like with us. We both admitted to not wanting kids unless we could entirely trust the other person. It already feels like we're on that track, though.

Austin kisses me, pausing my thoughts, before he escapes my arms and finds the kids who are unwrapping the gifts they've gotten from Santa. He easily sits cross-legged, "oohing and aahing" at the appropriate times when shown the gifts. I lose him for the next hour, sitting back in one of the sofa chairs, watching him. He isn't trying to prove to me he's a good partner. When he's good, he has a heart of gold. Somehow, throughout his childhood, he never lost hope that love exists.

The part of me that plots and plans imagines what our future could be. How many children would we have? What would the holidays look like arriving as a family unit, getting to experience Christmas from our children's perspectives? The thoughts nestle within me, sewing up the broken bits of my heart. I want to give Austin the world for as long as he'll allow me.

Chapter Twenty-One
Austin

The vibration is nearly silent from across the room, buried in my duffel bag—the last place Elijah saw me store my phone—but I can feel it in my bones. It's calling to me from the depths of my darkness.

The family Christmas dinner and caroling nearly had me forgetting. I allowed myself to drown in their happiness, but now my lifeline is calling.

Stick with the plan, Austin.

Elijah shifts beside me, turning toward the wall, pressing his backside ever so slightly against my thigh. If I place my pillow against him, he'll never know I've slipped out. I inhale, sliding from beneath the sheets. I situate the pillow and adjust the comforter back into position. As I step toward my duffel, the vibration grows in volume, yearning for me to make the worst mistake of my life.

It isn't that I want to; it's that I have to. There's a tether attached, ripping me from the inside out. I'll be empty in a few short hours, but I'll still have a family *and* Elijah.

I'll be back, I remind myself. The plan is to come back; always has been. My agreement with Elijah was until the 26th.

And I'll be damned if I miss Christmas. This was the point; the entire point. I needed an exit plan and Elijah was it. *Is* it.

I stare at my bag. It should stay here. A safety net. I'd have to come back to get my belongings.

What if Elijah changes his mind?

What if he thinks I'm a disgusting, pathetic person?

What if Mom rips down the defenses?

I lift my bag slowly, ensuring it barely makes a crinkle, and then I silently open and close the door behind me. I pause, listening for any slight noise within the house. Thankfully, Elijah's parents are at the backside. His sisters and their husbands are in their respective bedrooms, and the children are asleep in the den. Apparently, it's customary to spend the night of Christmas Eve. They've somehow convinced the children that Santa comes to Grandma and Grandpa's house. It's so disgustingly cute, and everything I want.

I'll be back.

The moment I escape out the front door, my stomach clenches and I double over in pain. I force one leg in front of the other, stumbling down the steps, and dash across the street to a bush. Heaving, I fist my eyes to stop the tears. *I am* choosing this. I *have* to do this.

When my stomach settles, I head toward town. I had scheduled a car, *just in case*, to pick me up at a 24/7 gas station. It was a pretty penny for private transportation three and a half hours away at one on Christmas morning, but without it, I wouldn't be able to escape. It's a sacrifice I choose to make.

The car is there waiting. I had requested for them to wait a solid thirty minutes, giving me time to stall or back out. Whether I showed or not, my account would have been charged.

I shouldn't get in. I should eat the charge for this car and then save my mother's tab. Put it into savings; toward a future.

My bag vibrates. Taking my phone out, I see a message from my mom.

> We need you. Starving away here. I can't believe you want your mom and sister to suffer.

It's all bullshit. It always is. Melodramatic guilt.
What if it isn't?
It's always been a fear to read about my sister's death. Not from drugs; that'd be her own doing. But I'd never be able to live with myself if she didn't have basic necessities.

With a deep breath, I get into the car and we're off before I can change my mind.

The car ride to my hometown is quiet, as requested. I try to sleep, lulled by the driver's monotone podcast softly playing. The highway encases the car in darkness, but each time I close my eyes, I see Elijah's smiling face.

I brought that smile to him. I have already started recognizing differences in his laugh. And gosh, his hands. His hands wrapped around me, cupping my cheeks, squeezing my ass, grazing my dick.

How is it even possible for someone to one day step into your life and flip it so drastically? I stepped directly into the fire, naïve enough to believe I could play a part and walk away without crumbling.

The thought of my ex invades my brain. His disappointed face; his screaming. I had his trust, and I stomped on it. The sound of the door slamming in my face. I can't . . . I can't have that same future with Elijah.

I'll be back. I'm just paying my dues. I'm just tying up loose ends.
This can be the last time. This has *to be the last time.*
The driver taps my leg, startling me. The neon lights of my

second home come into my periphery. My chest tightens as the letters flicker; The Diner.

"Let's go. This place gives me the creeps," the driver says, gesturing with his hand to get a move on.

I stretch my legs as I climb out of the car, placing my duffel on my shoulder. I curse my aging body and stressed demeanor. The place is packed. Barely a car in the parking lot, but the conversations and transactions have trickled outside. A few drunken Santas are still in uniform.

I toss the driver a tip after checking that my account was debited. He's out of the parking lot before I step closer.

"Whattada know, little A is back! Ready to come to the darkside, baby?" Jewels, my mom's friend, says as I near The Diner. For years, she took me under her wings to find me a girl; hell, she even attempted to find me a boy, too.

"Never can truly escape." I smile and nod toward her crew. I know my mom isn't outside; she never is. It's too cold for her brittle bones. Instead, she'll be cozy in a booth with someone who has less money than she does. She never quite understood the concept of a sugar daddy.

I walk up the cement stairs, making sure not to touch the rickety railing; I've seen firsthand the bodily fluids left on the metal. Miraculously, there haven't been any accidents from the drunken and drugged patrons leaving The Diner. It's the only place in this fucking town that's open all day, every day. Even Mo's closed a few hours ago.

Opening the glass door, cigarette and marijuana smoke escape the hotboxed diner. I hate how my body naturally inhales, relaxing under the cloud of my second home. As much as this place has stripped me of everything, it has also given me life. Literally. My mom had me in the back of a car in this fucking parking lot.

"A! Look at the time. Cutting it real close this year, huh?" Rick, the owner of The Diner, greets.

His words are like slime coating my heart, weighing me down. Everyone here knows the routine. I took my first steps in this shithole, and made it out alive. They know I give my mom money, and they always like to remind me how they wished they had a "me" in their life.

Rick's standing behind the counter, counting a wad of cash. Most diners wouldn't be caught dead doing that, but the patrons know Rick is strapped. If they wanna keep doing their business on the down low, then they must respect Rick's business. He's the grandson of my adopted grandma, Meryl. She never wanted her establishment to be for generations of junkies, but instead of fighting it, her mission was to keep them fed.

"Let me get you a drink. You earned it, as you're paying for it." Rick steps away from the register and toward the liquor wall. The good thing about the liquor here is it'll kill anything that might be growing.

My eyes find Meryl's picture, front and center, behind the counter. When I was young, she always made sure me and my sister had something to do while here. She was responsible for my Christmas morning meals and coloring. She was the one who taught me how to cook. She had dreams of being bigger than this diner. Her recipes were far more eloquent than this shithole, but she kept the menu small so the town could afford it and she could still make a living. She brought out her fancier meals a few times a year, but no one appreciated them. Meryl was my protector until she passed right before I left for college. She's the reason I strived so hard for a scholarship when things got hard. She motivated me. Her death was the final push; I wanted to accomplish her dreams.

"To Meryl," Rick says, nodding toward the picture frame. He hands me a shot of cheap ass tequila.

"To Meryl." I nod, and we both cheer before downing the

rubbing alcohol. Just enough liquid courage to complete my walk, and maybe leave this hellscape before the sun comes up.

"She's over in the corner booth; your sister's with her. Have a Merry Christmas, A," Rick says before going back to counting his cash.

Sure enough, they are in a rounded booth at the far corner of the diner. My mom's hanging on to Mika, my sometimes step-dad, when he feels like disciplining. With an unbuttoned shirt, he rests his head on the back of the booth, too strung out to hold it up. My mom filters through men like coffee grounds, but Mika's the only one that keeps coming back. My sister's on the booth's edge, carrying on a conversation. An entourage of people surround them; the same crew my entire life. The table is littered with half eaten plates.

I still have time to walk out, unnoticed. I can somehow catch a car back to Elijah's. Maybe sneak back in without him knowing I left. And if he did realize, I can apologize. Explain it all better than I have.

Tell him I want to invest in him. Deposit the cash back in the bank. Save it toward a future with him. For the first time, I really want to dream of a future without strings attached. Start a family. Give them everything I wish I could have had growing up.

The thought has me lightheaded. I lean on an empty booth. *Family.* I have the opportunity to create my own family, choose who gets to exist within my bubble. My hand shakes as I grip the torn fake leather seat. My duffel suddenly feels like it's weighed down by bricks.

I need to . . .

I have to . . .

My nerves are on fire; the tequila twists in my stomach. Her eyes connect with mine, and that fucking smile spreads across her face. I'm wrapped around her goddamn finger and she knows it. She raises her fingers in a gut-wrenching wave, and a tsunami of grief washes over me. My knees give out. I slide into the booth next to me, removing my bag from across my chest. Steadying my drenched forehead, I place my head in my hands, trying to blink away the blackout. Inhaling, I cough out the 80% smoke and 20% carbon dioxide.

This cannot be my future.

If it is, I might as well join them. I'm no better for having gotten out. It's a piece of me, one that controls my entire being.

"You better have enough for me this year." My sister slinks her half-naked body into the seat across from me. She's likely got enough money to cover her own tab with her bloodshot eyes and smeared makeup. Nausea creeps up my throat. She's chosen this life, allowing others to have their hands on her, all so she can get a little money to get high.

I swallow, gripping my duffel. Placing it on my lap. I don't have much here, but I can't afford to lose the little possessions I do have.

It feels like just the other day she was under my care, wanting the best for herself, looking at me for advice instead of as a bank. Now, those puppy dog eyes she used to give me light up as she looks behind me, likely zeroing in on her next paycheck, or drug deal.

"Holy fresh blood," she breathes, and the chatter silences around me. "He is delicious."

I glance at the other customers. The ones who have silenced have their eyes toward the door.

Before I can twist around, the voice sends a shiver down my spine. "Is there an Austin here?" Elijah asks, and I swallow the bile in my mouth.

Fuck. Fuck. Fuck.

"Hi, handsome!" my sister exclaims, waving her fingers. I sink into the corner of the booth. "I have an Austin right here."

I close my eyes, squeezing my duffel strap, wanting to get out of this fucking situation.

What the hell is he doing here? I had tested my movement in bed a few times to ensure he stayed asleep.

"Austin," Elijah says softly, but he isn't in my booth.

My eyes burn at the goddamn sadness in his voice. I clench them shut. If I have learned fucking anything from growing up, it's that men don't cry, particularly in this part of town.

"Hi, I'm Alana, Austin's sister. Who are you?"

"Elijah." His voice is stern. "May you please excuse us?" There's no room for discussion in his tone, but he also doesn't belong here, and if my sister chooses, she could get him removed in an instant.

I keep my eyes forward. The silence increases my heart rate, and I sneak a glance at Alana. She darts her eyes to the right of Elijah, and with a slight shake of her head, she shimmies out of the booth.

Her gaze cuts to mine; I hold in my exhale. "Our eyes are on you, Austin." I give her nod, maintaining eye contact until she breaks it. The moment she turns, I shut my eyes, exhaling slowly. There's a delicate balance between peace and chaos.

Elijah doesn't replace her spot; he shifts my cushion, his hand resting on my thigh underneath the table. "Can you please open your eyes?" he whispers, with a gentle squeeze of his palm. "I'm not upset with you."

I wait a breath cycle.

"H-how did you—?"

"I called Liza. She had given me her number, saying I might need it. I didn't understand why, but now I do."

The tears escape, and I instantly shove my fists onto my lids to stop them. Liza's never been here, but the compromise to keeping her in my life was telling her my mother's locations. If she couldn't stop me, she wanted to know where she could find me, just in case.

"I'm not here to stop you," he whispers.

All I want to do is fall into his arms, but we can't. Not here. They can't know how invested he is in my life. And he probably thinks I'm literally trash. At least the people in this diner know who they are, but me? I'm just a fucking fraud.

"I want to help this be your last payment. Give proper warning that this won't be happening again."

My eyes open, and the moment they connect with him, he grows blurry with another onset of tears. I ran from the softest eyes I've ever encountered, and still, they light up for me. "I've tried—"

"With no proper support," he interrupts. "If you'll have me, I can help you."

"B-but what if I . . . l-lose her?" I whisper. The confession drains me; my body sinks further into the cushion. Elijah's hand keeps me from sliding off the booth.

"Have you ever had her to begin with?"

My eyes cut to his. Red flashes and I swing. His reflexes grasp my hand mid-slap, clenching it between his, resting them on his lap.

Adrenaline rushes through me as I vibrate in place.

"Austin, baby, come here!" My mom's voice slithers into my cracks, giving power to protect her.

"Let's go pay her, tell her Merry Christmas, and inform her this will be the final payment, then I'll take you home."

I shove myself into the corner of the booth, yanking out of his grip to create as much goddamn space as I can. I gasp for air. He doesn't understand. How could he with his cookie cutter family? I can't just walk away. She needs me.

His hands caress me back into his arms; he holds firm. "Fight it, Austin. I'm not the one you're angry with. Take that anger, hone it in, and aim it toward her."

My body shakes. I'm so fucking angry. With her. With myself.

With him.

"No one stays," I whisper. "She . . . "

He leans his head down, hovering right above my forehead. A mere few inches would connect us. His eyes captivate mine, building pillars.

"I stay, Austin. I will stay. I'm here now, and I have no intention of leaving without you by my side."

I lean my head against the booth, steadying the nausea. I try to breathe as deep as I can, but all I manage are gasps.

The pillars collapse. This is all . . . too much.

She's robbed me of my goddamn happiness.

Chapter Twenty-Two

Elijah

Austin's feet are unsteady as we walk to the rounded corner booth; his mom is sitting center. His sister squeezed her way onto the left edge; those surrounding were not even kind enough to give her space.

My body is on high alert; I have one goal before I can shut down. Get Austin back home.

Home. The anxiety laced with fire in my bloodstream cools slightly at the thought of home. He belongs with me. With my family. We can be his home.

His sister's eyes bore into my own. If I wasn't absorbing Austin's energy, she might be able to sneak her way into my mind. His mother doesn't even notice me, her contact not wavering from Austin's; her smile only grows.

"About damn time. I thought you might have forgotten where you came from." His mom's words are laced with liquor, potentially even something else from her skin lesions, and the drugged out man on her arm.

I keep a safe distance from Austin, not needing to draw attention away from the core problem, but I swear he leans toward me with her words. This is uncharted territory. I'll never let him know, but I'm terrified. Before him, I never would have had the courage to walk into a place like this. I lived far too sheltered a life. In hindsight, I probably should have brought my dad for an additional body.

Austin unzips a corner of his duffel and pulls out a drawstring bag. He tosses it over, nearly hitting a plate of syrupy pancakes. Claws dig into the bag; perfectly wrapped cash is dispersed throughout the table. I force myself not to look at what bill starts the wad. I don't want to know the damage unless he specifically discloses that information, especially if this is his last payment.

"I'm done," Austin whispers.

I damn near have to restrain myself from squeezing his hand. He told me he has to be his own pillar.

"What?" his mom bites. Suddenly, the man beside her straightens, and the conversation from their group silences.

"I'm done. This is all I have. A bit extra than requested. I won't be back." His voice is steady, but I eye the tremor of his body. He grips the back of his jacket to stop his shaking hands.

The laugh his mother lets out is one from a horror movie. It rattles my bones. I want to pull Austin close to me, shower him with the love he deserves; the courage he needs, but I can't shake the fear of what could happen if I do.

"You said that last year, and here you are." His sister rolls her eyes, reaching across the table to down a drink. A person swats at her hand for stealing it, but his sister just waves toward the man behind the register.

Austin's fingers casually bump mine, similar to our first day hanging out. Catching his eyes is all the courage I need to speak up.

I straighten my shoulders, and for the first time, his mother looks at me. If she makes the connection that I might be the person from the phone, her face doesn't show it. "You heard what he said," I start, "use this wisely. He will not be back. You will not contact him again. You are now cut off."

Her eyes narrow, but not a single person steps closer as a threat. "Who the hell are you? You have no idea the type of arrangement we have."

"I do. And frankly, it interferes with mine. Contact him again, and I'll have your establishments shut down immediately. It will only take one call to the police for someone to investigate the number of violations happening. Pick your battle: your booze and drugs or potential jail time. I'm sure you've got a list of things the police might want to arrest you for."

"Half the police are in this diner every day," the man beside Austin's mom says. "They won't do shit."

I inhale, dusting off the names in the back of my mind. James can finally be good for something.

"Your local sector may not. But Lieutenant Moore, Sergeant Grant, and Sergeant Boone are close friends of mine. They work for the state police, trying to shut down these very establishments. I don't ask them for much, so you better believe they'll be here in minutes if I make a phone call. Should we see?"

"I suggest you leave and never show your face again." Austin tenses at the man's voice behind us. The guy from the register comes around Austin's side.

"R-Rick," Austin stutters.

I place my hand on the small of his back, steadying him. Tears escape his eyes as he looks at Rick. It isn't fear. Whatever it is has me swallowing my own emotion.

"It's time you go, Austin. Meryl would have stepped in ages ago. I'm sorry."

"Rick, what the fuck! This doesn't involve you," someone shouts at the booth.

Rick swivels, and silence clouds the diner. "You heard

Austin. If I hear that any of you are trying to ruin this kid's life, I'll personally call the police. Don't forget, I know all your damn secrets."

"Let's go," I whisper to Austin, turning us toward the door. His feet drag across the floor, my pressure the only thing keeping momentum.

"I thought you wanted to protect me!" his sister's shrill voice exclaims.

"I thought you loved me!" his mom screams.

I glance back as I push Austin's shaking body forward. Rick is blocking the table from moving. I look forward, quickening our pace. It isn't safe here; we need to leave.

When we are in the car, with the doors locked, and halfway down the street, Austin breaks down. I can't stop driving, but all I want is to wrap my arms around him so fucking tight and never let go.

I give him my hand. He squeezes it with everything he has as he curls up in a ball, resting his head against the passenger window, and sobs. My body begs me to shut down; my mind wants to process whatever the hell just happened. I can't do either. Possibly not until Austin is back at work. He needs my stability more than I need my sanity.

About two hours out from my parents, my phone startles us both. The sun is rising. I put my mom on speaker and her worried voice adds to the thick tension.

"Where are you guys? The kids are anxious to open gifts."

"Let them. We'll be back in an hour and a half."

"Elijah, it's Christmas morning."

"That's not important!" I snap, adrenaline still infesting my body.

As soon as Austin's hand is on my thigh, the fire starts to simmer.

"Excuse me?" my mom says.

Tears burn my eyes. I've never shouted at my mother

before. My heartbeat is erratic, and I grip the steering wheel. I don't know how to come down from this. The last hour in the car, all I tried doing was finding an equilibrium. Needing to protect Austin but having to protect myself. It's only heightened my awareness that nothing, and everything, is okay.

"I'm sorry," I say softly. I never left a note for my mom. There wasn't time. I had to find him. But I've also never missed Christmas; not even with James. "I promise this was important."

"What could possibly be so important . . . you two didn't break—"

"Mom," I interrupt. "Trust me. We had to take care of something. We are on our way back."

"We? Good," she sighs with relief. He's not going anywhere, if I have a say. "Okay. Austin's with you?"

"Good morning, Louise. I'm so sorry. It's my fault we're late. I'll make it up to you."

A wave of calm settles over me at the sound of his voice.

We are okay. We will be okay.

The pause on the other end has me questioning whether she's putting pieces together with the very minimal information she's been given. Austin's voice is hoarse, and if she remembers anything from the other day, she knows something serious is going on.

"You know you both can talk to me if you need to, right?"

"I know, and maybe someday," Austin offers. He shifts up in his seat, and I do everything to keep my eyes on the road. I don't want to startle him. "Right now," he continues, "I'd really love an Evergreen Christmas morning. Would that be okay?"

"Absolutely, sweetheart. I'll see you both soon."

The line drops. The tension consumes me again with the silence. The only thing regulating my heart is Austin's hand on my thigh.

"I'm sorry." His whisper is so low I almost believe it's my brain hoping he'd say those words, but the tight squeeze of his fingers tells me differently. "If you want to drop me at the bus station and never see me again, I understand. It's okay."

My vision blurs. I swerve immediately to the shoulder, trying my best not to slam on the brakes. Thankfully, there's no one around. When the car is in park, I open my door and make my way to the passenger side, unbuckling Austin's seatbelt and pulling him out of the car.

I wrap my arms around him as best as I can; his body is stone. He's built his walls back up.

"Austin," I lean back, cupping his cheeks, "I am falling in love with you. I don't plan to desert you. What I did back there? That is also an act of love. It doesn't have to be all fairy tale romances or picture perfect moments. I am choosing to be by your side. I want to help you fight your battles. I want to see the worst, best, and mediocre parts of you. I choose you, Austin. All of you."

"She might be dangerous," he whispers, eyes zoning out behind me.

"If she wanted to come after us, she could have. I don't doubt she'll try to contact you, but if you'd like to get a restraining order and/or change your number, we can. I'm not frightened of her."

That isn't entirely true, but his eyes connect with mine for the first time in over an hour, and I will myself to be courageous and patient. Austin has unraveled every part of me. All I want to do is upend my life; create a space for us.

"Do you really know those police officers?"

"Yes. I doubt they'd lift a finger for me; they were close with James, but it's a good threat."

Just as the local precinct is corrupt around that diner, the state police officers I know in the city aren't much better.

"Please don't shut it down." His eyes are glossy and his

contact drops from mine as I start to rub his back. "I took my first steps there. I grew up there. I learned how to cook there. A fucked up part of me feels connected to the idea that she chooses to spend her time there."

I place my palm on the back of his head, guiding it against me. I take a moment before responding. Trying not to be rash. I'll never truly understand the hold to a life like that. My first steps were in the grass in my parents' backyard, walking toward my dad. There's a home video of the bright and sunny day. And when I fell, the soft grass caught me. Austin likely fell on disgusting linoleum, sticky with god knows what.

My goal is to create a space he's safe in. A place he can shed his survival mode.

"I won't," I whisper, "but if she contacts you—"

"Then you can do whatever you need to protect me."

He finally relaxes in my arms, and I catch his limp body. A car zooms past; the first since I've stopped on the road. I tighten my hold. The silence settles into a calm.

Austin's chuckle a few minutes later startles me. "I'm supposed to show you what love is."

I breathe out a laugh, leaning back so I can look at him again. His eyes blink at the last bit of glossiness, crinkling slightly with his close-lipped smile. His rosy cheeks are blotched; his under eyes slightly swollen from the tears. Austin's hands make their way to the base of my neck, erupting goosebumps at his soft touch.

"You are showing me what love is," I whisper.

I want to catch the tongue that coats his lips. I walk forward a step, leaning him against my car's back door. My pelvis presses against his, holding him in place while my hands tangle themselves in the strands of his hair.

"I promise you," I breathe, hovering over his lips, "you being here. You being you. You're intoxicating." I brush my lips against his. My body shivers at his shaky exhale. "You've been my muse. I don't know where we go from here, but it's somewhere together. You've shown me love in your way, but it's a two-way street. It's multi-faceted. And I want to experience it with you."

His lips crash onto mine. I rest his head on the cold metal, pulling at his hair, devouring him, wishing there weren't so many layers between our bare skin. I want to take him in the backseat of my car, but we can't do that. Not yet. He deserves more than a heated hook-up.

No. This man deserves to be loved, kissed, sucked, and fucked until his mind shuts off, and he sleeps soundlessly.

I break our kiss, traveling down his neck and behind his ear. Brushing away some hair, I nip at his skin. He's hard against me; our bulges create friction between our jeans.

"Can you—I need—" His voice whimpers, and I suck the tender skin where I just nipped.

"Tell me what you need," I breathe against his neck.

"I need a release."

One hand tangles in his hair, my free hand squeezes between us, cupping him, eliciting the sweetest sound I've ever heard.

I need him. We have plenty of time for love and romance, but my god, my mouth needs to be wrapped around him, sucking him dry. I need a release from this anxiety and tension. Ecstasy to carry us over into Christmas morning.

"Get in the back seat," I murmur against his skin.

His eyes ignite before pushing me off of him and diving into the back seat. I lean in the front, turning the car on to blast the heat in the below freezing temperature.

"Lay down," I demand, standing outside. Before he's fully laying, I've already unbuttoned his pants and shimmied them down. Without warning, I suck him in, hitting the back of my throat. His groan has his pelvis lifting, pressing deeper into me.

My pace is rapid. With one hand, I steady his hips and my other hand releases my dick from its confines. I jerk off in time with my mouth. Lubricating my dick with my pre-cum and spitting on his, I watch him twist and flick his nipples, writhing beneath me.

"D-don't come," he moans. "I n-need to taste you."

The fucking phrase alone nearly has me blowing my load; instead, I release my hand and double down on him. I slide the tip of his dick back and forth on the ridge of my mouth as my free hand circles his rim. I lap up some pre-cum, coating his rim before pressing a finger in. His hips buckle; a guttural moan escapes his lips, and I all but choke with the hot liquid shooting down my throat. I swallow, continuing to fuck him with my finger, sucking him dry until his hand reaches for mine, pulling my finger out of him.

"Back up. I'm coming down on my knees." My dick throbs as his voice is thick with ecstasy. The moment his lips touch it, I'm going to lose it.

I step back, though, holding onto the car door to steady my wobbling legs. My ass is now in full view for anyone who might drive by. "Passenger side," I breathe.

He's pulling his pants up as I move between the open back and passenger doors. Slightly more privacy. The last thing we need is a ticket for public indecency.

I lean against the passenger seat cushion, gripping it as tight as I can. Austin's kneeling before me, my dick all but poking him in the face. His movements are slow, deliberate, and I'm ready to scream.

This release will be my equilibrium.

Two fingers press against my lips, and I open, my tongue coating them. In an instant, at a much different pace from his tongue barely touching my tip, he presses his fingers against my rim, dipping one in, sliding it all the way in before enveloping my dick with his mouth. My tip hits the back of his throat as the pressure of his second finger has me thrusting toward him. His fingers curl and stretch inside of me. My body vibrates on the sweet brink of coming.

He pulls his fingers out and slides my dick out into the frigid air. As I whimper, he says, "Look at me."

"F-fucking hell, Austin." My eyes connect with his as my legs shake. I'm so fucking close.

His eyes don't leave mine as he swirls his tongue around my dick. "I'm falling so deeply in love with you," he whispers. And in an instant, his mouth devours me and he fingers me. I hit the back of his throat, and I groan, squeezing my eyes shut. I'm lightheaded with my release. His mouth rides my aftershocks until I collapse toward him, his body barely catching me.

Austin lifts me up, settling us against the edge of the seat, his forehead meeting mine. "I don't think I'm falling. I think I *am* in love."

Chapter Twenty-Three
Austin

The front door swings open the moment Elijah and I step onto the porch. The children grip my hands, pulling me past Elijah. We are immediately consumed by so much happiness; it makes me want to cry. Though, I'm not sure how many more tears I have left.

Most of the car ride was a daze, aside from the mindblowing orgasm Elijah gave me. I can't seem to process what's happened and what consequences might be in store for me.

The kids throw clothes into our hands. Themed pajamas that seem to match the rest of his family—all of whom are sitting in the living room with their personalized mugs. Every single present is still underneath the tree.

It's nearly ten in the morning; our sex rendezvous, though necessary, delayed us further.

I breathe in, trying to settle my overwhelm. I had prepared to walk into a home of children busy playing with their toys. With the idea that unwrapping gifts already happened, despite his mother's promise to wait for us. The guilt that I made them wait weighs me down. I ruined their Christmas morning.

"How about you boys go get dressed? Breakfast is ready. We'll eat, and then have Christmas morning." Elijah's mom rests her hands on my shoulders.

"I'm so sorry, Louise," I whisper.

Her eyes aren't full of pity, but the level of understanding has me swallowing my tears. "Nonsense, my dear."

"After brunch, we all have to go back to bed!" Myles shouts. "It has to be *just* like Christmas morning."

Esme laughs, standing up from the couch. "We wouldn't dream of anything different. C'mon, let's help Grandma grab the food."

Elijah interlaces his fingers with mine, leading me down the hallway. Once settled behind the privacy of his door, the silence consumes us. After we had sex, it felt like we fell into an impending doom. What happened with my mom? What has happened with us? What happens after this? Where do we go from here? I had been trying to simmer the anxiety brewing with upending my life, going back to work, the New Year's Eve engagements, and love . . . god, love was almost the worst of it all. The chaotic, overwhelming feeling of happiness is too much and not enough.

I need to be present.

"My family must really love you," Elijah says softly, stripping off his clothes. "They *never* delay Christmas. Literally, one year I took too long in the bathroom and they couldn't wait for me."

A laugh breaks through my mental war at the ridiculousness. I can picture that. "They shouldn't have. Those kids are going to resent me." I place my bag down and change into the adorable Rudolph, the Red-Nose Reindeer flannel pajamas. I'm obsessed with them.

Elijah throws his head back in a laugh. "Resent you? They love you. I'm sort of jealous." He finishes buttoning his flannel shirt before closing the distance between us, mine still open.

"Careful about being too hot today," he whispers in my ear, his fingers trailing my waist band. "These pants don't hide anything." He steps back with a slight graze of my hardening boner. My breath hitches. He buttons my shirt, his fingertips brush my skin like little shocks of lightning.

With a peck on the forehead, he walks out of his bedroom door, leaving me breathless and wanting more.

Christmas morning is more than I could have imagined. Each minute was a distraction. From the children opening gifts from Santa to being gifted a collage photo frame filled with pictures of me and Elijah throughout our visit here. Elijah informed me his mother had a photo printer, which explains how a picture of us caroling the night before got mixed into it. His mother managed to print three pictures of us kissing in different corners of the home. She thought it would be the perfect gift to bring back to work, and I couldn't agree more. Elijah got the same gift, plus others; except, his photo collage was different *just in case* we happened to move in with one another. She didn't want her gifts to go to waste.

Once the gifts are unwrapped, and we eat seconds of breakfast, Elijah and I curl up on the living room couch with the rest of the adults as the children play with their toys. I can picture years of happiness under this roof. While the lead up was filled with grand moments of the holiday, it seems today is a slower pace.

"Hey," I whisper, leaning into Elijah, so he gazes down at me. "Could you tell me what was wrong earlier?"

When we had opened our collages, Elijah tensed momentarily before he blinked back tears. He seemed stunted by something.

"In the four years I was with James, I had three photos. We already have two collages." His hand dips beneath my waistband, resting on my thigh. It isn't sexual; just a need for physical contact. "The happiness in those photos," he breathes. "I haven't seen that pure joy on my face . . . god, I don't even know for how long."

I curl deeper into him, not responding. The joy is bubbling over at a rate that is terrifyingly close to spilling. This is exactly where I want to be here; present; in love.

But this isn't me, and we may be protected by the pheromones of Christmas. When the Christmas lights go down and we store away our rose-colored glasses, could there be a future between us?

I can't be responsible for Elijah's happiness. For not disappointing him. I want to showcase love, be in love, treat him like he deserves the world, because he does, but I'm broken. And I'm in a new career, one that has me testing my strengths in just a few days' time with these proposals, and I stress . . . a lot, when it comes to things I'm passionate about. He needs someone who can be there for his books, support him taking the next step, moving away from the negative reviews of his genre shift. He needs to heal.

His lips press against my scalp, his grip tightening ever-so-slightly on my skin.

"Breathe," he whispers. "What do you need?"

I need to avoid panicking about the fact that I only have a hundred dollars to my name before my next paycheck, and I know my mom isn't going to give up easily on the thousands I give her. I have to stop triple checking whether my recipes are good enough for someone's most important night until their wedding. I need to . . . backtrack to a couple of weeks ago when my world didn't get overturned. Where I was okay living paycheck to paycheck to give into my mom's needs. To not be forced to break away from that. It's unsettling. In my scheme of pretending to love Elijah, I naively didn't think it would challenge me to believe it's okay to be loved.

It's goddamn easier to think I'm not worthy of it.

"I need . . . I need to go." I try to sit up, but he clasps my thigh. If I'm not mistaken, he has a slight tremor.

"Where?"

"Home. I have to get ready for work."

"Austin, you don't work for another day and a half. You agreed to the 26th. I thought you already prepped?"

"I . . . I'm . . . I need to change the menus."

Elijah's free hand caresses my cheek, momentarily steadying my mind. "Let's go for a walk."

I barely nod before I'm off the couch, stumbling to the door to slip on my shoes and jacket. Snow started falling a few minutes ago, so it's likely colder than my layers will help, but maybe it'll make me numb. Distract me.

Elijah is saying we'll be back as I step out the front door. I'm a goddamn embarrassment of a partner to Elijah. I'm down the path and on the road before he shuts the front door, but he lets me be. I take advantage of the space, jogging up the road. There's a coating of snow on the ground already. I don't know how much it's going to snow, but it better not impact our commute home. *That* I don't have time for.

"I'm spiraling," I say once I hear he's behind me. The tears burn at my water line, the brisk air nearly freezing them in place. "I need it to stop." I shove my shaking hands into the flannel pants, pressing into my thighs with my fingertips. Closing my eyes, I tilt my head toward the sliver of sun peeking through the snow clouds.

He doesn't ask me to turn around, nor does he face me. "You've lost your control and you're desperate for it."

I nod, breathing the crisp air into my lungs.

"Do you want someone to take over the responsibility of your actions for a while? Or do you need to find something to control?"

"I need to . . . not think. My brain wants to self-destruct."

"I need you to answer one last question. Do you trust me?"

"Yes," I breathe, and I know it's true. It's subconscious.

What's happening is a result of my mother and my upbringing; I know that. But I can't logically think my way out of a spiral.

"Okay. We are going back to my parents' house. We will thank them for the holiday, grab our bags, and head to my home. You will spend the night. After a good solid edging, where I will finally make you mine, we will discuss your New Year's menus; we will figure out a schedule for us, and you'll let me loan you whatever money you may need to recoup."

My dick twitches at his tone. The hairs on my arm stand at attention. I've been into controlled play; it's not my first spiral, but even the ones who thought they could get me to stop talking to my mom failed.

"W-what about the three-hour drive home?"

He steps closer, hands on my hip bones, resting his pelvis against my ass. His breath sends shivers down my spine and his hand hovers tauntingly close to my dick. "Love, the edging starts right now." He palms my dick, pressing me against him, and lets out a groan as his dick grows beneath that very thin fabric.

This. This right here is very much of what I need. The anticipation. The focus. The *desire*.

He feather-kisses up my neck; I let my gaze unfocus, taking in the empty street around us. The only sound is his heavy breathing; but if we held our breath, we could hear the snowflakes settle. His chin rests on my shoulder, seemingly gazing out with me. As if we might be looking at the view from the resort. But instead, it's a regular snow-covered neighborhood. The road where my life changed.

🎄

This man will be the death of me. We're less than thirty minutes from his home, as per his sensual update of how many minutes it'll take before he's hovering over me. Claiming me as his. I've already got a pool of pre-cum in my boxers, so much so it's darkening my flannels; my legs shake in anticipation. But he's fucking good. We've carried on casual, silly conversations like ridiculous pop culture stuff that doesn't affect our lives one bit. Despite the conversations, my mind continues to travel back toward the negativity, and each time, without me recognizing I'm sloping, Elijah's hand caresses some part of me. I've never been so grateful to be in loose pants. The pajamas allow for easy access for his hand, and the ongoing boner I've sported the entire drive.

I try a few times to casually brush my hand up his hard on, but after a groan that nearly had him slamming on his brakes, he interlaced our hands and put a stop to it.

"I wish I had a butt plug." *Fucking hell.* "I wish you could have had one in you this whole drive to stretch yourself out for me."

I squirm. It's my play of choice, especially when I'm alone. I'll wear it throughout the day, building my excitement. That anticipation is such a part of the earth shattering experience for me.

"C-can I . . . I c-can—" I try repositioning myself so I can have access to my ass. I don't need a butt plug to prepare.

"Don't you dare." His voice turns husky, eliciting another twitch from my dick. His hand grips my upper thigh, holding me down. "That is my ass to prep."

I breathe in, closing my eyes. I have to make it past the foreplay. I can't lose it right here.

"This is Lake Juniper." His voice suddenly shifts back to normal, and I open my eyes.

It's dark now; half past five, but I can see we're driving through an adorable village. The main strip is lit by lamp posts with snowflake lights on top of the post. Shop windows are decorated for the winter season, with either spotlights on mannequins or the window laced with white string lights. It really is so similar to the village of his book series. I'm excited to get back to reading; something I never thought possible. There hasn't been any time to read over the past few days, but boy, does his written word give this place justice.

The flurries earlier today have continued through on our drive, but never amounting too much. Though, it's created a gorgeous backdrop against the faded brick buildings and cobblestone roads. The moment he mentioned the town name, our ride got slightly bumpier. Not a single car is in sight. Likely all the shops are closed.

"This is Isabella's Coffee; where Jemma works." He points to a storefront with two double-paned "snow frosted" windows and a cute metal sign.

"And they had a therapist for you?"

He gives me a bright smile, his eyes filled with shock. "You remembered."

My heart skips a beat, a gentle reminder of how the two of us came to exist. Throughout my own shit, I need to remember why this started.

"Will they be open tomorrow?" I ask. He nods as we take a turn left, the cobblestone ending. "May I take you out for coffee in the morning?"

He nods again, and this time, I place my hand over his on my thigh. I catch his exhale, but his focus remains forward.

Maybe we'll be good for one another because we can shift our dynamic. Just as powerfully as he can try to dominate me, I can bring him right back down.

"Elijah?" I lift his hand to my lips, kissing the backside gently. "Your words matter. I have every intention of remembering them."

I reach toward him, thumbing under his eye as a tear escapes.

Before me is the man from the novel. The one who's good at putting sex up as a front. Having sex heals things; and it can. Giving over complete and total control to someone else can be one of the most relaxing experiences. But he's still very much the broken and lost man when the experience ends. The bits in between the sexual encounters.

If possible, the car darkens; we're on a narrow drive surrounded by pine trees. Within a few seconds, we're pulling up to a small, one-story dark gray home. Just like he said, he's at the base of the mountain, in the woods, not a single home around us. There's a light on inside, lit string lights hang from the eave of the house, and there's a wreath on his front door. The simplicity is a stark difference from his childhood home.

"Did you turn those on?" I ask. Honestly, I hope I'm not walking into another tragic situation.

"Yes, I have an app to control the lights. Because of everything with James and living alone, I have an entire security system to reduce unnecessary anxiety."

I nod as Elijah turns the car off. He rests his palms on his thighs, breathing in.

"I want you here," he starts; his eyes closed, "but it's rare I bring guests. This is my safe place. Even Jemma and my parents have only been here a handful of times over the past year."

"We'll go at your pace, and if you want me to leave, just say the word." I rest my hand over his and give it a squeeze. "I understand."

We walk hand in hand to his front door, our bags over our shoulders. The snow is falling heavier now, coating the pavement. It's brisk the moment we step through the front door, and my eyes immediately search for a source of heat. I spot a small fireplace in the corner of his living room, an enclosed iron oval with a square glass view for the fire. *Jackpot.*

I can't say I'm surprised to see his house is monotone; the furniture is varying shades of gray, compared to his mother's vibrant home. It does make me wonder how he might have decorated if James never came into his life.

How he might decorate with me in his life.

Immediately to my right is the living room with a small hall that leads directly to a sliding glass door and porch, and to the left of that is an open kitchen; an island separating the two rooms. Not a kitchen table in sight, just two barstools. Off the kitchen, down a proper hallway, are three doors.

I don't know what to do first. I want to peruse the multi-pictured frames in his living room; I want to help him start a fire, so we can strip down in front of it; I want to explore his backyard, holding his hand as he opens up a little more, or go to his bedroom and crash in his bed.

Neither of us slept much the night before, and while I am excited to have sex with him, the lack of sleep and emotional turmoil is getting to me.

I hear the click of a lock behind me, then Elijah's hand runs up my back, lifting my duffel off, and places it on the floor. He comes back behind me; his one hand rests on my left hip bone while the other creeps beneath the flannel pajamas, dangerously close to my dick.

"Come with me," he whispers in my ear. I shiver, leaning into him. He interlaces our hands, leading me down the hallway. We enter the second door on the left, and the moment he flips the light switch, all I want is to spend my downtime here. I want to sink into his sleep-inducing down comforter and pile of pillows. His bed frame, specifically four-post, faces us and the right wall is an entire window.

An open door to the left presumably brings us to a bathroom, and there's a closed closet too.

Just like the rest of the home, his bedroom is shades of gray, but here, it sets the mood. I sink my toes into his plush carpet. He has two realistic-looking candle lights on each side of his bed. Elijah turns them on, and I swear the flicker looks real. Against the wall opposite the bed is a large, sleek, electric fireplace and a flat screen television hung above it.

I watch as he clicks the fireplace on, the flames igniting, creating a soft, golden glow on him. He then shuts off the overhead light.

"I'm going to start the real fire, the one that'll warm the rest of the home since I've been gone." He hovers behind me again, this time his hand wasting no time sinking beneath my waistline. His fingers trail the length of my dick under my boxers, inching toward my ass. "In the meantime," he whispers, licking my earlobe as he circles his finger around my rim, "you're going to choose a butt plug that you'll wear until I remove it and get in the shower. I want you to put the butt plug in and prep yourself." His lips kiss down my neck and a nip has me jumping; my cock leaking. "Do not wash your body." Another hard nip at the base of my collarbone has my head tilting on his shoulder. "Do not touch your dick. I'll be joining you shortly."

In an instant, his touch disappears and my skin yearns for more. He kneels down beside his bed, which has drawers beneath it, and he opens one, revealing a collection of sex toys. *Oh my fucking god.* The scenes in his book . . . I recognize some of the toys in his collection. Did he . . . has he experimented with all of these? He pulls out a tray and places it on his bed. There's a solid ten butt plugs to choose from.

He closes the distance between us as my mind is reeling, thinking of using each of these toys with him. His lips crash onto mine, his palm steadying my head. His free hand slips beneath my pants, clasping my butt, pressing us closer. The friction has me moaning into his mouth. Tonight, I get his dick inside me, and the thought alone has me wanting to blow. His fingers separate my butt cheeks, circling my rim once again.

"Choose whatever turns you on. I'll be back," he whispers against my lips. With a quick peck, his hands disappear and he's out of the bedroom before my body remembers to breathe.

I finger the silicone plugs of various sizes. Three look like a set pack, each one getting slightly longer and wider as you increase your stamina. My favorite kind is similar to anal beads, and he seems to have the perfect one.

I can hear his footsteps on the hardwood floor, then the sliding glass door opening and closing. The anticipation has my heart racing. I immediately grab my butt plug of choice and set the tray back in the drawer under his bed. So help me god, I hope I have the pleasure of coming back to his home and exploring *all* the toys he has.

He has a walk-in glass shower that steams the bathroom in an instant. The scorching hot water beats down on my skin. I lean my head toward the water spout as I work through stretching myself just enough for the butt plug, teasing to cleanse, before situating the plug deep within me. The pressure is enough to remind me of how goddamn long it has been since someone fucked me. A lifetime since someone made love to me.

My hand lazily grazes my dick; the sensation settling in the pit of my stomach.

"Looks like someone might need a punishment."

Elijah's voice has me squeezing the tip of my dick, swallowing a moan. I don't like punishments, but fuck; his husky voice when he's turned on is hot. Turning my head, I'm face to face with a naked Elijah, right outside the glass door.

"Remove your hand," he says as he opens the door; a rush of cool air awakens my nipples.

"I don't . . . I don't like punishments. That's not a—"

His eyes soften. He slowly disconnects my hand and places it on his dick instead. Then clasps mine. "No punishments," he whispers. Leaning in, his wet mouth grazes my earlobe, "But you will do as I say, and I forbid you from touching yourself."

Involuntarily, I grip his dick, leaning toward him.

His movements are languid; squeezing shampoo into his palm and massaging it into my scalp. My forehead rests comfortably on his shoulder as he works his fingertips in varying pressures. My only way to steady my balance is stroking his length, keeping my wobbly knees intact.

Once our hair is clean, he moves on to my body. He's meticulous and detailed, not missing an inch of skin. His fingers circle my nipples, graze around the butt plug, even so much as twisting it within me; resulting in me generously squeezing his balls to keep me from falling. His moans are music to my ears.

When he gets between my legs, the man drops to his knees, allowing my fingers to dig into his shoulders. Caressing my balls, he massages them between his palms. He waits for the water to rinse the soap before his head dives underneath my dick, tracing my ball sacks with his tongue. My dick yearns for a touch, a lick, a graze, but he expertly avoids the appendage. Instead, he sucks a ball into his mouth and experiments with pulling the butt plug out.

"My favorite," I think he mumbles around me, and slowly pushes the plug back in. I double over; the heat from the shower has me lightheaded with his movements.

He stands me upright, releasing his touch. My skin tingles at the loss, and our eyes lock. His gentle smile does more for me than any seductive or mischievous smirk.

In contrast to mine, his hands now race to wash his body

with soap, swatting my hands away with a lift of his brow when I try to return the favor.

Elijah reaches behind me to shut the water off, and my breath catches. We're about to take this to the next level; a step we can never get back. An experience with him I'm certain will exist in my memories for as long as I live.

Chapter Twenty-Four
Elijah

I'm not sure how I got so lucky to have this glorious dick staring at me, leaking, begging me to grab hold of it. Oh, how I'd love to be on the receiving end, but this night is all about Austin, and what he needs.

So instead, I consume the length of him, hollowing out my mouth before sucking in, my fingertip grazing where the plug and his asshole meet. Austin's body arches into mine, and I swallow him deeper, pausing through my gag before angling his tip to glide against the roof of my mouth. With a gentle tug, I pull the butt plug out before thrusting it back in time with my mouth's movements.

The body-twisting moan Austin releases tells me that his edging is going brilliantly. No matter where I touch, his nerve endings are on fire; I can relate. I've specifically kept my dick a far distance from Austin, in fear of spewing unexpectedly. Hell, the sight of him has me wanting to come.

I release his dick, watching as my saliva drips and mixes with the pre-cum.

"Eli?" Austin breathes. A wave of desire courses through me as my nickname falls from his lips. I rest my head on his stomach with a moan. He makes me weak; in all the best ways.

I kiss my way up his body, not forgetting to circle, then nip his nipples. When I reach his mouth, I kiss a "yes" on his lips.

"Can I top? I know you wanted . . . but I—"

I crash my lips against his, laying on him so our dicks collide and our burning skin connects. Thousands of my nerve endings electrify. This incredible man wants to take me as his. I break the kiss, smiling as he groans from the distance, but I sit back and straddle him.

How in the hell did I get here? He isn't a one-night stand. He's a terrifying prospect for my future.

Prospect. He isn't a prospect.

He's my boyfriend.

He could single handedly destroy me if he wanted.

"Please make love to me," I whisper, brushing our lips together.

In an instant, he is on top, pressing his tongue into my mouth, circling for dominance. He's got it; he's mine. His lips are ravenous, exploring my body like I kept him from doing all day. He twists and bites my nipples until I'm writhing beneath him. His tongue slides up and down my length, licking around my balls, making its way to my entrance. Hands separate my ass cheeks before his tongue presses against my rim, dipping into my sweet spot. Pre-cum leaks onto my cock as I jut my ass up.

"I'm clean; I've been tested."

Austin's eyes lock onto mine; his intensity alone nearly has me releasing. Instead of answering, his tongue presses further into me, slowly adding a finger at the same time.

"Holy fucking hell," I breathe, digging my head into my pillows, arching as high as I can. My legs tremble as he adds a second finger. Groaning against my skin, he sinks his fingers as deep as they can go. Just as he's about to add a third, while curling his other two, our eyes lock.

"I'm gonna," I inhale a shaky breath. "I need you to—"

Austin's eyes darken with a soft smile; his tongue and fingers disappear in an instant. My heart swells; tears brimming my eyes. My body vibrates. Any touch, gaze, taste would suffice. The desperation is utterly terrifying, and I clench my eyes shut. Fuck, he's going to be the death of me.

"I'm clean, too," he whispers, pecking a soft kiss on the base of my neck. "Boyfriend?" he questions, a fingertip brushing beneath my right eye. I flutter them open, blinking away the blur. "I have every intention of taking the very best care of you. You're safe with me."

He seals the declaration with a simple kiss. A momentary reminder that we exist outside these four walls.

Austin steps off the bed, kneeling to access the drawer underneath. He rummages as my body pulses, begging him to come back to me. He returns with the bottle of lube, and my god; my vibrating butt plug. Climbing back onto the bed, he makes a show of him removing the other plug, before shoving the slightly wider one in—one more resembling my girth. Once situated, I watch as his eyes roll back the moment he turns the vibration on. Austin then coats his uncut dick, lining it up with my throbbing entrance.

I breathe through the breach of my rim, not in pain, but to keep myself from climaxing. He's larger than any of my plugs—than James. The feel of the vibration in his ass, transferring to my own through his dick, is one of the most incredible feelings.

When he bottoms out, he paces his thrusts. I'm not going to last long. The desperation in our touches shoots electricity through our sensitive skin. Gripping, kissing, biting, moaning, I need the earth shattering climax. Tears burn my eyes; sensory overload. I've never felt so full. Emotionally, physically, mentally. A high I'm terrified to collapse from.

Austin quickens his pace. Hair slicked, head thrown back, he lets out a guttural moan. I reach out, drawing his body down. I need to be closer, connected in every way possible. Our sweaty skin smacks together and he cups my cheeks. "Come for me," he breathes against my lips.

I cry out, shooting streams onto my stomach. My vision blackens, only reawakened by his warmth coating my insides. He moans my name, burying his head in the crevice of my neck as he continues to thrust through his orgasm, ensuring we're both spent before he stills.

I barely have the energy to move, but Austin removes his softening dick before lifting my ass, lapping up his cum leaking from me. He then kisses his way up my body, licking every last drop of my cum.

After he swallows, Austin connects our lips and the taste of our musks nearly has me hardening once again.

We somehow switched roles as Austin climbs off the bed, heading to my bathroom. He comes back with a warm towel, wiping me down before removing his plug and cleaning himself.

When he crawls back into bed, my eyes are so heavy from the lack of sleep and being satiated, I can barely see him. Austin curls into my side, and I wrap my arms around his warm, naked body. Our dicks meet as he interlaces his leg with mine. I'm certain I've never been more comfortable. I swallow the emotion in my throat.

Austin is how I'll begin again; the start of something new. And as I drift off to sleep, my brain writes the rest of my newest romance novel.

The shrill of a phone has me bolting out of bed, barely grabbing my robe as I dart into the kitchen. I pick up the cordless house phone off its dock in the corner on my counter. My heart races as I try to figure out what time it is and what the hell is going on. No one ever uses this phone.

"Hello," I gasp before trying to slow my breathing.

"Elijah, I'm so sorry—" My shoulders relax and I shuffle back to my bedroom. "—but you needed to know." I miss half of what my assistant says as my mind tries to calm. No one is dying. No one is in the hospital.

"Hold on," I sigh, rubbing my face. I tap my bedroom light on and dim the brightness. Austin's awake, sitting up in bed, still naked, but wrapped in my comforter.

"Is everything okay?" he whispers.

I shrug because if everything is okay, this phone wouldn't be going off. My alarm clock says it's just after nine. We've been asleep for a couple of hours.

"Okay. Hi Sarah, why are you calling my house phone?" I ask, whispering to Austin that she's my assistant. He curls into my side.

"I'm so sorry. I know this is an emergency-only line, but you weren't answering your cell, and well, I think this is an emergency. I'm so sorry I didn't catch it sooner, but with the holiday—"

"Sarah, please. What's happening?"

"James made a statement."

My blood runs cold; my face flushes as I sit up straight. Austin's hand falls off my shoulders. I immediately put the phone on speakerphone. Without understanding what's going on, Austin's hand is on my back.

"With your book going viral, it seems to have gotten to a group of people James knows. The internet started investigating whether your book was autobiographical." I drop the phone onto the bed and Austin's dashing out of the room.

"They made the connection between you and James, and well, other people he's been with. His exes are speaking on behalf of similar behavior, but James is saying it's false."

"I don't . . . I don't understand."

Austin runs into the room and I wish I could admire how he comes to my rescue stark naked. My laptop bag is in his hands and he climbs back into bed with it.

"I sent you a few emails while I was waiting for a call back from you. Please read those and go through what I've provided. Then call me back and we can work on a game plan?"

"Thank you," I mumble, clicking the phone off.

Austin hands me my password-protected laptop. With shaking hands, I type in the password, but I'm too nervous to check my email.

How.

How could this happen? I was so fucking careful. I never shared anything personal. No one even knew I was in a relationship. I'm not even famous enough for this.

I hand the laptop back to Austin as my vision spots. "My email is already logged in through Gmail. Can you . . . can you go through everything?

"Are you sure?"

"Austin, please," I whimper, pressing my palms against my eyelids. I lean forward, pulling my knees up to rest against them.

My skin tingles; sensory overload. Everything touching me feels like pins and needles, or nails scratching against my skin. I can't run. I can't stand; I'll just fall over. I was supposed to be doing better. Healing. Moving forward.

I changed the character names. He didn't even fucking know I was successful.

"Goddamnit!" I scream, gripping the comforter and twisting it.

"Would you like me to show you the videos or would you like me to watch with headphones and I'll paraphrase?" His hand presses against my back, searing into my skin; I shimmy away.

I slept with another man.

I've finally moved forward.

It's like he fucking knows. Always one step ahead.

"I need to watch," I whisper. I dare a look back at him. The sadness in his eyes is too much. I have to remove myself from the situation; for just a moment. "I uh, I'll be right back. D-don't start without me."

He nods, and I dash out of bed, my un-tied robe flapping against the breeze. I find red wine in my wine cooler and uncork it, grab two wine glasses, and then I shuffle through my cupboard for white cheddar popcorn.

I can do this. He doesn't control me.

Not anymore.

I'm not his.

I'm not Austin's.

I am me. A romance author. A boyfriend. A son. A best friend. I am my own person, able to make my own choices and decisions. There is no part of the book that says it's him. I have done nothing wrong.

Once back in my bedroom, Austin smiles as he eyes my stress tactic. I hand Austin the wine and glasses and toss the popcorn on the bed before peeling off the robe. I'm way too overheated and overstimulated.

Austin pours the wine once I'm situated against the head-board. It almost feels like a powertrip to witness this with Austin; naked. He cannot control me anymore.

I open the popcorn, take a handful, and shove it into my mouth, allowing the superficial stress relief to settle my nerves.

He hands me a glass. "To everything being okay. Because you'll be okay," he says softly.

I tap my glass gently against his with a nod. *I'll be okay.*

Like ripping off a bandaid, we cycle through video after video my assistant sent me over. The videos start out with praises about my book. They are the viral videos I never allowed myself to watch at the resort. They then shift into the investigative work of my readers. Austin's expertly stayed away from the comments section, but we're down a rabbit hole of one specific creator who I've seen praise my work before. She's got a multi-part deep dive into everything that's happened.

When my book went viral, it naturally left my reader base, traveling through TikTok, Instagram, and Facebook. Popping up for all generations. An ex of James', I think they broke up a few months before we started dating, made a video talking about my book. The same day people speculated James' name. While he never liked social media, he still has a Facebook from back in the day that people traced back to him.

James' ex talked about how they could see themselves in my novel. How it brought back past traumas they thought they solved. That they had come across my book, not realizing I was James' next bait until they started contacting friends of friends still in contact with James. It got back to him.

In James' video, he calls me a pathological liar. He claims I was living a double life with him. He never had any idea that I was an author. He said I'm trying to ruin his name and his life. Each video we watch explicitly states that I never mention his name, not even one slip up. Though, one photo I posted on my author account was of a group of friends, and he's in it, but ironically, it's when he was with his ex and not me. The timeframes don't align.

He's put himself in a bad light. People are claiming he's victim shaming. The fear I had of people invalidating my experiences dissipates as people come out in droves, supporting me and the book. The question remains whether it was autobiographical or just relatively based on the experience.

My name is fucking trending. We manage to find James' original video, posted on his Facebook account. It was posted three days ago. I've been trending since. A few videos were just posted minutes ago.

"How are you doing?" Austin whispers as we fall into a lull of new information. He sets the laptop off to the side for a moment. "That was a lot. I didn't want to stop. I think it was necessary to see it all, but walk me through what's going on in your head."

I immediately give him my empty wine glass. An hour has passed since we've looked up. I was empty ten minutes in.

Austin refills the glass and shifts his body to face me. His hands remain cautious in his lap.

"People are on my side," I whisper. That's the only coherent thought repeating in my head. All of the fear and negative people on the internet outshine what we just consumed. The algorithm hasn't brought us to any creator who doesn't like me. They all claim to be avid readers of mine. The comments aren't all great, but for some reason, my mind is shifting toward the positives.

I am still here.

I am getting help.

I am persevering.

James . . . he, well, he's entirely unaware. Defensive and closed off. He isn't going to prosper. He isn't the future or community I want to surround myself with.

Austin places his hand overtop my comforter-covered thigh. "You have all the support, Elijah. You never mentioned his name. You never gave any indication it was about him. You wrote a fantastic book straight from your heart and that shows."

"I want to make a statement," I say before I change my mind. I climb out of bed, put my wine on the nightstand, and head to my closet.

"Wait, what?" Austin's not far behind me, his hand on my shoulder as I open the closet door.

"I need to reclaim ownership of my story. I can't give him power. I tried being private. It was never truly intentional until I started dating James. He talked down about social media and well, I didn't want anything to draw back to me personally. And maybe I don't like being 'on' all the time because it burns me out, but I like personal connections from other authors. If this can all happen while I've been my most private, what's the harm in being a bit more connected?"

I search through my hangers to find my favorite simple black T-shirt. I don't feel the need to impress, but the fabric has to soothe my skin.

"Should you contact Sarah first? See what she thinks?"

I shake my head as I grab a pair of fresh boxers, then sweatpants, from my dresser. No one needs to see past my chest.

"Will you take a video of me in the living room?" I turn to him once I'm dressed. If I wasn't so nervous about being bold, I'd laugh at his baffled expression. Just a reminder that despite our intense connection, there's still so much he doesn't know. I need strict plans, yet I can be spontaneously bold. Confident even. When I have a gut feeling, like right now, it's crucial I pursue it. It's almost always the right move.

"O-okay," he hesitates. "Let me get dressed."

When he leaves the room to grab his bag, I take a moment to look at my sales channels. My $95,000 went up to $110,000. Jesus fucking christ. Going viral has a cost, but lines my pockets.

I check my Instagram to see if my assistant has posted anything recently. The last post is wishing everyone a generic Merry Christmas. The post before that is the mixed drink from the cocktail night at the resort. James' specialty cocktail.

I click on the post, scanning the comments. Most of my followers find it funny, claiming it's so accurate. I've not a clue about that, but I'm glad I had the foresight to take the marketing photo. I click for recent notifications and see my follower count has skyrocketed.

No fucking pressure.

"Are you ready?" Austin calls out.

I grab our wine glasses and join him out in the living room. He has already turned on the lights and shifted my sofa chair so it'll have a backdrop of my author bookshelf. This man. He might not understand what's happening right now, but he's supporting me.

"For peace of mind, I need to ask again. Are you sure?"

I close the distance between us. He's dressed in his sweats and I can't wait for this to be over so we can go back to bed and sleep forever. We're both emotionally spent.

I lean my forehead against his. "Yes. I need to. May I mention I have a boyfriend if it feels natural?"

He kisses me, hands cupping my cheeks, before he pulls away. "I'd love that."

Within a few minutes, I'm sitting down with Austin standing in front of me; my iPhone in his hands, ready to record.

I nod before I begin.

Hi everyone, Elijah Evergreen here. I honestly can't remember the last time I made a video for you all. It's been a whirlwind of a few years, particularly this past one. I want to start by thanking everyone who has given me unwavering support. Whether through videos, comments, or reading my books, I truly wouldn't be where I am today without it.

Most of this past year, I took a massive step back from social media. While I rarely posted personal things, I did used to read all comments and communicate with you all. At the start of the year, I got out of a bad long-term relationship with the help of my best friend and my incredible therapist. To heal, I was told to write down my thoughts and feelings. What transpired was *Don't Forget to Breathe*. I never intended for it to be published until, well, I couldn't let it go to waste. It isn't that I wanted to help others with my story. I wish it was like that. It's truly because I had a self-imposed deadline that you guys have become aware of, and I didn't want to let a good piece of work go. I deserved to tell my side of the story.

I intentionally changed names and locations. Keeping it as discreet as possible. I wanted the book to stand on its own. The reason for the genre shift was because there was a shift in my life. I couldn't write sweet romances where everything has a happy ending because I didn't know what that looked like.

My books going forth won't have this tone, but I have taken your suggestions on the spice. I'll be adding much more of that in.

I wink at the camera; I love the breathy laugh that escapes Austin's lips. His eyes panic momentarily. I smile, looking directly at him.

If anyone heard that lovely laugh, that's my boyfriend. I want to be more transparent going forward. I want to connect with you all again. I'm doing better than I ever have. Otherwise, my name trending honestly would have had me spiraling. But I want you all to know that I'm happy, healthy, and I'm falling in love. I'm falling in love with love again, too.

In other news, the sequel to Ansel and Arlo's story will be coming this year. And if you're a fan of Christmas romances, next Christmas you'll have a wonderful surprise. A story about the man who rein-spired me.

I hope you all have a wonderful holiday season. We'll talk soon.

I end the video with a wave. Austin makes sure it saves, places my phone on the coffee table, and then jumps into my arms.

"You're amazing. Have I told you that?" he whispers in my ear, pecking below my lobe. "That was incredibly hot. I'm so proud of you."

I wrap my arms around his waist, breathing him in.

I feel good. Peace is creating a home within me again. I *am* healing.

"Let me post that, then let's go back to bed," I say.

Austin grabs my phone and settles back into my lap. He kisses up and down my neck while I navigate social media and post the video on all my accounts. Once complete, I send a quick text to Sarah with an apology about posting without discussing, and mention an extra holiday bonus for all her additional work. Then I leave my phone in the living room, carrying Austin back to bed.

Chapter Twenty-Five
Austin

Soft kisses on my neck have my eyes fluttering. The room is barely lit by natural light. I don't know what time it is, but I am surprisingly well-rested. As soon as we climbed into bed last night, we fell asleep instantly.

"Mmm, good morning," I murmur, curling toward Elijah. We're both tangled beneath his comforter. If I wouldn't get a caffeine headache, I'd argue to remain here for the day.

Instead of words, his lips connect with mine in a lazy kiss. "Thank you," he breathes, pulling me tight against him. I wrap him in my arms, tracing my fingers up and down his spine. His thanks is for everything and nothing at all. It makes me yearn to give him the world.

I can picture myself sliding out from this comforter, walking to the kitchen, and preparing a breakfast to bring back into bed. Maybe we snuggle with morning cartoons or energize ourselves with morning sexy time. I could see myself searching through the closet for my clothes; curled up on the couch in front of the fire, reading his latest book. Venturing into his backyard, hand in hand, as we explore the mountain and discover a new favorite place. I imagine a dog bounding through the house, maybe waking us up in the morning with her hovering gaze; a reminder she needs a cuddle in the morning, too.

It all feels too good to be true. My throat burns at the thoughts, and I press a kiss underneath his ear.

"I believe we have a date this morning. Are you up for some coffee?" I ask.

"After a quick shower with you, absolutely."

Despite my desperation for the steaming brown energy, we lazily shower, stealing kisses and feeling one another up. It never gets further than innocent touches, but as we're hopping into Elijah's car, we're both intoxicated with ecstasy.

The light in his bedroom was deceiving. As we pull out of his driveway, the warm winter sun greets us, as if Mother Nature is so happy we exist. My negativity wants to seep in, burn the happiness to dust, but I do my best to fight the feeling. Naming things in my head that I'm grateful for in the present moment. Elijah's hand interlaced with mine, his thumb caressing my hand being one of them.

Lake Juniper is more lively this morning. We have a short walk from a municipal parking lot in order to get to Isabella's Coffee, but the journey graces us with post-Christmas happiness. We're in the rare moments of the year where time slows and giddiness overflows. I want to walk through these cobblestoned streets all the time with my hand interlaced with his. Get to know the owners of each shop like his characters do in his novels. Create a new community for myself.

I always loved that I did grow up in a community. While intoxicated and drug-laced, most people know one another where I'm from. I might not have been raised well, but a village raised me.

I want the opposite of that. Supportive and loving. A community surrounding me that isn't contingent on chasing a high.

There's a squeal before the door to Isabella's Coffee shuts behind us. Suddenly, Elijah's best friend is standing before us, her hands on each of our shoulders. Jemma's gaze gives us a once—then twice—look over. Her eyes glow as she meets ours.

She grins. Her arms widen, and just as I think she's going in to hug Elijah, she wraps her arms tightly around my shoulders. I swallow my gasp, urging myself to remain neutral. "Welcome to the family. I cannot wait to get to know you better." I hug her back, but just as quick as she was to hug me, she steps back, her eyes narrowing.

"If I ever do anything to hurt him, you'll murder me, bury my body, and no one will suspect it was you?" I say with a grin, and Jemma glances at Elijah; both of them laugh.

"You can stay." She pats my shoulder.

Elijah squeezes my hand. Her acceptance solidifies a piece of me I didn't know was missing. It wasn't just Elijah I needed to win over; but the person who helped him out of his darkest place.

Her eyes then shift to Elijah. They seem to communicate without words. He wraps her in a hug, sinking into her touch. "I'm proud of you," she whispers. "That video took guts."

"We haven't checked—"

"The response is positive. Take the day with Austin. Get back to work when it's time. Crisis averted." Jemma then heads back behind the bar.

He leads me to the counter and I mentally shake off any concerns Elijah's video might have caused. We can focus on ourselves today. Hopefully nothing else interferes.

"What'll you be having?" she asks, shooing the barista away from the register and to the bar. She's already typing Elijah's order into the register.

I glance at the menu, grinning with the reminder that I can have espresso again. I missed that at Elijah's parents' house. Something I'll have to rectify next year. I smile at the thought. I then look at the pastry case; I'm ravenous. We never ate dinner last night before we fell asleep.

"A shaken espresso with oat milk, an everything bagel with cream cheese, a cinnamon bun warmed, and—" I glanced over at Elijah, locking eyes with him. His smile sends tingles down my spine.

Elijah's hand rests in my back pocket, and the grin on Jemma's face grows. "I'll have the same food."

Jemma jots it all down on the iPad, enters her employee discount, and before I can hand over my card, she's taking Elijah's. The reminder of my balance rolls in my stomach. He had mentioned something yesterday about giving me money, and I cannot for the life of me allow that to happen.

We settle ourselves at a table in the back corner of the cafe and sit in what feels like comfortable silence; though my mind is starting to race. We're in a final countdown. Customers come and go as we eat our food, but we have most of the cafe to ourselves.

"When will I see you next?" Elijah asks the moment we've finished our food.

Time stops.

This isn't goodbye.

I pull out my phone, opening up my calendar to look at the specific date. "I am home on January 10th for a week." While I'm excited to head back to work because I genuinely love my job, fourteen days feels like it'll be a lifetime. It's no longer a draw to have free accommodation.

Elijah's silent for a few moments, nursing his coffee mug. "I don't know how to do this," he admits.

My heart slowly cracks with each passing minute. I got us into this beautiful mess and I have to be strong enough to guide us through it. I reach across the table for his hand, swallowing the impending lump in my throat.

"Me either," I whisper, "but we need to be open with one another and tell each other how we're feeling, when we're feeling it. We both deserve that."

He nods, tightening his grip. "The separation terrifies me. I don't know if I can stop the thoughts from seeping in."

He hasn't seen them, but I received a few messages from my mom on our car drive to his place yesterday. I haven't had the courage to block her number yet, but his edging had kept me from spiraling.

What happens when our pillars disappear? Leaving us with our thoughts 24 hours a day? Sure, we can call, but not often, and a lot can be hidden through text.

"All I ask is that we try," I start. "I might not respond all the time as I keep my phone out of the kitchen, but I need you to know that is never a reflection of you. I can promise you I'll always respond by the end of the day."

I need to remain strong on my phone boundary. It isn't necessary in the kitchen and just because I have Elijah now doesn't mean I can allow him to be a distraction.

"I promise if I sink into the negativity, Jemma will reach out to you to explain."

A laugh escapes me involuntarily. I cover my mouth so quickly to not offend him, but he's grinning, too. I don't doubt that I'll be hearing from her, whether Elijah is good or not. Apparently, we both had the foresight to get each other's best friend's numbers before we left for his parents. He already cashed his in. I hope for Elijah's mental health, I never have to cash his in.

"I'm going to ask about the policy for visitors. Maybe you'll be allowed to stay with me every so often."

Elijah's eyes light up. He brings our hands to his lips and kisses the back of mine. "I would love to go back up there and write."

"Oh, sure, and I'm second best," I tease. Though, the idea

of an actually inspired Elijah writing at the resort, able to be found at any moment of the day, at the job I'm loving, sounds like perfection. I don't want to choose between them.

Elijah's ankle intentionally curls around mine. His eyes hold so much love in this moment, it has me holding my breath. I want so desperately to not wait for the ball to drop. I want to just exist in this world of ours. Embrace the love consuming us.

"Love," he whispers; my arm hairs stand at attention, "you aren't second best. You're the main character in my new novel. Literally and metaphorically."

My skin is on fire at his confession, and if this goddamn table wasn't between us, I'd be jumping his bones. That is single handedly one of the best compliments anyone has ever given me.

"Is this novel sweet or spicy?"

His hand reaches beneath the table, grazing my knee cap. "The best of both. What my readers have been asking for; what I've been experiencing."

I'm itching to go back to his place with the imagery of his words. I want him to make me his. Maybe role-play whatever he's written; you know, get some experience so he knows he's written it all correctly.

I want the memory of us, together as one, engraved in my soul, to replay over and over on the moments I need it the most, and if the universe were to separate us, I'd want the memory to haunt me forever.

The fireplace crackles, illuminating Elijah's living room in a soft glow. We're in our sweats, sitting in silence on opposite ends of his love seat, our feet intertwined.

After coffee, we traveled to my town to pack my bags for

my return to work. The original idea was for me to spend the night at Liza's, but as our coffee date grew more somber with the thought of separating, it only made sense that we spent as much time as we could together. Plus, the drive from Elijah's place to the resort is way shorter, lengthening our cuddle time in the morning.

Naturally, Liza wanted details on everything, so we stayed longer than anticipated. Driving separate cars back to Elijah's place was enough to have my mind spiral, so I requested red wine with dinner. It doesn't exactly go well with our Thai takeout, but it eases our anxieties as the sun sets.

"A penny for your thoughts," he whispers, tapping his toes against mine. He leans over to place his empty container on the coffee table and lifts his wine, cradling it against his chest.

"This is real, right? Like, I won't be driving away tomorrow, and we'll be wondering how the hell it all came to be and end it?"

Elijah takes my container and puts it next to his before handing me my glass of wine. He moves to the middle of the couch, and I meet him halfway, so our shoulders touch. The friction of our clothes shocks us, and tears brim my eyes.

"I don't know how it would be possible to fake this. We have a lot to learn about one another; sure. But this feeling? It's unlike anything I've known. I truly feel like you're a missing piece in the puzzle I didn't know I was completing. Though you walking out the door tomorrow is going to take more of me than I started with."

I lean my head against his shoulder, sipping the wine as I watch the fire spark. The strength to walk away, even if temporary, is going to strip my soul in the morning. This feels like home to me. I don't know what cabinets he keeps the Tupperware in, or if he has bandaids in his medicine cabinet, or if he even has a medicine cabinet. But I feel like I could climb off this couch and go search for something, knowing exactly where it is, as if I placed it there myself.

I want to stand at his kitchen island, preparing our dinner while he's finishing up a scene in his latest novel. Then we'd eat it on the back porch, watching the wildlife feel safe enough to roam near us.

"I'm waiting for it to crash and burn. For something to go wrong," I whisper, and his arm wraps around me so fast I nearly spill my wine. "People always leave. They don't . . . I don't know; people like who they think I am, instead of who I am. And I worry . . . I mean, you've seen portions of my worst, but what happens when you have time to reflect on that?"

"Austin." Elijah's voice is strong. His hand guides my chin toward his to connect our eyes. "I had a silent three and a half hour drive to a town I never heard of, walked into a run-down diner, and could have gotten the shit kicked outta me, if not worse, all for the hope that I found you. And I'm still here. No amount of silence is going to make me rethink wanting to build a life with you. As long as your actions remain true to who you've shown me, someone I don't believe you're lying about, then we'll be good."

I take another sip of wine, letting the liquid coat my mouth as I fear my next thought. The one that could break us. If his response is negative, I can always drive back to Liza's.

Swallowing the wine, I whisper, "What if I'm not strong enough to resist my mother's pull?"

Elijah's hold on me tightens, and a single tear escapes, trailing down my cheek.

"All I ask is that you're honest with me," he says, brushing the tears away. "Please, please don't hide anything about your family for fear that I'd end us. You lying? That'll end us. I can't . . . we can't have a relationship with lies."

Fuck. Has the clock already started? What's the difference between an outright lie and withholding information? He never directly asked.

"She's messaged me," I mumble. I want to lean away, create space from the vortex that makes my mouth want to spill every little secret of mine.

"That's to be expected." I hide the waterfall of relief flooding through me. "Anything of concern?"

I shake my head. They are all empty threats. She has the money for now. None of the bills I gave her are fake; directly from my bank. She should be on even ground with her bills and the extra will give her time to come up with a plan that doesn't involve me.

"Do you need money?" His fingertips travel to my temple, softly massaging the skin, and I shake my head again.

I have a full tank of gas. My only expense until my next paycheck. "The resort covers my food. I'm okay."

Elijah's eyes search mine, and I force myself to maintain the contact. I am okay. My mom got what she needed. My heart is conflicted by the overwhelming love and care I never grew up with.

How I became the person I am, one who felt ballsy enough to claim I could show Elijah love, is something I'll never understand.

"Tell me a happy story," he says, pulling us back toward his end of the couch, so I'm curled into his side; both of us comfortably able to sip our wine.

"In my childhood, on December 26th, Meryl, the woman I consider my grandmother, she owned The Diner, would take me and my sister to the toy store. They'd have marked down toys. We each got to choose one thing. My mom never put toys under the tree. She claimed the tree was enough of a gift. So choosing a toy on the 26th was one of the biggest decisions of my year."

"What was your favorite toy?" Elijah's hand caresses my thigh, and I can't imagine another place I'd rather be.

"When my sister was old enough to be interested in Barbies, they had a gift set with a knock-off Barbie RV. It came with two dolls, the RV, and accessories. We combined our gifts for it, and we were able to create stories about where we'd travel to if we lived a different life."

He presses a kiss to the top of my head. "And where would you travel?"

I smile, lifting my head off his chest to look him in the eyes. "To a Christmas tree farm. Those Hallmark Christmas movies always made it seem like Christmas cured everything. Everyone was always so happy." Elijah's gaze is intense, listening to every single word as if they all matter equally. "When I got to middle school, I learned more about my mother and started to understand why we were living the life we did. I tried my hardest to change things, and I suppose I still have been. I knew deep down nothing would fix our family if she didn't fix herself, but I never stopped chasing the idea that happiness like those movies could exist. Even for just myself." I cup Elijah's cheek with my hand. "Good thing, too. I mean, it brought me to you; to the goddamn Evergreen family." I laugh.

His eyes brighten as he laughs. "I hope you know you enhanced my family's Christmas."

I can't accept that compliment with words, so instead, I press my lips against his. Drinking in his warmth. In an ideal world, we're celebrating our one-year anniversary as we're walking into his parents' home next Christmas. A Christmas where it isn't interrupted with my family's bullshit; we're able to wake up bright and early with the presents underneath the tree.

"Hey," I breathe against his lips, "when would be our anniversary?"

"December 14th." His answer is immediate. I pull back so I can take him in entirely. "You essentially asked me out; to make your grandmother's lasagna, and while that didn't go according to plan, I like to think our hot tub session was a date. We were fooling ourselves to think it could ever be fake. So, December 14th." He grins, and I can't help but smile back. I like the sound of that. A perfect space between my birthday and Christmas. A moment we can experience all on our own.

"Speaking of," he continues, his grin turning into a smirk, "we'll be missing our two week anniversary, and well, as a romance author, it's mandatory to celebrate any and all things love . . ."

My face warms at his suggestion, and I lean my forehead against his.

"What do you say we take this to the bedroom and reenact our first time?" Elijah's hand tangles in my hair, tugging me close. His breath is on my lips, and I ground my hips onto him.

In a relatively swift motion, he's standing, lifting me off the couch before carrying me down the hallway. And when I'm lying on his comforter, his body hovering over mine, there is no doubt in my mind that this is where I belong.

Epilogue
Elijah

Fourteen days. Fourteen days of spotty text messages, dropped calls, and long, excruciating days. I never joined Austin at Enchanted Juniper Resort. His boss said in the future it would be okay, but not around New Year's. They didn't want him to have the distraction; especially with his promotion of truly running the kitchen. He is no longer in his probation period, which is wonderful, but boy does my heart ache. He was in my life for seventeen days before he disappeared.

Instead of trying to figure out how I could be so drawn to a person I've barely known for a month, I channeled all the feelings into the book inspired by Austin. I finished the first draft, revised it, and even started writing the sequel to the long awaited new series.

I had become a zombie; wanting to be awake whenever Austin might have a free moment. Luckily, it wasn't radio silent. I always got updates on his breaks, as well as good morning and goodnight messages. I hadn't wanted to miss a moment of communication, so I lived on the adrenaline of writing and coffee.

A rumble of the gravel in my driveway has me dashing to the front door. I had the wherewithal to shower this morning when Austin mentioned he was leaving the resort; something my non-stop writing schedule hadn't allocated for. First stop is me; then unfortunately, we have to travel to Liza's. It'll eat into our very short seven days we can potentially spend together; and that's hoping Austin doesn't have other plans. But of course he will, because seven days isn't a lot to recoup on your life. He naturally can't spend all of it underneath me in my bedroom.

His car stops right behind mine. I rush to his driver's side door when I see his goofy grin. I don't know when I became a lovesick fool, but the energy coursing through my system is too good to care. I haven't felt this alive in ages.

"Hi!" Austin exclaims, wrapping his arms around me as soon as he's standing. His grip is so fucking tight, I'm exhaling in relief. Not that I doubted we would be okay. But you know, I doubted it.

"Hi," I breathe, inhaling his scent, pressing a kiss against his neck as I bury my face in his nape. "God, I've missed you so much."

Austin's hands rest on my cheeks, lifting me to eye level. His eyes are soft, glistening slightly. "Elijah?" he questions, and I tangle my fingers in his hair. "I love you."

His words are so gentle, I have to replay them in my head to believe them. It's like a double layer of protection wraps around my heart. The puzzle piece connects.

I lean down, brushing my lips against his. I want to do so much more; but he needs a moment to settle. "I love you too," I whisper, before deepening the kiss, teasing my tongue on his lips.

"I need you to take me inside. Right now." His voice is deep; awakening my dick, and in an instant, our fingers interlace and I drag him up the path to my front door.

The moment the door closes, I push him up against it, pressing my pelvis into his. He's already hard, and I'm groaning, leaning my forehead against his shoulder.

I am in love.

When he first left, both of us admitted to jerking off to the memories of us in bed together. Five days ago, we agreed we wouldn't jerk off anymore, that the next time we both came would be together, in person. It was the single hardest and most exciting challenge I've done; particularly because not only was I imagining us together, but I had been actively writing intimate scenes.

Now I feel like if he touches me, I'll lose all restraint.

We strip our way down the hall and to my bedroom. It's mid-morning; the sun is starting to seep through the tree lines and onto my comforter. Bathing him in a soft glow as he sprawls across my comforter. He's naked in front of me, dick at attention, throbbing as his gaze admires me.

"Ride me," he whispers. At the start of this pact, I told him about a scene that was my favorite in the book he stars in. One where my character rides him; it's a position he hasn't done before, and I am all too willing to be his first, *and only,* to experience it with him.

When I climb on the bed, his hands squeeze my thighs, bringing me closer so his dick rests against my stomach. His one hand travels behind me, and the moment it touches the butt plug I have been preparing myself with, he thrusts up with a moan.

"Holy fuck, Elijah. You didn't tell me." His voice is raspy as he sinks his hips back down, twisting the plug inside me.

"Surprise." I grin. I knew I wanted him in me. We had plenty of time for more than one round, but I needed that act of love from him. One that solidifies he'll protect me; confirm this relationship. I just didn't know I'd have the added confirmation of the L-word.

His hand pulls the plug in and out, creating a perfect rhythm. I fall forward, bracing myself on my forearms, resting them on each side of his head. With his movements, our dicks rub against one another, the fiction enough for my vision to grow spotty.

"I need you," I say. "I need you now." I reach to my bedside table, grabbing the lube I had already set out, and squirt a generous amount into my palm.

He hisses as I coat his dick. Watching the way his body reacts to mine makes my heart swell. I'm overwhelmed by the happiness bubbling within me, but for the first time, I don't question when it'll disappear. Once he's lubed, and so is my rim, I lower myself onto his cock as he lets out a string of curses.

"Fuck, Elijah. You're . . . goddamn." His eyes roll back as I reach his base.

All of him is throbbing in me. Matching my own damn heartbeat. I'll never grow old of how he stretches me. Being as close as I'll ever be to him.

He jerks up, but I press his hips down with my own. His hand grasps my dick, stroking and squeezing his need for more.

"Elijah," he moans as he strokes my foreskin up, and drops it down slowly, showcasing my sensitive tip. What I would do to have his mouth on it.

I lift up and then down, giving him permission to set a pace he needs, one I'll take over for. His movements are desperate and erratic.

I bury my head in his neck, nipping at his skin, matching his pace. The moment I reach the skin beneath his ear, his nails dig into my ass cheeks, and his thrusts turn to pounds, chasing his release. He comes with the loudest moan I've heard from him, pinching the tip of my foreskin together as if it'd hold in my orgasm.

As my brain tries to process the emptiness as his dick pulls out of me, I'm flipped onto my back, and Austin's mouth is sucking me in. My hands yank him down. A deep-throated groan vibrates my cock, and I spew my hot liquid inside him. He sucks me until I tug his head away, growing sensitive, and he collapses beside me in our sex haze.

It takes everything to stand up and grab a warm washcloth to wipe us both down. Now that we are in the room, I don't want to leave. So I make sure once we are sufficiently clean to toss the cloth in the hamper and climb back into bed. We settle underneath the blankets, and I wrap him in my arms. His head rests above my heart, and I hope he can hear the rapid beats that are strictly for him.

"How is it I could go months without sex before you, and fourteen days just felt like a drought?" Austin sighs.

I chuckle and kiss the top of his head. "Move in with me," I breathe.

It isn't a rash thought. I ran through all the logistics in my head for days, but never expressed it with him. One, it makes no sense for him to be going back to a guest house; despite Liza being there, he's still alone. Two, I'm selfish. I want his home to be right here. For him to do laundry here. For him to unpack his belongings and not live out of Liza's guest room closet. For him to exist in a place he can call his own.

He sits up, looking down at me. It isn't fear in his eyes, more so contemplation. Society would tell me it's way too soon, but if they were feeling this, experiencing the intensity of what we've already expressed, society would know it's a month too late.

"I want you to have a home, Austin. I want this to be your home."

His eyes well up. His fingers trace up and down my chest as he composes himself. He hasn't told me if his mom has contacted him again, but it isn't anything I fear. I have already talked to the police department about filing a restraining order. When he is ready to discuss those options, I have the information.

"A-are you sure? Because . . . I can't . . . I can't have a home, then lose it. It's . . . I don't think—"

I press my finger against his lips. "Hold that thought," I whisper. I jump out of bed, grabbing my phone from the living room. I open Instagram, scrolling through my camera roll to find our first photo together at the resort. I frame it in the square and type a simple caption:

Meet Austin: head chef, romance enthusiast, and world-class boyfriend.

I post it before I can change my mind. Then I head back to my bedroom, tossing him my phone. A smile graces his lips at the photo.

Once in bed, I pull him into my arms, leaning our foreheads together. "Austin, I love you." I pause, letting the words seep into his mind. I seal them with a kiss before continuing. "I don't plan on losing you, love. I want this to be your home, just as much as mine. Or we search for a new home; I'm pretty attached to this one, but I'm open to options."

Austin chuckles, which causes the tears to escape his eyes. He glances back at the post. He's very well aware of how private my account has been. Since being away from me, he's admitted to keeping up with my socials in case anything crazy happens while he's gone.

"I think this one is perfect," he whispers. "I love you too."

My lips crash onto his before he finishes all his syllables. Grasping the base of his neck, I deepen our kiss, tangling my legs with his. I hover above him, and he gives me the cheesiest grin I've ever seen.

"Welcome home, Austin."

Thank you!

Thank you for reading *Arriving Home*. Elijah and Austin's story is the first in the Lake Juniper series! Be on the lookout for more coming soon!

If you enjoyed this novel, I'd love if you could leave a review.

Amazon

Goodreads

Interested in the Arriving Home universe? Check out *Underneath the Whiskey.* My debut novel, and the start of Isabella's Coffee and Cyan City. Read a sample with the QR code.

Interested in more holiday stories from Chelsea Lauren? **Use the QR code to read two short stories for free!**

"Happy Ex-Mas" is a short story about Carter and Aiden, two life-long best friends and boyfriends. While their holiday is usually filled with joy, this year takes a turn. Will Aiden's desperation for self-discovery be exactly what he needs, or will he push away the only person who has ever really known him?

This story takes place on Christmas Day.

"You Matter, Marley Mae" is a short story about Marley and Mason. Marley is suffering from a downward spiral of depression; she isn't sure who she can turn to, but a hot latte and a familiar face will have to do. Turns out, Mason might be able to understand. Maybe she isn't so alone after all.

This story takes place on New Year's Eve, and in the Isabella's Coffee and *Underneath the Whiskey* universe.

Acknowledgments

Thank you, thank you, thank you to each and every one of you who has made it this far. I hope you enjoyed *Arriving Home*!

First off, this story wouldn't be possible without D. Ally Howlett's #merrywipmas2022. This writing challenge is how the story manifested. What was meant to be 12 short Instagram posts turned into a novel and a drafted series.

Thank you to Brittany Evans. My best friend, critique partner, and incredible graphic designer. I mean, how cute is this cover?! Brittany, without your motivation, enthusiasm, and detailed notes, this story wouldn't be what it is today.

Tiffany, thank you for holding me accountable for getting this done! You're incredible to brainstorm with and I'm so grateful you're in my life.

To my husband, thank you for believing in me, supporting all my dreams, (and taking care of life when I couldn't pull myself away from the story). Also, thank you for naming Lake Juniper and Hemlock Lake. Your deep dive into evergreen trees was so fun.

To all my ARC readers, you're amazing and thank you for your honest reviews!

To all of my readers, thank you for your dedication and enthusiasm. I appreciate each and every one of you! I wouldn't be where I am today without you.

Also by Chelsea Lauren

Young Adult:

Simply An Enigma

Theodore's Work in Progress

Romance:

Underneath the Whiskey

Short Stories:

"All A-Boat You" from Because of You: A Represent Publishing
Anthology

About the Author

Chelsea Lauren is a contemporary romance author. Chelsea has been writing ever since she had vivid dreams in middle school. The only cure was to write them down, and only then, did Chelsea realize she could become an author.

She's an upstate NY native, establishing roots in her hometown with her husband and two pups.

Chelsea is the founder of Represent Publishing, a self-publishing company dedicated to helping authors strengthen their writing, edit, and publish their novels. Her passion lies in helping others accomplish their dreams.

When Chelsea isn't writing or working on her business, you can find her devouring books, snuggling with her pups, or having game nights with her friends.